Jonatha.. ....

Gulliver's Travels
In Plain and Simple English

(A Modern Translation and the Original Version)

Also Know As:
Travels into Several Remote Nations of the World, in Four Parts. By Lemuel Gulliver, First a Surgeon, and then a Captain of Several Ships

BookCaps™ Study Guides
www.bookcaps.com

© 2012. All Rights Reserved.

Table of Contents

About This Series

The "Classic Retold" series started as a way of telling classics for the modern reader—being careful to preserve the themes and integrity of the original. Whether you want to understand Shakespeare a little more or are trying to get a better grasp of the Greek classics, there is a book waiting for you!

The series is expanding every month. Visit BookCaps.com to see all the books in the series, and while you are there join the Facebook page, so you are first to know when a new book comes out.

Gulliver's Travels

The Publisher to the Reader

As given in the original edition

The author of this travel book, Mr.Lemuel Gulliver, is an old and close friend of mine, and we are also related on our mothers' side. About three years ago, Mr.Gulliver got fed up with the constant stream of curious visitors at his house at Redriff, so he bought a small piece of land, with a nearby house, near Newark, in Nottinghamshire, his home country. He lives there now, keeping to himself but well thought of by his neighbors.

Although Mr.Gulliver was born in Nottinghamshire, where his father lived, I have heard him say that his family came from Oxfordshire. This is backed up by the tombs and monuments of the Gulliver family that I have seen in the churchyard in Banbury, in that county.

Before he left Redriff he asked me to look after the following manuscript, saying that I could do whatever I thought was best with them. I have read through them carefully three times. The style is very plain and simple; the only fault I can find with it is that the author, like most travelers, includes too much detail. There is a feeling of truth throughout the document, and it is a fact that the author was so well known for his honesty that his neighbors at Redriff, if they wanted to say anything was the truth, were in the habit of stating it was "as true as if Mr.Gulliver had said it."

On the advice of several reputable people, to whom I sent these papers (with the author's permission), I am now publishing them for the public, in the hope that they will divert young noblemen from their usual reading of political and party nonsense.

This book would have been at least twice the size if I hadn't taken the liberty of removing many passages about the winds and tides, the different navigational challenges of each voyage, detailed descriptions of how to handle a ship in a storm, which could only interest a sailor; I've also removed much about latitude and longitude, and I understand Mr.Gulliver might not be too happy about this. But I wanted the work to suit the general reader, as far as possible. However, if my ignorance of nautical matters has led me to make mistakes then I am the one to blame. And if any traveler would like to see the original manuscript then I'll be happy to show him.

As for any other details about the author, the reader will get them from the first pages of the book.

RICHARD SYMPSON.

A LETTER FROM CAPTAIN GULLIVER TO HIS COUSIN SYMPSON.

WRITTEN IN THE YEAR 1727.

I hope that you will be ready to publicly admit, whenever asked, that you continually badgered me to publish a very sloppy and inaccurate account of my travels, telling me to hire some young gentleman from Oxford or Cambridge to put them in order and correct their style, as my cousin Dampier did, on my advice, to make his book, "A Voyage Round the World." But I don't remember telling you that you had permission to take anything out, and still less to put anything in. So, as for what you have added, I reject everything of that sort, particularly a paragraph about her majesty Queen Anne, of holy and glorious memory, whom I worshipped and respected more than any other human. But you, or your agent, should have thought that the reason I said that was that it was not fitting to rank any human being above my Houyhnhnm master.

And anyway, the actual fact was completely wrong, for as I was in England during part of her majesty's reign I know that she did rule through a chief minister, in fact through two in succession, lords Godolphin and Oxford, so you made me lie. Also in the story of the academy of projectors, and several passages of my conversation with my master Houyhnhnm, you have either left out some important point or chopped and changed the whole thing so much that I can hardly recognise it as my own work. When I said as much to you in a letter, you told me that you were afraid of getting into trouble, that people in power were keeping a close eye on the press and looked out for hidden meanings and punished anything which looked like it had a secret meaning. But please tell me how something I said many years ago, fifteen thousand miles away, under a different monarch, should now be taken as referring to any of the Yahoos, who now rule everybody, especially when at the time I had hardly thought that we would end up unhappily ruled by them. Shouldn't I be the one to complain, when I see Yahoos pulled along in carriages by Houyhnhnms, as if the second were the brutes and the first the thinking creatures? In fact I hated this horrible sight so much that it was one of the main reasons I retreated to this place.

I thought it was right to tell you what I thought of you, and of what you have done with the trust I gave you.

The next thing that upsets me is my own lack of judgement in giving in to the begging and false arguments of you and some others to have these travels published, which I really didn't want to happen. Please think how many times I asked you to think (when you said it was for the public good) that the Yahoos are animals which can't be changed either with rules or by setting examples. This has been proved; instead of all corruption and abuse stopping on this little island, as I had hoped, after more than six months I see no sign that my book has had the slightest effect which I planned.

I asked you to let me know by letter when parties and gangs had been abolished; when judges became clever and honest; lawyers trustworthy and quiet, with a little common sense, and when Smithfield became a bonfire of law books; when young noblemen got a different sort of education entirely; when doctors were exiled; when the female Yahoos became full of virtue, honor, truth and good sense; when the courts and meetings of great ministers have been thoroughly cleaned up; when sense, merit and learning are rewarded; when all those disgraceful writers of prose and poetry are sentenced to eat nothing but their own paper, and drink their own ink.

Your encouragement led me to believe that these and a thousand other changes would take place, as they were so clearly laid out in the instructions in my book. And you must admit that seven months would be long enough to eliminate all vice and stupidity in Yahoos, if they were at all wise or virtuous. But your letters have been so far from what I expected, on the contrary every week the postman is loaded down with worthless books of all sorts, and I find inside them that I am accused of attacking the mighty, mocking human nature (so they still call it) and of abusing women. I also find that the writers of all this can't agree amongst themselves; some say that I didn't write my travels, and others say I wrote other books which I have never even read.

I also find that your printer has been careless enough to mix up the dates and times of my voyages and returns; he hasn't given the right year, month or day, and I hear that the original manuscript has been almost destroyed since publication, and I don't have a copy. However, I have sent you some corrections which you may put in if there's a second edition. But I can't swear to their accuracy, and I'll leave it up to my sincere and discerning readers to make the changes if they want.

I hear some of the Yahoos who go to sea criticize my nautical language, saying it is wrong or old fashioned. I can't help that. When I first went to sea I was young and was taught by the oldest sailors, and learned to speak like them. But I've found since that sailor Yahoos, like the ones on land, like to use newfangled words (the land ones change theirs every year, so that when I got back to my own country their speech was so changed I could hardly understand them. And I have seen that when a Yahoo comes from London to visit me at my house, out of curiosity, we can hardly make ourselves understood to each other).

If the criticism of the Yahoos could affect me in any way I would have every reason to be upset, as many of them think that my travels are all made up, and have dropped hints that Houyhnhnms and Yahoos are as imaginary as the citizens of Utopia. I must admit that I have never heard a Yahoo so cheeky as to doubt the existence of the people of Lilliput, Brobdingrag (that's how it's spelt, not the mistaken Brobdingnag) and Laputa, because every reader can see they are real at once. Is the existence of the Houyhnhnms or Yahoos any less likely, particularly as there are many thousands of Yahoos in this country, who only differ from their brothers in Houyhnhnmland in that they have a sort of rough speech and wear clothes? The unqualified praise of the whole lot of them would mean less to me than the neighing of the two lowly Houyhnhnms I keep in my stable, for low as they are I can still teach them to get better, and they have no vices.

Do these miserable animals have the cheek to think that I'll stoop to their level to defend the truth of my work? Though I'm a Yahoo it's well known throughout Houyhnhnmland that through the teachings and example of my great master I was able within two years (though I admit with great difficulty) to lose the awful habit of lying, evasion, deceit and equivocation which is so ingrained in all my kind, especially the Europeans.

I have other things to say about this matter, but I won't trouble you or myself any further. I must admit that since I came back some of the bad parts of my Yahoo nature have resurfaced through mixing with some of my own species, and particularly my own family, through necessity. If they hadn't I wouldn't have been so stupid as to try to reform the Yahoo race in this country, and I've certainly given that up forever now.

APRIL 2, 1727

Part I: A Voyage to Lilliput

Chapter I

[The author writes about himself and his family. What first made him travel. He is shipwrecked and has to swim for his life. He reaches the shore of Lilliput safely and is made a prisoner and taken into the country.]

My father had a small estate in Nottinghamshire, and I was the third of his five sons. He sent me to Emanuel College in Cambridge when I was fourteen, and I stayed there for three years, working hard. However, his lack of money meant he could no longer support even the small allowance I had, so I became an apprentice to Mr.James Bates, a famous London surgeon, and I stayed with him for four years. My father occasionally sent me small sums of money, which I invested in lessons on navigation and other types of mathematics which would be useful to a traveller, which is what I always thought I would end up doing at some time. When I left Mr.Bates I went to my father and he, my Uncle John and various other relations raised a sum of forty pounds for me and promised me thirty pounds a year to go to Leiden in Holland; I studied medicine there for two years and seven months, knowing it would come in handy on long voyages.

Soon after my return my good master, Mr.Bates, got me a place as ship's surgeon on the Swallow under the command of Captain Abraham Pannel. I stayed on that boat for three and a half years, making a trip or two to the Eastern Mediterranean and other places. When I came back I decided that I would settle down in London; my master, Mr.Bates, encouraged me, and sent me several patients. I rented part of a small house in the Old Jewry, and having been advised to change my lifestyle I married Mrs.Mary Burton, the second daughter of Mr.Edmund Burton, a tailor in Newgate Street, and I got four hundred pounds as a dowry. But my good master Bates died two years later and as I had few friends my business began to fail, as I would not follow the sharp practice of others in the same profession. After I consulted with my wife and others I knew I decided that I should go to sea again.

I was surgeon on two different ships, making several voyages, for six years, to both
the East and West Indies, which improved my bank balance. I always had a good number of books with me and spent my free time reading the great authors, ancient and modern; when I was ashore I would spend my time observing the customs and characters of the people, and learning their languages, which I was very good at, having an excellent memory.

The last of these voyages was not very happy, so I was tired of the sea and decided to stay at home with my wife and family. I moved from Old Jewry to Fetter Lane, and from there to Wapping, hoping to get some business amongst the sailors, but I couldn't make a profit. After three years of hoping for things to get better I accepted a generous offer from Captain William Pritchard, Master of the Antelope, who was making a voyage to the Pacific. We set sail from Bristol on May 4th 1699, and at first our trip was very profitable.

This is not the place to bother the reader with all the details of what happened in those seas; it's enough to say that as we made our way to the East Indies a violent storm drove us to the north-west of Tasmania. By taking measurements we found we were at a latitude of 30 degrees 2 minutes south. Twelve of our crew were dead from exhaustion and lack of food; the others were all very weak. On the 5th of November, which is when summer begins in that region, the weather was very hazy and the sailors spotted a rock very close to the ship. The wind was so strong that we were driven straight on to it and holed. Six of the crew, including me, let down a boat and strained to get away from the ship and the rock.

By my reckoning we rowed about ten miles, until we could do so no longer, having been exhausted by our efforts on board the ship. So we let the boat drift, and in half an hour we were overturned by a sudden gust of wind from the north. What happened to my companions in the boat, as well as the ones who got on to the rock or stayed with the ship, I cannot tell, but I assume they were all drowned. For me, I trusted to luck and was driven along by the winds and tide. I often tried to stand but could not touch bottom, but when I was almost exhausted and unable to go on I found I was within my depth, and the storm had greatly calmed. The slope of the seabed was so shallow that I walked almost a mile in the sea before I reached the shore, at what I guessed was about eight o'clock in the evening. I then walked on about half a mile, but there was no sign of houses or people, or at least, being in such a state, I didn't see them.

I was exhausted, and that, the heat of the weather and the half pint of brandy I had drunk as I left the ship, made me feel very much like sleeping. I lay down on the grass, which was very short and soft, and had a better sleep than I ever remembered in my life for, I thought, about nine hours, for when I woke up it was just daybreak. I tried to get up, but couldn't move, because, lying on my back, I found that my arms and legs were strongly tied down, and my hair, which was long and thick, was fastened in the same way. I could also feel several thin ropes across my body from my armpits down to my thighs. I could only look upwards, and the sun started to grow hot and the light hurt my eyes. I heard a hubbub around me, but in the position I was in I could only see the sky.

In a little while I felt some living thing on my left leg, coming gently over my chest and almost up to my chin. Looking down as far as I could I saw that it was a human, less than six inches high, with a bow and arrow in its hands and a quiver on its back. In the meantime I felt at least forty of the same kind (so I thought) following him. I was amazed, and shouted so loudly that they all ran backwards in fright, and some of them, I was told later, were hurt falling from my sides to the ground. However, they soon came back and one of them, coming far enough to get a good look at my face, cried out in a high but clear voice, "Hekinah degul"; the others repeated the same words several times but I didn't know what they meant. I lay there for a while, extremely uneasy as you can imagine.

Eventually, struggling to get loose, I managed to break the strings and pull out the pegs holding my left arm to the ground. By lifting it up to my face I could see the way I was tied, and at the same time with a great heave, which was very painful, I managed to loosen the strings which held down my hair on the left hand side, so that I could turn my head about two inches. The creatures ran off again before I could grab them, and then there was a loud shout in a very high voice, and after that I heard one of them cry, "Tolgo phonac!" and I felt over a hundred arrows hit my left hand at once, which were like a hundred needle pricks. They also shot another flight into the air, as we do with missiles in Europe, and I assume many fell on my body (though I didn't feel them) and some fell on my face, which I at once covered with my left hand. When this shower of arrows had finished I was moaning with fear and pain, and then as I struggled to get free they fired another volley, larger than the first, and some of them tried to stick spears in my sides. Luckily I had on a leather waistcoat and they couldn't get through it.

I thought the best thing to do would be to keep still, and I planned to stay like that until nightfall when, with my left hand already loose, I could easily free myself; as for the inhabitants, I thought that I could beat the largest army they could send against me, if they were all the same size as the one I saw. But fate had other plans.

When the people saw that I was quiet they didn't fire any more arrows, but by the noise I heard I could tell that more of them had arrived. About four yards away, next to my right ear, I heard a knocking for over an hour, like people working. Turning my head that way as much as the pegs and strings would allow me I saw that a stage had been built about a foot and a half from the ground, which could hold four of the inhabitants, and there were two or three ladders to let them climb up on it. From here one of them, who seemed to be some sort of nobleman, made a long speech to me, which I didn't understand a word of. But I should have said that before the main person began his speech he shouted out three times, "Langro dehul san!" (these words and the ones I heard before were later explained to me); at that at least fifty of the inhabitants came forward at once and cut the strings holding the left hand side of my head, which allowed me to turn my head and observe the gestures and the appearance of the speaker.

He seemed to be middle aged, and taller than the three others with him, one of whom was a page, about the length of my middle finger, holding up his cloak, and the other two stood either side in support. He made all the gestures of an orator, and I could see that sometimes he was threatening and other times making promises and offering pity and kindness. I answered with a few words in a humble manner, lifting up my left hand and turning my eyes to the sky as if begging him to believe me. As I was almost starving, having not eaten since several hours before I left the ship, I found my hunger was so strong that I could not keep myself from (perhaps a little rudely) pointing frequently at my mouth, to show I wanted food. The Hurgo (this is what they call a great lord, as I later learned) understood me clearly. He came down from the platform and ordered that several ladders should be leaned on my sides, and over a hundred of the natives climbed up them and walked towards my mouth carrying baskets of meat; these had been got and sent there on the orders of the king, when he first heard about me. I saw that there were several kinds of meat, but I couldn't tell them apart through taste. There were shoulders, legs and loins, shaped like those of a sheep and very well cooked but smaller than a lark's wing. I ate then two or three at a time, and had three loaves at a time which were about the size of musket bullets.

They brought the food as quickly as they could, showing absolute amazement at my size and appetite. Then I made another gesture to show that I wanted a drink. They had seen from my eating that I needed large quantities, so, being very ingenious people, they pulled up, very cunningly, one of their largest barrels, then rolled it to my hand and beat the lid in. I drank it straight down, for it wasn't more than half a pint; it tasted like a weak Burgundy, and was much more tasty. They brought me another barrel, which I tossed off again, and made signs for more, but that was all they had. When I had done these things they shouted with joy and danced on my chest, repeating over the thing they had said at first, "Hekinah degul." They signalled me to throw down the two barrels, first warning the people below to stand clear by shouting, "Borach mevolah!". When they saw the barrels in the air there was a great shout of "Hekinah degul!"

I must admit I was tempted, as they walked to and fro over my body, to grab the first forty or fifty that came within reach and smash them to the ground. But remembering what they had done before, which might not be the worst they could do, and my promise to behave – that was what I meant by my humble behavior – I soon gave up the idea. Besides, I felt I was now bound to behave as a guest, as they had treated me with such generosity. However, I couldn't help but be amazed at the nerve of these tiny people, who dared to climb and walk on my body whilst I had a hand free without trembling at the sight of what must seem, to them, an enormous creature. After some time, when they saw I stopped asking for food, a high-ranking court official came to me.

His excellency, having climbed up the back of my right knee, walked up to my face with about a dozen of his followers. He showed me his credentials with the royal seal, holding them close to my eyes, and spoke for about ten minutes without showing any anger, but with a kind of set determination, often pointing ahead which, I later found, was the direction of the capital city, about half a mile away; it had been decided by his majesty and his ministers that I was to be taken there. I answered in a few words, but they were not understood, so I made a sign with my free hand, moving it over him (though going high over his excellency's head to avoid hurting him or his followers) and then over my own head and body to show that I wanted to be freed. It seemed that he understood me, but he shook his head and made a gesture to show that I was to go as a prisoner. However, he also made signs that I was to be given plenty of food and drink and would be well treated. I thought again of breaking the ropes, but when I thought of the pain of their arrows on my face and hands, which were all blistered, with many arrows still sticking in them, and realising that there were many more of them than before, I gave signs that I would do as they ordered.

At this the Hurgo and his followers withdrew, with great politeness and smiles on their faces. Soon after I heard a great shout, with frequent repetition of the words, "Peplom selan!", and I felt that many people were on my left side, loosening the cords so I could turn on my right and urinate, which I did, copiously, to the amazement of the people, who had guessed what I was about to do and ran to the right and left to avoid the torrent with came from me with such noise and violence. But before this they had dabbed a pleasant smelling sort of ointment on my face and hands which removed all the pain of their arrows in a few minutes. This, and the refreshment I had from their food and drink, made me feel much better and feeling like sleep. I slept for about eight hours, I was told afterwards, and no wonder, for his majesty's doctors had mixed a sleeping potion into the barrels of wine.

It seems that as soon as I was found sleeping on the ground, after I landed, the emperor was alerted very quickly by an express messenger, and he had decided with his ministers that I was to be tied up as I described (which they did in the night as I slept), that I should be sent plenty of meat and drink and that a machine should be built to carry me to the capital city.

This decision might seem very daring and dangerous, and I am sure there isn't a prince in Europe who would do the same in the circumstances. However, in my opinion, it was a very good decision, as well as being generous. Supposing they had tried to kill me with their spears and arrows, when I was asleep; I should certainly have been woken by the first prick, and that might have so enraged me that I could have broken the ropes they tied me with, and then they would have been at my mercy.

These people are very clever mathematicians, and have developed great mechanical skill, through the patronage and encouragement of the emperor, who is known for sponsoring education. The prince has several wheeled machines to carry trees and other heavy weights. He often builds his largest warships, some of which are nine feet long, in the woods where the timber grows and then has them carried on these machines the three or four hundred yards down to the sea. Five hundred carpenters and engineers immediately began to prepare their biggest machine. It was a wood frame raised three inches off the ground, about seven feet by four and moving on twenty-two wheels. The shout I had heard was to greet the arrival of this machine, which it seems had set off four hours after I landed. It was brought up alongside me.

The great difficulty was to lift me and put me in this vehicle. Eighty poles, each a foot high, were put up for this, and very strong cords, about as thick as packthread, were fastened with hooks to many bandages which the workmen had tied around my neck, hands, body and legs. Nine hundred of the strongest men pulled on these cords, using pulleys fastened to the poles, and so in less than three hours I was hoisted onto the machine and tied down. I was told this later, as I was asleep through the whole procedure due to the sleeping potion they had put in my wine. Fifteen hundred of the emperor's largest horses, each one about four and a half inches high, were used to pull me to the city, which as I said was half a mile away.

About four hours after we began the trip I was woken by an absurd accident. The machine had stopped for a while, to adjust something that was out of order, and two or three youngsters wanted to see what I looked like asleep. They climbed up on the machine and sneaked quietly up to my face; one of them, a guards officer, put the sharp end of his spear far up my left nostril, which tickled my nose and made me sneeze violently. They sneaked off unobserved and for three weeks I didn't know what had made me wake so suddenly. We kept marching for the rest of the day, and rested at night with five hundred guards on each side of me, half with torches and half with bows and arrows, ready to shoot me if I moved. The next morning at sunrise we carried on and by noon we were two hundred yards from the city gates. The emperor and all the court came out to meet me, but his officers would not let him risk climbing on my body.

Where the machine had stopped there was an ancient temple, thought to be the largest in the kingdom. It had been polluted some years before by a murder taking place inside it, so according to the religion of these people it was no longer holy but used for everyday things, with all the sacred objects removed. It was decided that this was where I would stay. The great gate facing north was about four feet high and two feet wide, so I could easily creep in. On each side of the gate there was a small window, only about six inches above the ground, and through the left one the king's blacksmith carried ninety one chains, almost the size of a European lady's watch chain, and these were locked to my leg by thirty six padlocks. Opposite this temple, twenty feet away on the other side of the highway, there was a turret at least five feet high.

The emperor climbed up here, with many of the great men of his court, to have a look at me (I was told this, as I could not see them). It was thought that over a hundred thousand townspeople came out to have a look as well, and in spite of my guards (I think there weren't less than ten thousand, on and off) some climbed up on my body with ladders. A proclamation was soon issued, banning this on pain of death. When the workmen found I couldn't escape they cut off all the ropes which held me, and I stood up, feeling as fed up as I ever had in my life. You cannot imagine the noise and amazement of the people at seeing me get up and walk. The chains on my left leg were about two yards long and allowed me to walk to and fro in a semicircle, and also, as they were fixed four inches from the gate, they allowed me to creep in and lie down at full length in the temple.

Chapter II

[The emperor of Lilliput, with several noblemen, comes to see the author in his imprisonment. The emperor is described. Wise men are appointed to teach the author their language. His quiet nature impresses them. His pockets are searched and his sword and pistols are taken from him.]

When I got to my feet I looked round me, and I must say I never saw such a charming sight. The country looked like a garden, with the enclosed fields, which were usually around forty feet square, looking like flowerbeds. The fields were mixed with woods about ten feet square, and the tallest trees, as far as I could judge, were about seven feet high. I looked at the town on my left, which looked like a city painted on the backdrop of a theatre.

I had for some hours been bothered by the call of nature, which was no wonder as it was two days since I had last relieved myself. I was torn between necessity and embarrassment. The best thing I could think to do was to creep into my house, which I did, and I shut the gate, went as far in as my chain would allow, and shed my body's burden. This was the only time I ever did such an unpleasant thing, and I hope that the fair reader will, after he has sensibly and impartially thought about it, make allowances for the distress I was in. From then on it was my custom to do that business in the open air, as far from my house as the chain would allow. It was made sure that every morning, before any company came, the offensive matter was carried off in wheelbarrows by two servants chosen for the task. I wouldn't have spent so long explaining this, which might not look that important at first glance, if I didn't think it was necessary to demonstrate my hygienic practices to the world, because I have been told that some of my detractors have seen fit to call them into question at various times.

When the business was over I came back out of the house, needing some fresh air. The emperor had already come down from the tower and was coming towards me on horseback, which could have cost him dearly, because the horse, not used to what must have seemed like a mountain jumping up ahead of him, reared up. However, the prince is an excellent horseman and he stayed seated until his attendants could run in and hold the bridle while he dismounted. When he had got down he walked round me, looking on admiringly, but he was careful not to get within reach. He ordered his cooks and butlers, who were standing ready, to give me food and drink, which they pushed forward on carts. I took these carts and had soon emptied them all; there were twenty full of meat and ten of drink; each cart gave me two or three good mouthfuls, and I emptied the drink from ten earthenware vessels into one cart and drank it off in one go, and I did the same with the rest. The empress and young princes of the blood of both sexes, with many ladies-in-waiting, sat some way away in their chairs, but when the emperor had the mishap with his horse they got down and came near to him. I am now going to describe him. He is taller, almost by the width of my fingernail, than any of his court, which is enough to give onlookers a great respect for him.

His features are strong and manly, with a protruding jaw and arched nose, he has an olive complexion, upright bearing, a well proportioned body and limbs, graceful movements and a regal carriage. He was then past his prime, being twenty-eight and three quarters; he had ruled for about seven of those years with great success and victory in battle. To see him better I lay on my side, with my face looking into his, and he stood just three yards away. I have held him in my hand many times since and so I know the description is accurate. His clothes were very plain and simple, a mixture of Asian and European styles; but on his head he had a light gold helmet, decorated with jewels with a plume on top. He had his sword to defend himself in case I got free: it was almost three inches long and the hilt and scabbard were made of gold studded with diamonds. His voice was high but very clear and precise, and I could still hear it well when I stood up. The ladies and the courtiers were splendidly dressed, so that where they stood it looked like there was a petticoat embroidered with gold and silver figures spread out on the ground. His majesty said a lot to me, and I answered, but neither of us could understand a word.

There were several of his priests and lawyers there (as I guessed they were from their clothes) who were ordered to speak to me. I spoke to them in all the languages I knew, being High and Low Dutch, Latin, French, Spanish, Italian and English, but got nowhere. After about two hours the court left, and I was left with a strong guard to stop the cheekiness and probably the violence of the rabble, who wanted to get as near to me as they dared. Some of them had the cheek to fire their arrows at me, as I sat on the ground by my front door, and one only just missed my left eye. The colonel ordered six of the ringleaders be seized, and thought the best punishment was to give them to me, so some of the soldiers pushed them within my reach with the blunt ends of their pikes. I took them all in my right hand and put five into my coat pocket; I made a face as if I was going to eat the sixth alive.

The poor man gave an awful squeal, and the colonel and his officers were terrified, especially when they saw me take out my penknife, but I soon eased their worries, for I looked gentle and cut the strings he was tied with and put him softly on the ground, and he ran off. I did the same with the others, taking them out of my pocket one by one, and I saw the soldiers and the people were very pleased with this show of mercy, and this played very well for me when it was reported to the court.

Towards nightfall I got into my house, with some difficulty, where I slept on the ground as I did for about a fortnight; during that period the emperor gave orders that a bed should be made for me. Six hundred ordinary sized beds were brought in carriages and joined together in my house; there were a hundred and fifty together to make up the length and width, and they were four deep. However, this didn't give me much protection from the hard floor, which was smooth stone. Using the same measurements they gave me sheets, blankets and quilts, which were good enough for one as used to hardship as I.

As the news of my arrival spread through the kingdom there were large numbers of rich, idle and curious people who came to see me, so that the villages were almost emptied. There would have been a great neglect of farming and household business if this had gone on, but his majesty took precautions, through several proclamations and official orders, against it. He ordered that all those who had already seen me should go home, and nobody was to come within fifty yards of my house without a permit from the court (these made a good profit for the king's officials).

In the meantime the emperor had many meetings to debate what should be done with me. Afterwards I was told by a special friend, a very high ranking man who was as involved in these discussions as anyone, that I gave the court a lot of trouble. They were worried that I might break loose, and that feeding me was going to be very expensive and could cause a famine. Sometimes they decided they should starve me, or shoot me in the hands and face with poisoned arrows, which would soon finish me off, but then they thought that such a large corpse, rotting, could cause a plague in the city which would spread across the country.

In the middle of this debate several army officers went to the door of the meeting room and the two who were admitted told them how I had behaved with the six criminals mentioned before. This made such a favourable impression on his majesty and his counsellors that a royal order was sent out making all villages for nine hundred yards around the city bring in every morning six beef cattle, forty sheep and other food for me, with a matching quantity of bread, wine and other liquors. His majesty gave orders for the payment of this from his treasury; he generally lives on his own property and rarely raises any taxes on his people, who are obliged to fight in his wars at their own expense.

It was also ordered that six hundred people be enrolled as my servants, with their room and board paid for, and tents were set up for them handily on either side of my house. It was also ordered that three hundred tailors should make me a suit of clothes in the style of the country, that six of the king's greatest scholars should be employed to instruct me in their language and that the emperor's horses, and those of the noblemen and army, should be exercised often in sight of me, so that they would get used to me. All these orders were duly obeyed, and in about three weeks I had made great strides in learning their language. During this time the emperor frequently honored me with visits, and helped my teachers. We began to be able to talk to each other, and the first words I learned were to ask him to set me free, which I begged him every day on my knees.

His answer, as far as I could understand, was that this would take time, and couldn't be undertaken without consultation with his advisers, and that first I must 'Lumos kelmin pesso desmar lon emposo', that is, swear to be peaceful to him and his kingdom. He did say that I should be treated as kindly as possible, and he advised me to get the good opinion of himself and his subjects through patience and quiet behavior. He asked me not to be offended if he asked some of his officers to search me, for I might well have several weapons on me which would have to be very dangerous things if they were in proportion to my size. I told him that I was happy to strip myself and turn out my pockets.

I told him this partly through words and partly through signs. He answered that by the law of his kingdom I must be searched by two of his officers, and he knew this couldn't be done without my help and agreement. He said he had such a good opinion of my kindness and sense that he would trust these officers in my hands, and that anything which was taken from me would be returned when I left the country, or paid for at the price I set. I picked up the two officers and put them in my coat pockets, then in all my other pockets except my fobs and another secret pocket which I didn't want searched, in which I had a few bits and pieces that were of no use to anybody but me. In one of my fobs there was a silver watch, and in the other a little gold in a purse. These gentlemen, having pen, ink and paper, made a precise inventory of everything they saw, and when they were finished they asked me to put them down so they could give it to the emperor. I have translated this inventory into English, and this is it, word for word:

"Firstly, in the right hand coat pocket of the great man-mountain [this is how I interpret the words Quinbus Flestrin], after the closest search, we only found one great piece of rough cloth, big enough to make a carpet for your majesty's biggest room. In the left pocket we saw a huge silver chest, with a lid of the same metal, which we could not lift. We asked for it to be opened, and as one of us stepped in he found himself up to his knees in some sort of dust, which started a fit of sneezing in both of us when it flew into our faces. In his right waistcoat pocket we found a great bundle of thin white things, about the size of three men, folded over one another, tied with a strong rope and marked with black figures. We humbly assume that there are writings, with each letter being half a hand's breadth high. In the left there was some sort of machine, from the back of which were sticking twenty long poles, like the railings outside your majesty's palace; we assume he uses this to comb his hair, we didn't ask as we found it very difficult to make ourselves understood.

"In the large pocket, on the right side of his middle cover [this is how I translate the word 'ranfulo', meaning my breeches] we saw a hollow iron pillar, about the length of a man, fastened to a strong timber larger than the pillar. On one side of the pillar there were huge pieces of iron sticking out, cut into strange shapes which we could not understand. In the smaller pocket on the right hand side there were several round flat pieces of white and red metal; some of the white pieces, which seemed to be silver, were so large and heavy that my comrade and I could hardly lift them. In the left pocket were two unevenly shaped black pillars; we couldn't easily reach the top of them when we stood at the bottom of his pocket. One of them was covered and seemed the same all over, but at the end of the other there was a round white ball of something, twice the size of our heads. Each of these had a great steel plate inside, which we ordered him to show us, as we thought they could be dangerous weapons. He took them out of their cases and told us that in his own country one was used for shaving and the other for cutting meat.

There were two pockets we could not enter, which he called his fobs. They are two large slits cut into the top of his breeches, held tight by the pressure of his stomach. Out of the right fob there hung a great silver chain, with an amazing machine at the end of it. We ordered him to pull out whatever was on the end of the chain; it seemed to be a globe, half silver and half some transparent material. On the transparent side there were some strange figures drawn round in a circle, and we tried to touch them but found our fingers were blocked by the clear substance. He put this machine by our ears, and it made a never-ending noise, like a watermill; we assume it is either some strange animal, or the god that he worships. We think the latter is more likely as he told us (if we understood correctly, for he expressed himself very poorly) that he hardly ever did anything without consulting it. He called it his guide, and said that it told him when to do things. From the left fob he took out a net, which was almost large enough for a fisherman but opened and shut like a purse, which is what he used it for, we found several heavy pieces of yellow metal in there which, if they are real gold, must be worth a fortune.

"Having, as your majesty instructed, searched his pockets carefully, we saw a belt round his waist made from the skin of some great animal; on the left hand side there hung a sword as long as five men, and on the right there was a bag or pouch split into two compartments, each one capable of holding three of your majesty's subjects. In one of these compartments there were several balls of a very heavy metal, about the size of our heads and needing a strong man to lift them. The other compartment held a heap of black grains which didn't have much size or weight, for we could hold fifty of them in our hands.

This is an exact inventory of what we found on the man-mountain, who treated us very kindly and with all due respect for your majesty's orders. Signed and sealed on the fourth day of the eighty-ninth month of your majesty's prosperous reign.

Clefrin Frelock, Marsi Frelock."

When this inventory was read to the emperor he ordered me, though very politely, to hand over the things mentioned. First he asked for my sword, which I took out, scabbard and all. In the meantime he ordered three thousand of his best troops (who were with him) to surround me at a distance and to be ready to fire their bow and arrows, but I didn't notice this as I was watching his majesty. He then asked me to draw my sword, which, although it had got some rust from the sea water, was mostly very shiny. I did as he asked, and at once all the troops gave a shout of terror and surprise, for the sun was shining brightly and the reflection dazzled them as I waved it to and fro. His majesty, who is a very noble-hearted prince, was less afraid than I had thought he would be; he ordered me to put it back in its scabbard and throw it on the ground as softly as I could about six feet from the end of my chain.

The next thing he asked for was one of the hollow iron pillars, by which he meant my pocket pistols. I took it out, and as he asked I explained to him, as well as I could, how it was used. I loaded it just with powder (which due to the tightness of the pouch had not got wet, a precaution taken by all sensible sailors), told the emperor not to be afraid and fired in the air. The astonishment here was much greater than at the sight of my sword; hundreds collapsed as if they were dead, and even the emperor, though he stood his ground, was quite shaken for a while. I handed over both my pistols in the same way as I had my sword, and then my powder and bullet pouch; I begged him to keep the powder away from fire, for it would catch light from the smallest spark and would blow his palace to smithereens.

I also handed over my watch, which the emperor was very curious to see, and he ordered two of his tallest guards to carry it on a pole between their shoulders, as deliverymen in England carry a barrel of beer. He was amazed at the continual noise it made, and the movement of the minute hand, which he could easily make out, as their sight is much sharper than ours. He asked his learned men what they thought of it, and their opinions were different and off the mark, as you can well imagine without my telling you (though I couldn't understand them well). I then gave up my silver and copper money, my purse, with nine large gold pieces and some smaller ones, my knife and razor, my comb and silver snuffbox, my handkerchief and diary. My sword, pistols and pouch were taken in carriages to his majesty's storerooms, but the rest of my goods were handed back. As I said before, I had one private pocket they didn't find, which held a pair of spectacles (which I sometimes use for my weak eyes), a magnifying glass and some other bits and pieces, which, as they would be of no interest to the emperor, I didn't think I was obliged to show him, and I thought they might be lost or damaged if I gave them up.

Chapter III

[The author entertains the emperor, and his aristocrats of both sexes, in a very unusual way. The entertainment at the court of Lilliput is described. The author is freed, on certain conditions.]

My quiet manner and good behavior had made such a good impression on the emperor and the court, and indeed on the army and the people in general, that I began to hope I would shortly be freed. I did everything I could to increase their good impression of me. The natives gradually became less frightened of me. I would sometimes lie down and let five or six of them dance on my hand, and eventually girls and boys used to come and play hide-and-seek in my hair. I had now got on well with understanding and speaking the language. The emperor decided one day to entertain me with some of the fairground shows of the country, which are better than I've seen anywhere else, both for agility and excellence. Nobody impressed me so much as the tightrope walkers, who performed on a thin white thread, about two feet long, a foot above the ground. If the reader will allow I would like to say a little more about this.

This entertainment is only practised by those people who are in the running for top jobs and preferment at court. They are trained in the art from childhood, and they are not always of noble birth or great education. When a great office is open, either through death or disgrace (which often happens), five or six of these candidates will ask permission to entertain his majesty and the court with a tightrope dance, and the one who jumps highest, without falling, gets the job. Very often the chief ministers are ordered to perform themselves to show their skill and to convince the emperor they have not lost it. Flimnap, the treasurer, is agreed to be able to jump at least an inch higher on the rope than any lord in the empire. I have seen him perform somersaults several times in succession on a plate fixed to a rope which is no thicker than a normal thick thread in England. My friend Reldresal, the principal secretary for private affairs, is, in my opinion if it's not biased, second best after the treasurer, and the rest of the great officers are all about the same.

These entertainments are often the cause of fatal accidents, of which there have been a great number in history. I personally have seen two or three candidates fracture a limb. The danger is far greater when the ministers are ordered to show their skills, as in trying to excel themselves and beat their fellows they try so hard that hardly any of them have not fallen, some of them two or three times. I was told that a year or two before I came there Flimnap would certainly have broken his neck if his fall hadn't been broken by one of the king's cushions which had happened to be lying there.

There is another entertainment which only takes place in front of the emperor and empress, and the first minister, on special occasions. The emperor puts three fine silk threads, each six inches long, on the table. One is blue, one red, and the third green. These threads are offered as prizes for the people the emperor wants to specially reward. The ceremony is held in his majesty's great chamber of state, where the candidates have to undergo a test of skill very different from the one just mentioned, which I haven't seen the like of in any other country in the new world or the old. The emperor holds a stick in his hands, level with the ground, and the candidates come on one by one, sometimes jumping over it, sometimes creeping under it, to and fro several times, depending on whether the stick is held high or low. Sometimes the emperor holds one end of the stick and the first minister the other, and sometimes just the minister holds it. Whoever performs with the greatest agility, and keeps up the leaping and creeping the longest, gets the blue silk; the red is given to the next best and the third gets the green. They wear the threads wrapped twice round their middles, and you don't see many great people in the court who aren't wearing one of these belts.

The horses of the army, and the ones from the royal stables, were no longer shy of me as they had seen me every day, so they would jump right up to my feet without running. The riders would jump them over my hand as I put it on the ground, and one of the emperor's huntsmen, on a large hunter, jumped my foot, shoe and all, which was a really impressive leap. I was lucky enough to amuse the emperor one day in a remarkable way. I asked him to order that several sticks, two feet high and as thick as an ordinary cane, should be brought to me, so he gave instructions for this to be done to his chief forester. The next morning six foresters arrived with six carriages, with eight horses to each one. I took nine of these sticks and fixed them to the ground in a square, two and a half feet on each side. I tied four other sticks into a square across these, about two feet from the ground, then I put my handkerchief over the nine upright sticks and pulled it on all sides until it was tight as a drum, and the four parallel sticks, rising five inches higher than the handkerchief, made railings on each side.

When I was finished I asked the emperor to let a troop of his best horses, twenty-four of them, come and exercise on this plain. He agreed to this, and I picked them up one by one, armed and mounted and with officers to direct them. As soon as they were lined up they split into two parties, performed mock fights, fired blunt arrows, drew their swords, attacked and retreated, and all in all showed the best military skill I had ever seen. The parallel sticks stopped them and their horses falling over the edge, and the emperor was so pleased that he ordered the entertainment to be repeated on several days, once being lifted up to give the word of command. With great difficulty he even managed to persuade the empress to let me hold her in her sedan chair just two yards from the stage, where she got a good view of the whole show. It was lucky for me that no accident happened during these shows. Just once a lively horse, that belonged to one of the captains, pawed with his hoof and made a hole in the handkerchief, and as his foot slipped he and his rider fell. But I saved them at once, and covering up the hole with one hand I put the troop down with the other, just as I had lifted them. The horse that fell strained its left shoulder, but the rider was not hurt, and I repaired the handkerchief as well as I could. However, I wouldn't take a chance on its strength any more in such dangerous games.

About two or three days before I was set free I was amusing the court with this sort of demonstration when an express messenger arrived to tell his majesty that some of his subjects, riding near the place I was found, had seen a great black object on the ground. It was very oddly shaped, as wide as his majesty's bedchamber and as high as a man in the middle. It was not a living creature, as they first thought, for it lay on the grass without moving. Some of them had walked round it several times, and climbing on each other's shoulders they had reached the top which was flat and even, and stamping on it they had found that it was hollow inside. They thought it might be something belonging to the "man mountain", and if his majesty wished they could bring it using five horses. I soon knew what this meant, and was very happy to hear of it. It seems that when I first made the shore after our shipwreck I was so confused that before I got to the place I fell asleep my hat, which I had tied to my head with a string while rowing, and which had stuck on my head all the time I was swimming, fell off after I landed. The string must have broken by some accident which I never noticed, and so I thought I had lost my hat in the sea.

I begged his imperial majesty to order that it be brought to me as soon as possible, telling him what it was, and the next day the carters arrived with it, but it was not in very good shape: they had drilled two holes in the brim, an inch and a half from the edge, and put hooks in the holes; these hooks were tied to the horses with long ropes, so my hat was dragged over the ground for more than half an English mile. However, the ground in that country was very smooth and level, so it took less damage than I expected.

Two days after this happened the emperor took a fancy to amusing himself in a very unusual way: he ordered the part of the army quartered in the town and nearby to get ready, and asked me to stand like a Colossus, with my legs as far apart as they would comfortably go. Then he ordered his general (an experienced old leader, and a great supporter of mine) to line up the troops in close order and march them under me, the foot soldiers twenty-four abreast and the horses sixteen, with drums beating, colors flying and pikes at attention. The whole lot came to three thousand foot soldiers and a thousand cavalry. His majesty gave strict orders, on pain of death, that every soldier as he marched should show me the greatest respect; however this didn't stop some of younger officers looking up as they passed under me, and I must admit that my breeches were so ragged that they did cause some amusement and joking.

I had sent so many memos and pleas asking for my liberty that his majesty finally mentioned the matter, firstly in cabinet and then to the full council, and nobody objected except Skyresh Bolgolam, who had decided, without provocation, to be my mortal enemy. But everyone else was against him and the emperor backed the decision. Bolgolam was Galbet, or admiral of the realm, very trusted by the king and very knowledgeable but of a gloomy and sour demanor. However, he was eventually persuaded to agree, though he insisted that the terms on which I should be set free would be written by himself. The conditions were brought to me by Skyresh Bolgolam in person, with two under-secretaries attending him and several notable people. After they were read I was told to swear that I would obey them, firstly in the style of my own country and then in the way their laws demanded, which meant I had to hold my right foot in my left hand, put the middle finger of my right hand on the top of my head and my thumb on the tip of my right ear. Because the reader might be curious about the unique style of expression of those people, and also might like to see the contract which set me free, I have made a translation of the whole thing, word for word, as close as I could, which I offer here.

"Golbasto Momarem Evlame Gurdilo Shefin Mully Ully Gue, most mighty Emperor of Lilliput, delight and terror of the universe, whose kingdoms extend five thousand blustrugs (about twelve miles round) to the edges of the world, king of kings, taller than all men, whose feet reach the center of the earth and whose head touches the sun, at whose nod princes give way at the knee, lovely as the spring, warm as the summer, fertile as autumn and dreadful as winter: his most wonderful majesty offers to the man-mountain, who lately came to our heavenly kingdom, the following contract, which he shall stick to through a solemn oath:

"1st, The man-mountain will not leave our kingdom, without a passport with the imperial seal.

2nd, He shall not enter our capital city without being explicitly invited, and when he is the inhabitants will be given two hours' notice to stay indoors.

"3rd, The man-mountain will only walk on our main roads, and will not walk on, or lie down in, a meadow or a cornfield.

4th, As he walks along these roads, he shall take the greatest care not to trample on any people, horses or carriages, and he shall not pick any people up without their permission.

"5th, If an express message requires particular speed, the man mountain will carry the messenger and his horse in his pocket for a six day journey, once a month, and he shall bring the messenger back (if necessary) safely to the emperor.

"6th, He shall be our ally against our enemies on the island of Blefuscu and do all he can to destroy their fleet, which is currently preparing to invade us.

"7th, The man-mountain shall, when he has spare time, help our workmen to lift up certain great stones needed to cover the walls of the main park and other royal buildings.

"8th, That the man-mountain shall, in two months' time, give us an exact measurement of the circumference of our kingdom, counted in his own paces around the coast.

"Lastly, when he has given his solemn assent to all the above, the man-mountain shall have a daily allowance of meat and drink equivalent to the amount needed for 1724 of our subjects and he shall have free access to the emperor and other sins of our favor. This is ordered at our palace at Belfaborac on the twelfth day of the ninety first month of our reign."

I swore to obey this contract very happily, though some of the conditions were rather more demeaning that I would have liked; these were the ones included through the malice of Skyresh Bolgolam, the high admiral. Then my chains were unlocked and I was completely free. The emperor did me the honor of being next to me in person throughout the ceremony. I showed my gratitude by bowing down at his majesty's feet, but he told me to rise and after many flattering words (which I shall not repeat, to avoid being accused of vanity) he added that he hoped I would be a useful servant and be worthy of all the favors he had already given me as well as the ones he might give me in the future.

The reader might like to note that in the last article of my freedom contract the emperor rules that I should have enough meat and drink to support 1724 Lilliputians. Some time after I asked a friend at court how they had chosen that exact number. He told me that his majesty's mathematicians, having measured my body using a quadrant had found that I was twelve times bigger than them, and as our bodies were similar mine must hold at least 1724 of theirs, and so I would need the same amount of food as would be needed to support that number of them. This shows the reader how clever those people were, as well as the careful and precise economy of their great prince.

Chapter IV

[Mildendo, the capital city of Lilliput, is described, along with the emperor's palace. The author and a principal secretary discuss matters related to the empire. The author offers to serve the emperor in war.]

The first thing I asked after I was set free was for permission to see Mildendo, the capital city. The emperor was pleased to give permission, but specifically said that I must not harm the inhabitants or their houses. The people were warned in a proclamation that I was coming to visit. The wall which runs round the town is two and a half feet high and at least eleven inches across, so that a coach and horses can be easily driven along it; it is bordered with strong towers, ten feet apart. I stepped over the great western gate and shuffled along very carefully along the two main streets. I was only wearing my short waistcoat, as I was worried that the skirts of my long coat might damage the eaves and roofs of the houses. I walked extremely carefully to avoid treading on any stragglers who might still be in the streets, though they had strict orders to stay indoors for their own safety. The attic windows and rooftops were so packed with people that I thought I hadn't seen such a crowded place in all my travels. The city is an exact square, with each side of the wall being five hundred feet long. The two main streets which run across it and split it into quarters are five feet wide. The lanes and alleys which I saw as I passed but could not enter are between twelve and eighteen inches wide. The town can hold five hundred thousand people, the houses are between three and five stories high, and there are plenty of shops and markets.

The emperor's palace is in the center of the city where the two main streets meet. It is surrounded by a wall two feet high, twenty feet away from the buildings. I had his majesty's permission to step over this wall, and as the space between the wall and the palace was so wide I could walk round and view it from all angles. The outer court is forty feet square, and includes two more courts; the royal apartments are in the inner court; I was very keen to see these but it was very difficult to do so as the great gates from one court to the other were just eighteen inches high and seven wide. The buildings of the outer court were at least five feet high and it was impossible for me to step over them without causing great damage to the stonework, though the walls were made of solid cut rock and four inches thick. At the same time the emperor was very keen for me to see his palace, but I could not do so until three days later; I spent these days cutting down some of the largest trees in the royal park, which was a hundred yards away, with my knife.

I made two stools from these trees, each one about three feet high and strong enough to take my weight. With the people being warned a second time I went through the city to the palace carrying my two stools. When I came to the wall of the outer court I stood on one stool and picked up the other; I lifted this one over the roof and gently put it down in the space between the first and second court, which was eight feet wide. I then stepped easily over the building from one stool to the other, and pulled the first one up behind me with a hooked stick. By using this method I got into the inner courtyard, and lying down on my side I looked in through the windows of the middle storeys, left open on purpose, and found the most splendid rooms imaginable. I saw the empress and the young princes in their different quarters, with their chief attendants. The empress smiled graciously at me and put her hand out of the window for me to kiss.

But I shan't give the reader too much information about all this, as I am keeping them for a larger work which is now almost ready for printing, which has a general description of the empire from its first days down through a succession of kings; it has detailed accounts of their wars, politics, laws, education and religion; their plants and animals and their unique habits and customs, along with other matters both strange and instructive. At the moment all I'm concerned with is giving an account of the events which took place during the nine months I stayed in the empire.

One morning, about a fortnight after I was set free, Reldresal, principal secretary (as they call it) for private affairs, came to my house with just one servant. He ordered his coach to wait some way away, and asked if I would talk with him for an hour. I gladly agreed, due to his nobility and personal merits as well as the many favors he had done me when I was petitioning the court. I offered to lie down so that he might be able to speak into my ear more easily, but he chose to let me hold him in my hand as we talked. He began by saying how pleased he was I was free, and said that he might take some credit for it. However he added that if things were different at court I might not have been freed so soon, for, he said, "As prosperous as we might appear to foreigners, we are troubled by two great problems: there are violent rebels at home and we are in danger of being invaded by a very powerful enemy from abroad.

"As for the first you must understand that for about seventy months there have been two competing parties in this empire, called Tramecksan and Slamecksan, who identify themselves by wearing high and low heeled shoes respectively, which is where they get their names. It is alleged that our country's tradition is to wear high heeled shoes, but whatever the truth of that his majesty has decided that he will only allow low heels in the government and in all the positions he has to give, as you must have seen. His majesty's heels are at least a drurr lower than those of any of his court (a drurr is about a fourteenth of an inch). There is so much hatred between these two parties that they will not eat, drink or talk with each other. We calculate that the Tarmecksan, or high heels, outnumber us, but we have all the power. We think that his imperial highness, the heir to the throne, has some sympathy towards the high heels; at least, we can plainly see that one of his heels is higher than the other, which makes him limp as he walks.

Now, in the middle of these internal struggles, we are threatened with invasion by the island of Blefuscu, which is the other great empire in the universe, almost as large and powerful as his majesty's. Our philosophers doubt your story that there are other kingdoms and states in the world inhabited by people as large as yourself, and they would sooner believe that you dropped from the moon or one of the stars, because it is certain that a hundred of you could quickly lay waste to his majesty's whole kingdom and empire. Besides, our histories go back five hundred years and they don't mention any regions except the great empires of Lilliput and Blefuscu. These two great powers have, as I was saying, been fighting a very hard war for the last thirty-six months.

It began in this way. Everyone agrees that the traditional way of breaking eggs before eating was at the large end, but the current king's grandfather, when he was a boy, happened to cut one of his fingers doing this. So his father, the emperor, ordered that all his people, on pain of great punishment, should break their eggs at the small end. Our histories show that the people resented this so much that there have been six rebellions caused by it, in one of which an emperor was killed and in another one was overthrown. These rebellions were always stirred up by the kings of Belfuscu, and when they were put down the exiles always ran to that empire. It is calculated that at various times eleven thousand people have been killed, rather than break their eggs at the small end. Many hundreds of weighty books have been written about the controversy, but the books of the Big-enders have been banned for a long time and it is against the law for them to have jobs. During all these troubles the emperors of Belfuscu frequently sent messages via their ambassadors saying that we were causing a division in religion, by going against a fundamental law of our great prophet Lustrog, in the fifty fourth chapter of the Blundecral (which is their holy book). However, we think this is twisting the text too far, as the actual words are, "all true believers crack their eggs at the best end."

"What the best end is seems, in my humble opinion, best left to every man's conscience, or at least to the chief magistrate, to decide. Now, the Big-ender exiles have got such a good place in the emperor of Blefescu's court, and had so much secret assistance and encouragement from their comrades who are still here, that a bloody war has raged between the two empires for three years, with varying results. During that time we have lost forty of our battleships, and many more smaller ones, along with thirty thousand of our best sailors and soldiers; it's thought the enemy has suffered even more heavily. However, they have now built a great fleet and are preparing to attack, and his imperial majesty, having great trust in your strength and bravery, has asked me to tell you how things stand."

I asked the secretary to offer my humble respects to the emperor, and to tell him that I thought it would be improper, as a foreigner, to meddle in internal affairs, but I was ready to risk my life to defend him and his country against all invaders.

Chapter V

[The author, through an extraordinary tactic, prevents an invasion. He is given a very noble title. Ambassadors arrive from the emperor of Blefuscu and want to negotiate a peace treaty. The empress' rooms are set on fire by accident; the author saves the rest of the palace.]

The empire of Blefuscu is an island to the northeast of Lilliput, separated by a channel only about eight hundred yards wide. I had not seen it, and once I had news of this intended invasion I avoided showing myself on that side of the coast in case I was seen by some of the enemy's ships; they knew nothing about me, as all communication between the two empires during the war had been forbidden on pain of death, and our emperor had banned all shipping. I told his majesty of a plan I had to seize the whole of the enemy's fleet, which our scouts had told us was waiting in the harbor, ready to sail with the first favourable wind. I consulted the most experienced sailors about the depth of the channel, which they had often measured. They told me that at high tide it was, in the middle, seventy glumgluffs deep, or about six feet by European measurement; the rest of it was not more than fifty glumgluffs. I walked over to the northeast coast, near to Blefescu, and lying down behind a mound I took out my little telescope and looked at the enemy's fleet in the harbor. It was made up of about fifty warships and a great number of troop carriers; I then came back to my house and ordered (which I had permission to do) a large amount of the strongest rope and iron bars.

The cable was about as thick as twine and the bars were the size of a knitting needle. I twisted three lengths of cable together to make it stronger, and for the same reason I twisted three iron bars together to make a hook. Having fixed up fifty hooks and cables I went back to the northeast coast, took off my coat, shoes and stockings and walked into the sea in my leather waistcoat about half an hour before high tide. I waded as fast as I could, and swam about thirty yards in the middle until I touched bottom again. I got to the fleet in less than half an hour. The enemy was so frightened by the sight of me that they leapt from their ships and swam to shore, where there couldn't have been fewer than thirty thousand of them. I took my tackle and fastened a hook into the hole on the prow of each boat, then tied all the cords together at the other end. While I was doing this the enemy fired several thousand arrows, many of which stuck in my hands and face and besides the pain this caused it put me off my task.

My greatest concern was for my eyes, which I would surely have lost if I hadn't thought of a plan. Amongst other things I kept a pair of spectacles in a private pocket which had not been searched by the emperor's men. I took these out and fixed them as firmly as I could on my nose, and armed like this I carried on with my work, in spite of the arrows, many of which hit the glass of my spectacles but had no other effect apart from slightly scratching them. I had now fastened all the hooks and I took the end of the cords in my hand and began to pull. However not a ship moved, as they were all firmly held by their anchors, so the biggest part of my plan was not done. So I let go of the cord, left the hooks in the ships and with my knife I determinedly cut the cables that held the anchors, getting about two hundred arrows in my face and hands. Then I picked up the knotted end of the cables which were tied to my hooks and very easily pulled fifty of the enemy's largest warships behind me.

The Blefuscudians, who had had no idea of what I was up to, were at first stunned with amazement. They had seen me cut the cables and thought I just meant to set the ships drifting or make them crash into each other, but when they saw the whole fleet moving together, with me pulling on the cables, they set up a scream of sorrow and despair which it is almost impossible to describe or imagine. Once I was out of danger I stopped to pull out the arrows that had stuck in my hands and face and rubbed on some of the ointment I have mentioned before, that was given to me when I first arrived. Then I removed my spectacles and after I waited an hour for the tide to drop I waded through the middle with my ships and arrived safely at the royal port of Lilliput.

The emperor and his whole court stood on the shore, waiting for the outcome of this great adventure. They saw the ships coming on in a large semicircle, but they couldn't see me as I was chest-deep in the water. When I got to the middle of the channel they were even more worried, as I was up to my neck, and the emperor assumed I had drowned and that the enemy's fleet were approaching to attack. However, his fears were soon calmed, for as the channel got shallower the nearer I got I was soon within earshot. I held up the end of the cable holding the fleet and shouted loudly, "Long live the mighty king of Lilliput!" This great prince welcomed me as I landed with all possible praise, and he made me a Nardac on the spot, which is their highest title.

His majesty asked that I would carry on and bring all the rest of his enemy's ships into his ports. Princes have such overwhelming ambitions that he seemed to want nothing less than to turn the whole empire of Blefuscu into a province and govern it with his own agent, and kill the Big-ender exiles, forcing people to break their eggs at the small end and so become king of the whole world. I tried to put him off this plan with arguments based on both politics and justice. I told him that I would never allow myself to be used to bring a free and brave people into slavery, and when the matter was debated in council the wisest ministers agreed with me.

This open and clear statement of mine was so against the schemes and politics of his imperial majesty that he would never forgive me. He mentioned it in a very cunning manner in council, where I was told that some of the wisest seemed to share my opinions, as they kept silent. However, there were others who secretly hated me, and they said some things which obliquely referred to me. From this time a plot began, led by his majesty and a group of his ministers, which was maliciously aimed at me. It came to a head within two months, and could have ended with my death. That's how little your service to a prince counts, when set against any refusal to let them have what they want.

About three weeks after this adventure ambassadors came from Blefuscu, humbly asking for peace, and a treaty was very soon agreed on very favourable terms for our emperor which I won't bother the reader with. There were six ambassadors, with about five hundred attendants, and their entry was very magnificent as was fitting for the status of their master and the importance of their business. When the treaty was agreed (in which I helped them on several points, using the credit I had, or appeared to have, at court) their excellencies, who had often privately thanked me for my friendship, paid me a formal visit. They began with many compliments about my bravery and kindness, invited me at the emperor's request to visit their kingdom, and asked me to show them some demonstrations of my great strength, of which they had heard so much. I was glad to do this, but I won't bother the reader with the details.

When I had entertained their excellencies for a while, to their great enjoyment and astonishment, I asked them to do me the honor of giving my humble respects to their emperor, whose goodness was well known and admired throughout the world, and whom I had decided to visit before I returned home. So the next time I had the honor of seeing our emperor I asked him permission to visit the Blefuscudian king. He granted me permission, but I noted that he did so in a very cold manner. I couldn't guess why this was, until a certain person told me that Flimnap and Bolgolam had implied that my talk with the ambassadors was a sign of treachery, of which I am sure my heart was completely free. This was the first time I began to see that courts and ministers were not always perfect.

It should be noted that these ambassadors spoke to me through an interpreter, the languages of the two empires being as different as any two in Europe, and each nation prided itself on the age, beauty and energy of their own language and scorned the other. But our emperor, having the upper hand through the seizure of their fleet, made them present their credentials and make their speeches in Lilliputian. It must be admitted that due to the great interchange of trade and commerce between the two kingdoms, from the exiles going to and fro, and from the custom of sending the young nobles and gentlemen out to see the world and learn about men and manners, there are very few decent people, or merchants, or sailors who live near the coast who can't hold a conversation in both languages. I discovered this some weeks later when I went to pay my respects to the emperor of Blefuscu, which as I shall tell you in the right place was a very happy trip for me, in the middle of hard times caused by the malice of my enemies.

The reader may remember that when I signed the contract which gave me back my freedom there were some conditions I did not like, as they were demeaning, and I only agreed to them out of extreme necessity. But now I was a Nardac, holding the highest rank in the empire, those tasks were seen as beneath me, and to be fair to the emperor he never mentioned them to me. However, it was not long before I was able to do his majesty a great service (or so I thought). I was woken at midnight by the cries of many hundreds of people at my door, and I was frightened at being so suddenly woken.

I heard the word "burglum" repeated over and over; several of the emperor's court made their way through the crowd and begged me to rush to the palace, where the empress' palace was on fire due to the carelessness of a maid of honor, who had fallen asleep while reading a romance. I leapt up at once, and as it was a moonlit night and orders were given to clear the way ahead of me I managed to get to the palace without trampling anyone. I found that there were already ladders up against the walls and there were plenty of buckets, but the water was some way away. These buckets were about the size of thimbles, and the poor people passed them to me as fast as they could, but the fire was so strong that they did little good. I might have easily smothered it with my coat, but unfortunately I had left it behind in my hurry and came out in just my leather waistcoat.

The situation seemed desperate and doomed, and this magnificent palace would definitely have been burned to the ground, if I had not, thinking unusually quickly for me, thought of a plan. The evening before I had drunk a lot of a very delicious wine called Glimigrim (the Belfuscudians call if Flunec, but ours is thought better) which is very diuretic. By the greatest luck I had not passed water since. The agitation of being so near the flames, and of the work I had done to put them out, made the wine produce urine, and I got rid of it in such a quantity, so well aimed, that in three minutes the fire was completely out, and the rest of that noble building, which took so many centuries to construct, was saved from ruin.

It was now daylight, and I retuned to my house without waiting to celebrate with the emperor, because although I had done a very great service I wasn't sure if his majesty would object to the way in which it had been achieved. It's a set law of the kingdom that it's a hanging offence for anybody, of whatever class, to urinate within the palace grounds. But I was a little comforted by a message from his majesty that he would give orders to his supreme court to give me a formal pardon. However, I did not get this, and I was told privately that the empress was revolted by what I had done and had moved right over to the other side of the palace, said that the buildings should never be repaired for her use and, in the presence of her most trusted advisers, swore to have revenge on me.

Chapter VI

[About the inhabitants of Lilliput, their knowledge, laws and customs and how they educate their children. How the author lived in that country. He defends a great lady.]

Although I am going to leave my description of this empire to another work, in the meantime I am happy to give the curious reader some general impressions. The normal size of the natives is under six inches, and all other animals, and the plants and trees, are exactly in proportion. For example, the largest horses and oxen are between four and five inches high, the sheep about an inch and a half or so, the geese are about the size of a sparrow, and so it goes down in size until you get to the smallest which were almost invisible to me. Nature has adapted the Lilliputians' eyes so they can see everything they need: they have very sharp vision but cannot see very far. To show how sharp their vision is to nearby objects, I have been delighted to watch a cook jointing a lark which was not as big as an ordinary fly, and see a young girl threading an invisible needle with invisible silk. Their tallest trees are about seven feet high: those are the ones in the royal park, which I could just about touch the tops of with a clenched fist. The other vegetables are in proportion to this, but I'll leave that to your imagination.

I will only mention their learning for now, which has flourished in all its forms amongst them for centuries. Their way of writing is very odd, not going from left to right like Europeans, nor right to left, like Arabians, nor up and down like the Chinese, but diagonally, from one corner of the paper to the other as that of English ladies does.

They bury their dead head downwards, because they believe that they will all be resurrected in a thousand years' time. They believe that at that point the earth (which they think is flat) will be turned upside down, so that when they come back to life they will be standing upright. The educated amongst them admit that this idea is absurd, but the practice carries on in agreement with popular superstition.

There are some laws and customs which are quite unique to this empire, and if they weren't so directly opposite to those of my own dear country I would be tempted to say a little in their defence. I only wish that there enforcement was as good. The first thing I shall mention is the law related to informers. All crimes against the state are punished very severely, but if the person accused clearly proves his innocence at his trial then the accuser is immediately given a shameful execution. Out of the accuser's goods and land the innocent person is compensated four ways: for the loss of his time; for the danger he faced; for the suffering of imprisonment; and for all the expenses he has incurred in his own defence. If the fortune of the accuser isn't big enough then the king makes up the difference. The emperor also gives the innocent man some token of his favor, and his innocence is proclaimed throughout the town.

They regard fraud as a worse crime than theft, and so usually punish it with death. They feel that care and vigilance and common sense is enough to keep a man safe from thieves, but that honesty has no defence against superior cunning, and as there must always be buying and selling, and dealing on credit, if fraud is permitted or ignored, or isn't punished by the law, the honest dealer will always lose out and the scoundrel will prosper. I remember once I was pleading with the emperor on behalf of a criminal who had cheated his master of a great sum of money, which he had been entrusted with and then run off; I told his majesty, by way of an excuse, that it was only a breach of trust. The emperor was horrified that I should use as a defence what to him was the worst feature of the crime, and I must say I didn't really have an answer, apart from the old cliché that different countries have different ways, and I must admit I was thoroughly embarrassed.

Although we usually regard reward and punishment as the foundations of government I have never seen any nation except Lilliput put this into practice. Anyone who can give proper proof that he has strictly observed the country's laws for seventy-three months can claim certain privileges, according to his rank and employment, and by the same criteria he is awarded a sum of money out of a fund set up for that purpose. He is also given the title of Snilpall, or legal, which is added to his name, though it cannot be inherited. These people thought there was a great weakness in our system when I told them that our law was only enforced through punishment, without any reward for good behavior. It is for this reason that the statue of Justice, in their law courts, is shown with six eyes, two in front, two behind and one each side, to show she looks at everything, and she has an open bag of gold in her right hand with a sheathed sword in her left, to show that she is more inclined to reward than to punish.

In choosing people for state jobs, they are more interested in good morals than great ability. They believe that government is a natural part of human nature, so normal human minds are well able to cope with ruling positions. They do not believe that God intended government to be a mystery only understood by a few people of outstanding genius, for there are rarely three of those born in a generation. They assume that truth, justice, mercy and so on can be shown by every man, and they think that by exercising these powers, helped by experience and good intentions, any man is capable of being in government, except in those posts where a course of study is needed. In fact they think that a lack of moral virtue can never be compensated by superior intelligence, so they try to keep jobs out of the hands of the highly intelligent, thinking that the mistakes made by a virtuous man through ignorance will never be so disastrous as those of a corrupt man who has the ability to order, increase and justify his bad deeds.

In the same way, a lack of belief in God disqualifies a man from public office. Lilliputians say that as kings say they are representing God there is nothing more ridiculous than a king employing someone who does not believe in the God he represents.

In telling of these and other laws I am only referring to the original institutions, not the terrible state they have fallen into through the corrupt nature of man. The reader should note that absurd practices such as gaining jobs by dancing on the tightrope, or titles and favors by leaping over sticks and creeping under them, were first introduced by the current emperor's grandfather, and they have reached their modern importance through the spread of parties and factions.

Ingratitude is punished in their system with death, as we have read it is in some other countries. They reason that a person who cannot be grateful to his benefactor will be an enemy of the rest of mankind to whom he owes nothing, and so such a man does not deserve to live.

Their ideas about the relationship between parents and children are very different to ours. The Lilliputians say that as the joining of men and women is driven by the law of nature, to continue and increase the species, men and women are joined together by desire like other animals, and that their fondness for their children comes from the same natural laws. For this reason they do not regard a child as owing anything to his father for creating him or to his mother for bringing him into the world. Considering the misery of human life it was not a favor to him, and his parents didn't mean it to be, for when they had sex they were thinking of something quite different. Through these thoughts and similar ones they think that parents are the last ones who should be trusted with the education and upbringing of their children, so every town has public nurseries where all parents, excepting cottagers and laborers, have to send their children to be raised and educated when they get to the age of twenty months, when they have reached a point when they should have some basic understanding. There are different types of schools for different abilities and both sexes. They have teachers who are skilled in preparing children for a life which will suit them according to their parents' rank, their own abilities and their inclinations. I'll say something about the male nurseries first, and then the female.

The nurseries for males of noble or high birth have serious and learned professors and their assistants. The children's food and clothes are plain and simple. They are taught the principles of honor, justice, courage, modesty, mercy, religion and patriotism. They are kept busy at all times except for eating and sleeping (which they only have short periods for) and two hours for physical exercise. They have servants to dress them until they are four years old, then they have to dress themselves, however noble they are. The female servants, the equivalent of our fifty year olds, only do the most menial tasks. They are never allowed to talk to servants but go together in small or large groups to their lessons, always accompanied by a professor or one of his assistants. In this way they avoid the early harmful ideas of stupidity and vice which our children pick up. Their parents are only allowed to see them twice a year for an hour. They may kiss them in greeting and saying goodbye, but a professor, who is always present on these occasions, will not allow them to whisper, or use any baby talk, or bring any presents of toys, sweets and so on. If a family fails to pay the correct price for the education and care of the child the king's officers collect it from them.

The nurseries for children of ordinary gentlemen, merchants, traders and craftsmen are managed in the same way, in proportion, except that those who are destined to go into trade are apprenticed at eleven years old, whereas the children of people of quality continue their academic exercises until they are fifteen (which is the same as twenty one for us); in the last three years they are not so strictly controlled. In the female nurseries the young girls of quality are educated much as the males are, except they are dressed by servants of their own sex, always in the presence of a professor or deputy, until they start to dress themselves at five years old.

If it is found that these nurses ever try to entertain the girls with terrible or silly stories or any of the other nonsenses practised by our chambermaids then they are publicly whipped three times round the city, imprisoned for a year, then banished for life to the most desolate part of the country. So the young ladies are as ashamed of being cowards and fools as the men are, and they reject all personal decoration apart from decency and cleanliness. I didn't see any difference in their education due to their sex, except that the lessons for the girls weren't quite as difficult, and that they were taught some rules about household matters, and they were not taught such a variety of subjects. The thinking amongst people of quality is that a wife should always be an intelligent and stimulating companion, as she will not always be young. When the girls are twelve years old, which amongst them is a marriageable age, their parents or guardians take them home, giving much thanks to the professors, and it's rare for the girls and their friends not to cry.

In the nurseries for females of a lower type the children are taught all kinds of work appropriate for their sex and their position: those sent to be apprentices leave at seven years old, and the rest are kept to eleven. The lower families who have children at the nurseries are obliged, in addition to their annual fee, which is kept as low as possible, to give the steward of the nursery a small monthly percentage of their earnings to pay for the child, so all parents have their finances limited by the law. The Lilliputians feel that nothing is more wrong than people bringing children into the world and then, so they have enough to enjoy themselves, asking the public to pay for their upbringing. As for the upper classes, they guarantee a certain amount for each child according to their status, and these funds are spent wisely and fairly.

The cottagers and laborers keep their children at home, as all they do is plough and harvest, so it's not of public benefit for them to be educated, but the old and diseased amongst them are cared for by hospitals, and begging is unknown in the empire.

Here it might amuse the curious reader to hear about my servants, and the way I lived in the country for nine months and thirteen days. Being of a practical turn of mind, and being forced by necessity, I made myself a nice enough table and chair out of the largest trees in the royal park. Two hundred seamstresses were employed to make me shirts, and bed and table linen, all of the strongest and thickest kind of material they could get, though even this they were forced to sew together in several thicknesses, as the thickest was considerably thinner than gauze. Their linen is usually three inches wide, and sold in lengths of three feet. The seamstresses measured me as I lay on the ground, one at my neck and another by my knee, each holding the end of a strong cord which a third measured with a ruler an inch long. Then they measured my thumb, and wanted no other measurements, for they calculate that twice round the thumb equals once round the wrist and so on for neck and waist, and by looking at my old shirt which I laid on the ground for them as a pattern they got my measurements perfectly.

Three hundred tailors were employed in the same way to make me clothes, but they had another way of measuring me. I kneeled down and they put a ladder up from the ground to my neck; one of them climbed up this ladder and dropped a plumbline from my collar to the floor, which was good for the length of my coat, but I measured my arms and waist myself. When my clothes were finished (they were made in my house, as none of their houses were big enough to hold them) they looked like the patchwork made by ladies in England, except that it was all one color.

I had three hundred cooks to prepare my food, in little huts built close to my house where they lived with their families, and each prepared me two dishes. I picked up twenty waiters in my hand, and put them on the table; a hundred more waited on the ground, some with dishes of meat and some with barrels of wine and other liquors on their shoulders. All of this the waiters on the table drew up by a very ingenious arrangement of cords, just as we draw a bucket out of a well in Europe. One of their plates of meat made a good mouthful, and a barrel of their drink was a fair swig. Their mutton isn't as nice as ours, but their beef is excellent. I have been given a joint so large that it took me three bites to eat it, though this was rare. My servants were amazed to see me eat it bones and all, as we eat a lark's leg at home. I usually ate their geese and turkeys in one mouthful, and I must admit they are far better than ours. I could fit twenty or thirty of their smaller birds on the end of my knife.

One day his imperial majesty, having been told about my lifestyle, asked that he and the empress, as well as the young princes of the blood of both sexes, might have the pleasure (that's what he called it) of dining with me. So they came, and I put them on the table on their thrones next to me with their guards around them. Flimnap, the lord high treasurer, also came with his white rod, and I could see that he looked at me with a sour expression, but I pretended not to notice. I ate more than usual, to show the prowess of men from my country and to impress the court. I have some secret reasons to believe that this visit from his majesty gave Flimnap a chance of doing me a bad turn with his master. He had always been my secret enemy, although he was nicer to me than his gloomy nature usually permitted. He told the emperor that the treasury was in a bad way and that they had to borrow money at very unfavourable rates, and that I had cost his majesty over a million and a half sprugs (their biggest gold coin, about the size of a sequin) and on the whole the emperor should take the first good chance of getting rid of me.

I must here clear the reputation of an excellent lady, who suffered innocently on my account. The treasurer became jealous of his wife due to the gossip of some evil people, who told him that her grace had become violently in love with me, and there was a great rumor in the court that she had paid me a private visit. I solemnly swear that this is a scandalous lie, completely without foundation other than that her grace was kind enough to be my friend. I admit she often came to my house, but always publicly and never with fewer than three others in the coach, usually her sister, young daughter and some good friend. Many other ladies of the court did the same. And I appeal to my servants to say if they ever saw a coach at my door without knowing who was visiting.

On these occasions, when a servant had alerted me, it was my custom to go to the door at once, and after I had greeted my visitors I would pick up the coach and two horses very carefully in my hands (if there were six horses the coachman always unharnessed four) and put them on the table where I had put a moveable rim, five inches high, to prevent accidents. I have often had four coaches and horses on my table at once, full of guests, while I sat on my chair and bent my face down towards them. When I was engaged with one set the coachmen would gently drive the others around the table. I have spent many agreeable afternoons in these conversations. But I defy the treasurer or his two informants (I'll name them, and let them make of it what they will) Clustril and Drunlo to prove that any person ever came to visit me secretly, apart from the secretary Redresal, who was sent at his majesty's orders, as I have said before.

I would not have written so much about this if it wasn't for the fact that the great lady's reputation is concerned, not to mention my own, even though I was a Nardac which the treasurer is not; all the world knows he is only a Glumglum, a title one step down, as in England a Marquis is a step down from a Duke – though I admit he was ahead of me in terms of his position as treasurer. These false rumors, which I heard about afterwards through a source it's not proper for me to mention, made the treasurer be very against his lady for a time, and against me even more so. Although at last he learned the truth and was reconciled with her he never forgave me, and I found that meant I started to lose favor from the emperor himself, who was too easily influenced by his favorite.

Chapter VII

[The author is informed of a plan to accuse him of high treason, so he escapes to Belfuscu. How he is welcomed there.]

Before I go on to tell of my leaving Lilliput, the reader should know about a secret plot which had been brewing against me for two months.

Up until now, in my whole life, I had not been involved with royal courts, as I was from humble stock. I had heard and read plenty about the behavior of great princes and ministers, but I never expected to find it played out in such a terrible fashion in such a remote country which I thought was governed by very different rules to those of Europe.

When I was preparing to make a visit to the emperor of Belfuscu a high up person of the court (whom I had given great help to at a time when he was very much in his majesty's bad books) came secretly to my house at night in a closed sedan chair, and without giving his name he asked to be let in.   The chair carriers were sent away and I put the chair, with his lordship in it, in my coat pocket and gave orders to a trusted servant that callers were to be told I was not feeling well and had gone to sleep. I locked the door, put the chair on the table as I usually did and sat down by it. When the usual greetings were done I saw that his lordship was looking very worried, and when I asked him why he asked me to patiently hear him out, as he had news which concerned my honor and my life. I made notes of his speech shortly after he left, and this is what he said:

"You should know," he said, "that several council committees have recently met, very secretly, to discuss you, and two days ago his majesty came to a decision. You know that Skyresh Bolgolam [Galbet, or high admiral] has been your mortal enemy almost ever since you arrived. I don't know how this started, but his hatred has increased greatly since your great victory over Befuscu, which overshadowed his glory as an admiral. This lord, in conjunction with Flimnap the high-treasurer, who everybody knows hates you because of the rumors about his wife, Limtoc the general, Lalcon the chamberlain and Balmuff the chief justice have drawn up accusations against you of treason and other crimes.

This introduction made me so cross, knowing my own merits and innocence, that I was going to interrupt him, but he begged me to be quiet and carried on:

"Out of gratitude for the favors you have done me I got information about the whole business, and a copy of the impeachment, so I'm risking my neck for you.

"Articles of impeachment against Quinbus Flestrin [the Man-Mountain]

"Article I
"By a law that was passed in the reign of his imperial majesty Calin Deffar Plune it is the law that anyone who urinates within the precincts of the royal palace shall be punished for high treason; in spite of this the Quinbus Flestrin, openly breaking this law, disguising his behavior as an attempt to put out the fire in the apartments of his majesty's dear empress, maliciously, traitorously and devilishly urinated, put out the fire in the apartments, which are in the precincts of the palace, and so he was breaking the law.

"Article II

"The said Quinbus Flestrin, having brought the imperial fleet of Blefuscu into the royal port, and having been told by his imperial majesty to seize all the other ships of that empire and reduce it to a province to be ruled by his viceroy, and to kill all the Big-ender exiles as well as all the people in that empire who would not immediately give up the Big-ender heresy, he, the aforementioned Flestrin, like a false traitor against his most wonderful, placid imperial majesty, asked to be excused from this duty, pretending that he did not wish to force innocent people to act against their will or destroy their lives or freedoms.

"Article III
"That when certain ambassadors arrive from the court of Blefuscu to negotiate a peace treaty with his majesty the aforementioned Flestrin acted like a false traitor in helping, encouraging, comforting and entertaining these ambassadors, even though he knew they were servants of a prince who had recently been openly hostile to his imperial majesty and waged war against him.

"Article IV.
"That the aforementioned Quinbus Flestrin, ignoring the duties of a faithful subject, is now preparing to make a journey to the court and empire of Blefuscu, which he has only had verbal permission for from his majesty, and he intends, under the cover of this permission, falsely and traitorously to help, comfort and encourage the emperor of Belfuscu, who as mentioned before was so recently an enemy and in open war against his majesty.

"There are some other clauses, but these are the most important, and I have read you a summary of them.

"In the many debates about this impeachment, it must be admitted that his majesty gave many signs of his mercy; he often mentioned the service you had done for him, and tried to soften your crimes. The treasurer and admiral insisted that you should be given the most painful and shameful death, by setting fire to your house at night with the general standing by with twenty thousand men, armed with poisoned arrows, to shoot you in the face and hands. Some of your servants were to be given secret orders to spread poison on your shirts and sheets, which would make you tear at your own flesh and die in agony. The general was of the same opinion, so for a long time there was a majority against you, but his majesty wanted, if possible, to spare your life, and at last brought the chamberlain round.

"When this happened Reldresal, principal secretary for private affairs, who has always proved to be your true friend, was ordered by the emperor to give his opinion, which he did, and what he said justified your good opinion of him. He admitted that your crimes were great, but said that there was still room for mercy, the greatest quality of a prince and one for which his majesty was so rightly famous. He said that your friendship was so well known that the most honorable jury might think he was biased, but he would freely offer his opinions as he had been asked to do. He said that if his majesty would acknowledge the services you had done and follow his own merciful nature by sparing your life and just ordering that you be blinded, he thought that justice would be done to an extent and the whole world would applaud the emperor's mercy, as well as the fair and generous nature of those who had the honor to be his counsellors. He also said that the loss of your eyes would not affect your strength, so you would still be of use to his majesty, and that blindness could add to courage by hiding dangers from us; the worry for your eyes was the greatest problem you had in bringing over the enemy's fleet, and it would be enough for you to see through the eyes of the ministers, which is all the greatest princes did.

This proposal met with furious objections from the whole board. Bolgolam, the admiral, couldn't keep his temper but jumped up in fury and said he didn't know how the secretary dared to propose saving the life of a traitor; that the services you had done in fact made your crimes worse; that you, who could by passing urine put out the fire in her majesty's apartments (which he mentioned with horror) might at some other time do the same thing and drown the whole palace; that the strength you had used to bring over the enemy's fleet could just as well be used, as soon as you were unhappy, to take it back; that he had good reason to suspect that you were a Big-ender at heart, and as treason begins in the heart then you were a traitor and you should therefore be executed.

"The treasurer thought the same; he showed what a burden you were on his majesty's finances and argued that soon you would be impossible to keep. He also said that the secretary's proposal of putting out your eyes would make things worse rather than better, because you would be like certain types of bird which, when blinded, eat faster and become fat quicker. His sacred majesty and the council, who are your judges, were fully satisfied that you are guilty, and that should be enough to condemn you to death without the formal proofs the strict law demands.

"But his imperial majesty, who was completely against your being executed, said that if the council thought losing your eyes wasn't punishment enough then some other punishment could be inflicted afterwards. And your friend the secretary, humbly asking to say something more, to answer the treasurer's objections, said that his excellency, who had sole control of the emperor's funds, could easily stop that evil by gradually cutting back your rations. That way you would gradually become weak and faint, lose your appetite and starve to death in a few months, and the threat of disease from your corpse wouldn't be so dangerous, as it would only be half the size. As soon as you died five or six thousand subjects could, in two or three days, cut the flesh from your bones and carry it away in carts to be buried far off, to prevent disease, and your skeleton could be left as a marvel for history.

"So, by the great friendship of the secretary, the whole business was compromised. It was strictly ordered that the project of gradually starving you should be kept secret, but the sentence of blinding you was entered into the minutes, with none disagreeing except Bolgolam the admiral who, as a crony of the empress, has always been pushed by her to ask for your death, as she has always hated you because of the infamous and illegal way you put out the fire in her apartment.

"In three days your friend the secretary will be told to come to your house and read the indictment to you and tell you that to show the great mercy and favor of his majesty and his council you will only be blinded, and his majesty doesn't question that you will humbly and gratefully agree to this. Twenty of his majesty's surgeons will come to see that operation is done well; they are going to fire arrows with very sharp points into your eyes as you lie on the ground.

"I leave it up to you what you do about this, and to avoid suspicion I must go as secretly as I came."

His lordship left, and I remained alone, very doubtful and confused. It was a custom for this prince and his ministers (things were very different, I was told, in earlier days) that, after the court had ordered any cruel execution, either to satisfy the monarch's resentment or the malice of a favorite, the emperor would make a speech to the whole council telling how merciful and kind he was, and that this was recognised throughout the world. This speech was published at once throughout the kingdom, and nothing terrified the people so much as this praising of his majesty's mercy. It was noted that the more the king was praised the more inhuman the punishment was, and the more innocent the victim as well. I must say that I personally, not being cut out by birth or education to be a courtier, was such a bad judge of these matters that I could never see the mercy and kindness in the sentence and thought (perhaps wrongly) that it was harsh rather than kind. I considered asking for a trial, as although some of the facts in the indictment we true I hoped I could show that there were extenuating circumstances. But as I had read many accounts of state trials, which always ended up the way the judges wanted them to, I didn't dare rely on such a risky business in such a tough spot, with such powerful enemies against me. At one point I was very keen on fighting back, for while I had my freedom the whole of that empire could hardly beat me, and I could easily smash their city to pieces with stones. However, I soon rejected the idea, horrified, thinking of the promise I had made the emperor, the kindness I had had from him and the high title of Nardac he had given me. And I hadn't got into the habits of courtiers so much to think that his current harshness to me meant I was freed from my previous obligations.

At last I hit on a plan which might let me in for some criticism, possibly rightly; I must admit that the saving of my sight and so my freedom is down to my own hastiness and lack of experience. If I had known then what I have since learned from observing other courts what princes and ministers were like, and how they treated criminals who had committed lesser offences than mine, I would quickly and willingly have accepted such a light punishment. But I had the impetuousness of youth, and as I had his imperial majesty's permission to visit the emperor of Blefuscu I took the chance, before the three days were up, of sending a letter to my friend the secretary telling him that I was setting out for Blefuscu that morning, as I had been given permission to do. I didn't wait for an answer but went round to the side of the island where our fleet lay. I grabbed a large battleship, tied a rope to the prow and, unhooking the anchors, I stripped off and put my clothes (including my quilt, which I had carried under my arm) into the boat and pulled it after me, wading and swimming, until I arrived at the royal port of Blefuscu, where the people had been expecting me for a long time. They gave me two guides to show me the way to the capital city, which has the same name. I carried them in my hands until I got within two hundred yards of the gate, when I asked them to tell one of the secretaries I had arrived and that I was waiting for his majesty's orders. In about an hour I got a reply that his majesty, with his family and the highest court officials, were coming out to meet me. I went forward a hundred yards. The emperor and his attendants got off their horses, and the empress and her ladies got out of their coaches, and I couldn't see that they were frightened or worried. I lay on the ground to kiss the emperor and empress' hands.

I told his majesty that I had come as I said I would, with the permission of my master the emperor, to have the honor of meeting such a great king and to offer him any service I could which did not clash with my duties to my own prince. I didn't tell him about my conviction, because I had not been officially informed about it and could pretend to be completely ignorant of it. Also I didn't think that the emperor would find out that I knew, while I was away, but I soon found out I was wrong.

I won't bother the reader with a detailed account of my reception at this court, which was what one would expect from the generosity of such a great prince, nor of the inconvenience of not having a house or a bed, so I was forced to sleep on the ground, wrapped up in my quilt.

Chapter VIII

{The author has a stroke of luck which enables him to leave Belfuscu, and after some troubles returns safely to his homeland.]

Three days after I arrived I walked, out of curiosity, to the northeast coast of the island. I saw, about a mile and a half off in the sea, something that looked like an overturned boat. I pulled off my shoes and stockings and walked in two or three hundred yards, with the object being driven towards me by the tide. I could then clearly see that it was a real boat, which I guessed might have been washed off a ship in a storm. I immediately went back to the city and asked his majesty to lend me twenty of the biggest ships he had left, after the loss of his fleet, and three thousand sailors under the orders of his vice-admiral. This fleet sailed round the coast, while I went the most direct way, to the place where I had first seen the boat. I found the tide had driven it even closer. The sailors were given ropes, which I had already twisted to a suitable thickness. When the ships arrived I stripped off and waded in until I came within a hundred yards of the boat, after which I had to swim to reach it. The seamen threw me the end of the cord, which I fastened to a hole at the front of the boat, and I fastened the other end to a warship; but I found I couldn't do as I wished, as I was not able to work, being out of my depth.

Because of this I was forced to swim behind and push the boat forward as often as I could with one hand. The tide was in my favor, and I managed to get far enough that I could just touch the bottom with my chin above water. I rested for two or three minutes and then gave the boat another push, and carried on like that until the sea was no higher than my armpits, and now, with the hardest part being done, I took out my other ropes, which were stored in one of the ships, and fastened them first to the boat and then to nine of the ships which had followed me. The wind was blowing in the right direction, so the sailors pulled and I shoved until we got forty yards from the shore. By waiting until the tide was out I had the boat on dry land, and with the help of two thousand men, with ropes and machines, I managed to turn it the right way up and found it was hardly damaged.

I won't bother the reader with the trouble I had, with the help of some oars, which took me ten days to make, to get my boat to the royal port of Blefuscu, where a great crowd gathered to greet my arrival, full of amazement at the sight of such a huge vessel. I told the emperor that good luck had sent me this boat to take me to some place where I could get a passage back to my homeland, and begged him to order that I be given materials to repair it, and to give me permission to leave. After some polite attempts to dissuade me he was pleased to give me permission. I was very surprised throughout this time that I didn't hear of any messengers being sent from my emperor to the court of Blefuscu. But I was told privately afterwards that his imperial majesty, never guessing that I had any warning of his plans, believed that I had only gone to Blefuscu to keep my commitment to make the visit he had given me permission for, which everyone at our court knew about, and that I would come back in a few days. But eventually he became worried at my long absence, and after consulting with the treasurer and the rest of the conspiracy a nobleman was sent with a copy of the indictment against me. This messenger had instructions to tell the king of Blefuscu about the great mercy of his master, who was pleased to punish me no further than blinding me. He also had instructions to tell him that I was a fugitive from justice and that if I did not return within two hours that I would be stripped of my title of Nardac and declared a traitor. He also added that in order to keep peace and friendship between the two empires his master expected that his counterpart in Blefuscu would order that I be sent back to Lilliput, tied hand and foot, to be punished as a traitor.

The emperor of Blefuscu, having taken three days debating with his advisers, sent back an answer full of politeness and excuses. He said that his brother knew it was impossible to have me tied up, and though I had deprived him of his fleet he was very much in my debt for the favors I had done him in negotiating the peace terms. However, both of them would soon be able to relax, for I had found a great boat on the shore which could carry me on the sea, and he had given orders to refurbish it, with my help and instructions, and he hoped that within a few weeks both empires would be freed from such a great burden.

The messenger went back to Lilliput, and the king of Blefuscu told me everything that had happened. At the same time he told me (in strict secrecy) that he would be glad to protect me if I carried on serving him. Although I believed that he was sincere I had decided that I would never again trust a prince or his ministers if I could help it, and so I humbly asked him to excuse me, though I thanked him for his kindness. I told him that as luck, whether good or evil, had thrown a boat in my path, I had decided to risk the ocean rather than cause conflict between two such great kings. I didn't find the emperor at all unhappy about this, and I discovered accidentally that he was very glad of my decision and so were most of his ministers.

These events made me speed up my plans for departure, and the court, wanting to see me gone, were very happy to help. Five hundred workmen were employed to make two sails for my boat, under my instructions, by sewing together their strongest linen, folded over thirteen times. I took great care over making ropes and cables by twisting ten, twenty or thirty of their thickest and strongest ones. I happened to find a great stone on the seashore, after a long search, and I used that as an anchor. I had the fat of three hundred cows to grease my boat and other things. I had great work cutting down the largest trees to make oars and masts, though I was greatly helped by his majesty's ship carpenters who helped me sand them down after I had cut them into the rough shapes.

In about a month, when everything was ready, I asked his majesty to give me his orders and to say goodbye. The emperor and royal family came out of the palace, I lay down on my face to kiss his hand, which he was kind enough to give me, and the empress and young princes of the blood did so too. His majesty gave me fifty purses with two hundred sprugs in each one, as well as a full length picture of him, which I immediately put in one of my gloves to stop it being damaged. The ceremonies of farewell were too many to bother the reader with at the moment.

I put the carcasses of a hundred oxen and three hundred sheep in the boat, with a matching quantity of bread and drink, and as much ready prepared meat as four hundred cooks could provide. I took six live cows and two bulls, and the same number of ewes and rams, meaning to take them to my country and breed them. To feed them I put in a good bundle of hay and a bag of corn. I would have liked to take a dozen natives, but the emperor would not allow this by any means, and as well as ordering a careful search of my pockets his majesty put me on my honor not to take away any of his subjects, even if they agreed and wanted to go.

Having got everything ready as well as I could, I set sail on the twenty fourth of September 1701 at six in the morning. When I had gone about twelve miles north, the wind coming from the southeast, at six in the evening I spotted a small island, about a mile and a half to the northwest. I went on and anchored on the sheltered side of the island, which seemed to be uninhabited. I ate and then slept. I slept well for about six hours, as I guessed, for the sun rose about two hours after I woke. It was a clear night. I ate my breakfast before sunrise, and having raised the anchor and with a favourable wind I set off in the same direction I had taken before, guided by my pocket compass. I was trying, if possible, to reach one of the islands which I believed lay northeast of Tasmania. I found nothing all that day, but the next day, at about three in the afternoon, when I had as I reckoned sailed about seventy miles from Blefuscu, I saw a sail going southeast. I shouted to her but got no answer, but as the wind dropped I started to catch her up. I put up as much sail as I could, and in half an hour she spotted me, then she raised her flag and fired a gun. I can hardly explain how happy I was at the hope of seeing my beloved country again and the dear people I had left there. The ship took down her sails and I reached her between five and six in the evening on September 26th, and I was thrilled to see she flew the English flag. I put the cows and sheep in my coat pockets and climbed on board with all my little store of provisions. The ship was an English trading ship, coming back from Japan via the Pacific and Atlantic; the captain, Mr.John Biddel of Deptford, was a very kind man and an excellent sailor.

We were now in the latitude of thirty degrees south. There were about fifty men in the crew, and among them was an old friend of mine, Peter Williams, who told the captain I was a good man. He treated me kindly, and wanted me to tell him where I had come from and where I was going. I told him briefly but he thought I had been turned mad by the trials I had suffered. Then I took my black cattle and sheep out of my pocket, and after he got over his astonishment he was convinced I was telling the truth. Then I showed him the gold the emperor of Blefuscu had given me, and his majesty's full length portrait, and some other strange things from that country. I gave him two purses of two hundred sprugs and promised that when we got to England I would make him a present of a pregnant cow and a sheep.

I shall not bother the reader with a detailed account of this voyage, which was generally very pleasant. We got to England on the 13th of April, 1702. I had only one piece of bad luck, which was that one of the rats on board stole one of my sheep; I found her bones in a rat hole, picked clean. I got the rest of my cattle safely ashore and put them out to graze on a bowling green at Greenwich, where the fineness of the grass made them eat very well, which was not what I had feared. I couldn't possibly have kept them alive for such a long voyage if the captain hadn't given me some of his best ship's biscuit which, ground to a powder and mixed with water, was their constant food. In the short time I stopped in England I made a good profit by showing my cattle to the gentry and others, and before I made my second voyage I sold them for six hundred pounds. When I finished my last voyage I found that the breed has flourished, especially the sheep, and I hope that the fineness of the fleeces will be very useful to the woollen industry.

I stayed just two months with my wife and family, as my hunger to see foreign countries wouldn't let me stay longer. I left my wife with fifteen hundred pounds and settled her in a good house in Redriff. I took the rest of my wealth with me, partly in money and partly in goods, hoping to improve my fortunes. My eldest uncle, John, had left me some land near Epping, which brought in about thirty pounds a year, and I had a long lease on the Black Bull inn on Fetter Lane, which brought in as much again, so there was no danger that my family would need to be looked after by the parish. My son Johnny, named after his uncle, was at grammar school and a good child. My daughter Betty (who has now made a good marriage and has children) was then helping with the house. I left my wife and the boy and the girl, with tears on both sides, and boarded the Adventure, a three hundred ton merchant ship, headed for Surat in India. Captain John Nicholas of Liverpool was the commander. But the story of this voyage must wait for the second part of my book.

Part II: A Voyage to Brobingnag

Chapter I

[A great storm is described. A longboat is sent to get water and the author goes with it to look at the country. He is left on the shore, taken by one of the natives and carried to a farmer's house. There is a description of the welcome he found there and several accidents which took place. The inhabitants are described.]

As I have been assigned, by my nature and my luck, an active and restless life, two months after I came home I left my homeland again and joined a ship off the coast of Kent on June 20th 1702. The boat was the Adventure, commanded by captain John Nicholas, a Cornishman, heading for Surat. We had a very favourable wind all the way to the Cape of Good Hope, where we stopped for fresh water; but finding a leak in the boat we took off our cargo and spent the winter there, then the captain fell sick with a fever and we could not leave the Cape until the end of March. We then set sail, and had a good voyage until we passed the Straits of Madagascar, but once we got to the north of that island, on a latitude of about five degrees south, the winds, which in that region blow equally from north and west from December to May, began on April 19th to blow much stronger and more from the west than usual, for twenty days in a row. During this period we were driven a little way east of the Maluku Islands, about three degrees north of the equator, as our captain found through an observation he made on May 2nd. At that time the wind dropped and it was perfectly calm, which I was very happy about. But he, being a man with much experience of those seas, warned us all to get ready for a storm, which came the next day; the southern wind, called the southern monsoon, had begun. It looked as though it could overturn us, so we took down our sprit-sail and got ready to take in the fore-sail; we checked that the guns were all tied down and took in the mizzen. The ship lay very broad off, so we thought it better spooning before the sea, than trying or hulling.

We brought in the fore-sail and set it, and hauled back the fore-sheet – the helm was hard over. The ship stood up well. We belayed the fore down-haul; but the sail was split, and we hauled down the yard, and got the sail into the ship, and unbound all the things clear of it. It was a very fierce storm, and the sea was wild and dangerous. We hauled off upon the lanyard of the whipstaff, and helped the helmsman with the wheel. We could not get our topmast down but left it up which was better for the ship and ran better through the sea. When the storm was over we put up the fore-sail and main-sail and brought the ship round. Then we put up the mizzen, main top-sail and the fore top-sail. We were sailing east northeast with the wind coming from the southwest. We got the starboard tacks aboard and cast off our weather-braces and lifts; we set in the lee-braces, and hauled forward by the weather-bowlings, and hauled them tight, and belayed them, and hauled over the mizen tack to windward, and kept her full and by as near as she would lie.

[Editor's note: Swift is here deliberately lampooning the incomprehensible talk of sailors, which makes a full rendering in modern English both impossible and pointless]

During this storm, which was followed by a strong west-south-west wind, we were carried, by my reckoning, about fifteen hundred miles to the east, so that even the oldest sailor on board could not judge where we were. We had plenty to eat, our ship had held up well and our crew were all healthy, but we were desperate to get drinking water. We thought it would be best to carry on the same course rather than turn to the north, which might have brought us to the northwest of central Asia and so on to the Arctic.

On the 16th of June 1703 the boy on lookout duty saw land. On the 17th we saw a great island, or continent (we didn't know which), on the south side of which there was a small spit of land sticking out into the sea, and a creek too shallow to hold a ship which weighed over a hundred tons. We anchored within a couple of miles of this creek and the captain sent a dozen men out in a longboat, well armed, with jugs to collect fresh water, if there was any. I asked if I could go with them, to see the country and see what I could find. When we came to the shore we could see no river or spring, nor any sign of inhabitants. So our men wandered around on the shore looking for a stream running into the sea while I walked about a mile the other way where I found that the country was bare and rocky. I started to feel tired, and as there was nothing to see of any interest I strolled back towards the creek. I had a clear view of the sea and I saw that our men were already in the boat and rowing furiously for the ship. I was going to yell after them, though it wouldn't have been much use, when I saw a huge creature walking after them into the sea, as fast as he could. He went not much deeper than his knees, and took great strides, but our men had a lead of a mile and a half and as the sea was full of sharp pointed rocks the monster could not catch them. I was told this afterwards, for I did not stay to see how events panned out but ran as fast as I could the way I had come. I then climbed a steep hill, which gave me a view of the countryside. I found that it was all farmland, but what surprised me was the length of the grass; in the fields which seemed to be used for growing hay it was about twenty feet high.

I got onto a main road, which is what I thought it was, though for the inhabitants it was only a footpath through a barley field. I walked on here for some time, but I could not see much on either side as it was nearly harvest time and the corn was at least forty feet high. It took me an hour to get to the edge of this field, which was fenced with a hedge at least a hundred and twenty feet high, and the trees were so tall I could not figure out their height. There was a stile to get from this field into the next one. It had four steps and at the top there was a stone one had to climb over. It was impossible for me to climb this stile, as every step was six feet high, and the stone on the top was about twenty high. I was trying to find a gap in the hedge when I saw one of the natives in the next field, coming towards the stile. He was the same size as the person I had seen in the sea chasing our boat; he was as tall as a normal church tower with a spire, and as near as I could guess he took ten yards with each step. I was both utterly amazed and completely terrified, and I ran to hide myself in the corn, from where I saw him on the top of the stile looking back into the next, right hand field. I heard him call with a voice many times louder than a megaphone, but it was so high up in the sky that at first I thought it must be thunder.

At that seven monsters of the same type came towards him with sickles in their hands, and each one was about the size of six scythes. These people weren't as well dressed as the first one, and they seemed to be his servants or laborers, for when he spoke to them they came to cut the corn in the field where I lay. I kept as far from them as I could, but it was very difficult for me to move, as the stalks of corn were sometimes less than a foot apart, so that it was nearly impossible for me to get between them. However, I managed to get through to a place where the corn had been twisted by rain and wind. I couldn't go a step further, as the stalks were so tangled that I could not get through, and the ears of corn were so sharp and pointed that they stabbed through my clothes into my skin. At the same time I could hear the reapers less than a hundred yards behind me. Being absolutely exhausted by the effort, and completely overcome with sorrow and despair, I lay down between two furrows and wished I was dead.

I wept for my sad widow and fatherless children. I cursed my own stupidity and recklessness in trying a second voyage against all the advice of my friends and relations. With my mind whirling I couldn't help thinking of Lilliput, whose inhabitants thought I was the greatest thing to have ever appeared in their world, where I could pull along an imperial fleet by hand and do other things that will always be remembered in that empire, and those who come after will hardly believe them, though millions witnessed them. I thought how terrible it would be for me to be as insignificant in these parts as a Lilliputian would be in our country. But I thought that this would be the least of my worries, for as we know that human beings are more savage and cruel the bigger they get what could I expect but that I would just make a snack for the first of these enormous barbarians who found me? The philosophers are certainly right when they tell us that nothing is big or small except in comparison to other things. It might have been the case that the Lilliputians could find some country where the people were as small in comparison to them as they were to me. Who knows, maybe there is somewhere we haven't yet discovered where even this enormous race would seem equally small.

Sacred and confused as I was I could not keep out these thoughts, when one of the reapers, coming within ten yards of the furrow where I was lying, made me realise that at his next step I would be squashed to death underfoot or cut in two with his sickle. So when he was about to move again I screamed with the strength of fear, which made the huge creature break stride; he looked around him for some time and at last spotted me on the ground. He looked at me for a while, like someone who is trying to grab a small dangerous animal but be careful that it can't scratch or bite him, as I have sometimes done myself with a weasel in England. Eventually he grabbed me round the middle from behind, between his forefinger and thumb, and carried me up to three yards in front of his eyes where he could get a better look at me.

I guessed what he was doing, and luckily I had the common sense not to struggle at all as he held me in the air over sixty feet above the ground, although he pinched my sides painfully, for fear of slipping through his fingers. All I did was turn my face to the sky and place my hands together as if I was praying, and speak some words in a polite sad voice which suited my condition, for I feared that any moment he would smash me to the ground as we usually do with any horrid little animal which we want to destroy. But luckily he seemed pleased with my voice and gestures and looked on me as a novelty, being amazed to hear me speaking, although he couldn't understand the words. In the meantime I couldn't stop myself groaning and weeping and turning my head towards my sides, to show him how much he was hurting me with the pressure of his thumb and forefinger. He seemed to understand me, for he lifted up the lapel of his coat, gently put me in it, and ran straight to his master, who was a well-to-do farmer, the same person I had seen in the first field.

The farmer having (as I imagined from their conversation) been told about me by his servant, took a small piece of straw, about the size of a walking stick, and lifted the lapels of my coat, which he seemed to think was some sort of skin nature had given me. He blew my hair aside to get a better look at my face. He called his workers together and asked them (I later learned) if they had ever seen any other little creatures like me in the fields. He then gently put me on the ground on my hands and knees, but I got up at once and walked slowly to and fro, to show them that I had no plans to escape. They all sat around me in a circle to get a better look at me. I took off my hat and made a low bow to the farmer. I fell on my knees, lifted up my hands and eyes, and spoke several words as loud as I could. I took a purse of gold out of my pocket and meekly presented it to him. I put it into the palm of his hand and he held it up close to his eye to see what it was, then turned it over several times with the point of a pin which he took from his sleeve, but he couldn't work out what it was. So I signalled that he should put his hand on the ground. I then took the purse and, opening it, poured out all the gold into his palm. There were six Spanish four pistole coins and twenty or thirty smaller ones. I saw that he wet the tip of his little finger with his tongue and picked up one of the largest coins, and then another, but he still seemed to have no idea what they were. He signalled that I should put them back in my purse and the purse back in my pocket, which, after offering it to him several more times, I thought I had better do.

The farmer, by this time, was convinced I was a thinking creature. He often spoke to me, but the sound of his voice battered my ears like the noise of a watermill, though his words were shaped well enough. I answered as loudly as I could in several languages, and he often put his ear two yards away, but it was all useless, for we were completely incomprehensible to each other. He then sent his servants off to their work and took his handkerchief out of his pocket; he folded it over and put it on his left hand, indicating that I should step into it, as I could easily do for it was not over a foot thick. I thought I should do as he asked, and so I wouldn't fall I laid down full length on the handkerchief; he wrapped me up in the edges and carried me home to his house like this. When he got there he called his wife and showed me to her, but she screamed and jumped back, as English women do when they see a toad or a spider. However, when she had watched me for awhile, and seen how well I obeyed the signs her husband made, she soon came round and bit by bit grew very fond of me.

It was about twelve noon, and a servant brought in dinner. It was only one large course of meat (suitable plain farmer's food) in a dish about twenty-four feet in diameter. At the table were the farmer, his wife, three children and an old grandmother. When they had sat down the farmer put me some way from him on the table, which was thirty feet from the floor. I was very afraid, and kept as far as I could from the edge out of fear of falling. The wife minced up some meat and crumbled some bread on a plate then put it in front of me. I made a low bow to her, took out my knife and fork and began to eat, which pleased them greatly. The mistress then sent her maid for a little shot glass, which held about two gallons, and filled it with drink; I picked this cup up in both hands with much difficulty and respectfully drank to her ladyship's health, speaking as loudly as I could in English. This made all of them laugh so heartily that I was almost deafened by the racket. The drink tasted like a weak cider, and was not unpleasant. Then the master signalled that I should come to the side of his plate, but as I walked on the table, being absolutely amazed all the time, as the kind reader will find easy to imagine and forgive, I stumbled over a crust of bread and fell flat on my face, though I wasn't hurt.

I got up at once, and seeing the good people were very worried I took my hat (which I was holding under my arm for politeness) and waving it over my head I gave three cheers to show that I was not hurt. But as I went forwards towards my master (that is what I shall call him from now on) his youngest son, who sat next to him, a little rascal of about ten, grabbed me by the legs and held me so high in the air that I shook all over. But his father grabbed me off him and at the same time gave him such a slap on the left ear that it would have knocked down a dozen horses in England, and he ordered that he be taken from the table. But I was worried the boy might take his revenge, and knowing how naturally spiteful our children are to sparrows, rabbits, kittens and puppies I fell on my knees and pointed to the boy, making my master understand, as much as I could, that I wanted him to forgive his son. The father agreed, and the lad sat back down, so I went to him and kissed his hand, which my master took and made him stroke me gently with it.

In the middle of dinner my mistress' favorite cat jumped into her lap. I heard a noise behind me like a dozen weavers at work, and, turning, I found it was the purring of that animal, which seemed three times larger than an ox, as I judged from what I could see of her head and one of her paws as her mistress stroked and fed her. The fierceness of this creature's face shook me greatly, although I was at the opposite end of the table and her mistress held her tight to make sure she didn't spring at me and grab me in her claws. But it turned out there was no danger as the cat took no notice of me, even when she put me down within three yards of her. As I have always been told (and I've found it true on my travels), running or showing fear in front of a fierce animal is the best way to provoke an attack, so I decided, at this moment, to show no fear. I walked boldly to and fro in front of the cat's face, coming within half a yard of her, and she backed off as if she was the one who was afraid of me. I was less worried about the dogs, of which three or four had come into the room, as they usually do in farmer's houses. One of them was a mastiff, the same size as four elephants, and another was a greyhound, rather taller but not so bulky.

When dinner was almost over the nurse came in with a one year old child in her arms, which saw me at once and began a wail which you could have heard from London Bridge to Chelsea, as children usually do, wanting me as a toy. The mother, indulging her child, lifted me up and held me out to it. He grabbed me by the middle and put my head in his mouth, which made me roar so loudly that the child was scared and dropped me, and I would definitely have broken my neck if the mother hadn't caught me in her apron. The nurse, to quiet the child, tried to amuse it with a rattle which was a kind of hollow drum filled with great stones, fastened to the child's waist with a rope. Nothing worked, and she was forced to use the last resort of suckling it. I must say that nothing has ever disgusted me as much as the sight of her monstrous breast, and I don't know what I can compare it to to give the curious reader and idea of its size, shape and color. It was at least six feet high and couldn't have been less that sixteen feet round. The nipple was about half the size of my head, and the color of that and the aureole, covered in spots, pimples and freckles, couldn't have been more disgusting; I had a good view of it, as she sat down to be more comfortable as she breastfed and I was standing on the table. This made me think about the lovely skins of our English ladies, which only look so beautiful to us because they are our size, and their flaws can only be seen through a magnifying glass, which experience shows us makes the smoothest and whitest skins look rough, coarse and an unpleasant color.

I remember when I was in Lilliput the complexion of those little people seemed to me to be the loveliest in the world. When I spoke of this with a close friend of mine there, a clever man, he said that my face looked much fairer and smoother when he looked at me from the ground than it did up close when I picked him up in my hand, which he said was at first a very shocking sight. He said that he could see great holes in my skin, that my stubble was ten times stronger than boar bristles, and my complexion was made up of several unpleasant colors; I must say in my defence that I am as good looking as most of my countrymen, and have very little sunburn from my travels. On the flipside when we spoke of the ladies of the emperor's court he would tell me that one had freckles, another's mouth was too big, a third had a big nose, all flaws which I couldn't make out. I suppose that this is obvious enough, but I had to make it clear in case the reader might think that these huge creatures are actually deformed; I must in fairness say that they are an attractive people and the features of my master's face when I looked at him from sixty feet away seemed very well shaped. When dinner was over my master went out to see his laborers and, as I guessed from his voice and gestures, told his wife to take good care of me. I was very tired and wanted to sleep. My mistress realised this and put me down on her own bed and covered me with a clean white handkerchief which was larger and rougher than the mainsail on a warship.

I slept about two hours, and dreamed that I was at home with my wife and children, which made my sadness worse when I woke up and found myself alone in a massive room, between two and three hundred feet wide and over two hundred high, lying in a bed twenty yards wide. My mistress was doing her household chores and had locked me in. The bed was eight yards from the floor. The call of nature meant I had to get down; I didn't dare to shout out and if I had it would have been pointless, given how small my voice was and how great the distance from the room where I lay to the kitchen where the family were. While I was in this plight two rats crept up the curtains and ran sniffing to and fro over the bed. One of them came up almost to my face, and I jumped up in a fright and drew my sword to defend myself. These horrible animals had the nerve to attack me from both sides at once, and one of them put his forefeet on my shoulders, but I was lucky enough to cut his belly open before he could do my any mischief. He fell down at my feet, and the other one, seeing what had happened to his comrade, made his escape, but not without a good wound to his back which I gave him as he fled which made the blood run from him. After this adventure I walked to and fro on the bed for a while, to get my breath back and get over my fright. These creatures were about the size of a large mastiff, but much more agile and fierce, so that if I'd taken off my sword-belt before I went to sleep I would definitely have been torn to pieces and eaten. I measured the tail of the dead rat and found it was an inch short of two yards. It made me feel sick to drag the carcass off the bed, where it was lying bleeding; I saw it still had some sign of life, but I quickly got rid of it with a strong slash across the neck.

Soon after my mistress came into the room, and seeing me all bloody she ran to me and took me up in her hand. I pointed to the dead rat, smiling and making other signs to show I had not been hurt. She was overjoyed, and called the maid to pick up the rat in a pair of tongs and throw it out of the window. Then she put me on a table, where I showed her my bloody sword, wiped it on my lapels and put it back in its scabbard. I had to do more than one thing that nobody else could do for me, and so I tried to make my mistress understand that I wanted to be put on the floor. When she had done this my shyness meant that I couldn't express myself any further, except to point to the door and bow several times. The good woman, with much difficulty, eventually understood what I meant and picked me up in her hand and took me into the garden, where she put me down. I went about two hundred yards away and, signing that she should not follow or look at me, hid between two sorrel leaves and did my business.

I hope that the polite reader will forgive me for dwelling on this and other details, which, however insignificant they might seem to low and vulgar minds, will certainly fire the thoughts and imagination of thinking men, and make them use their conclusions beneficially in private and public life, which was my only intention in presenting this and other accounts of my travels to the world. That's why I have been scrupulously truthful, without putting in any showy elements of scholarship or style. But the whole of this voyage made such a great impression on me, and is so clear in my memory, that in writing it down I didn't leave out a single thing that happened. However, on carefully rereading it, I crossed out several less important things in my first draft for fear of being criticised as being dull and shallow, which is what travellers are often accused of, perhaps not without reason.

Chapter II

[A description of the farmer's daughter. The author is taken to a market town, and then to the capital. The journey is described.]

My mistress had a nine year old daughter, an advanced child for her age, who was very good at needlework and skilled at dressing the baby. She and her mother fitted up the baby's cradle for me for sleeping; the cradle was put in a small drawer from a cabinet and the drawer was put on a shelf on the wall to keep off the rats. This was my bed the whole time I stayed with those people, though it was gradually made more comfortable as I began to learn their language and was able to tell them what I wanted. This young girl was so dextrous that after she had seen me undress once or twice she was able to dress and undress me, though I never asked her to if she left me to do it myself. She made me seven shirts and some other things out of the finest available cloth, which was coarser than sackcloth, and she always washed them for me herself. She was also my teacher to help me learn the language: when I pointed to anything she told me what it was called in her language, so that in a few days I was able to ask for anything I wanted. She was very good natured and less than forty feet high, as she was small for her age. She called me Grildrig, and the family started using the name and afterwards the whole country did. The word is the equivalent of "nanunculus" in Latin, "homunceletino" in Italian and "manikin" in English. She was the main reason I stayed alive in that country, and we were never apart the whole time I was there. I called her my Glumdalclitch ("little nurse") and I would be most ungrateful if I didn't mention her care and affection for me, and I sincerely wish that I could repay her as she deserves, instead of being the unhappy, though innocent, reason for her disgrace, which I fear is what I was.

It was now known and talked about in the neighborhood that my master had found a strange animal in the field, about the size of a splacnuck, but shaped exactly like a human being in every way. It was also said that he copied humans in all his actions, seemed to have a little language of its own and had already learned several words of theirs, walked upright on two legs, was tame and gentle, would come when it was called, do whatever it was told, had the most delicate limbs in the world and a smoother complexion than the three year old daughter of a nobleman. Another farmer, who lived nearby and was a close friend of my master, made a visit specifically to ask if this was true. I was immediately produced and put on a table, where I walked up and down as instructed, drew my sword, put it away again, bowed to my master's guest, asked him how he was and said "You are welcome", just as my little nurse had taught me. This man, who was old and shortsighted, put on his spectacles to see me better; I couldn't help laughing, as his eyes looked like the full moon shining into a room through two windows. When the family found out what I was laughing at they joined in with me, and the old fellow was stupid enough to be put out and angry. He was known as a great miser, and it was my bad luck that he deserved the reputation, because he gave my master the devilish advice that he should show me as a curiosity in the next town which was half an hour's ride away, about twenty two miles from our house.

I guessed that there was some mischief afoot when I saw my master and his friend whispering together, and my worries made me imagine that I could hear and understand some of what they were saying. The next morning Glumdalclitch, my little nurse, told me the whole business, which she had cunningly wheedled out of her mother. The poor girl held me to her chest and wept with shame and grief. She feared that some accident would happen to me at the hands of common and vulgar people, who might squeeze me to death, or break one of my limbs by picking me up. She also knew how modest I was and how much I valued my honor, and how undignified I would find it to be exhibited to the common rabble for money as a public entertainment. She said that her mother and father had promised that Grildrig should be hers, but now she discovered that they were going to do the same as they had last year, when they had pretended that a lamb was a present to her but as soon as it was fat they had sold it to a butcher. I can honestly say for myself that I was less bothered than my nurse. I had great hopes, which never left me, that one day I would escape and be free: as for the disgrace of being exhibited as a freak I thought that I was a foreigner in that country and I could never be mocked for it if I returned to England, since the king of Great Britain himself, in my situation, would have faced the same fate.

My master, following his friend's advice, carried me to the nearby town in a box the next market day. He took his little daughter, my nurse, along on the back of his saddle. The box was closed on all sides, with a little door for me to go in and out and a few airholes. The girl had carefully put the baby's quilt in it for me to lie down on. However, I was terribly shaken up and discomforted during this journey, though it only took half an hour, because the horse went around forty feet with every step and trotted with such a high gait that the shaking was like being on a ship in a hurricane, though much more frequent. Our journey was a little farther than the trip from London to St.Alban's. My master stopped at an inn where he was well known, and after talking with the innkeeper and making some necessary arrangements he hired the Grultrud (town-crier) to announce throughout the town that there was a strange creature to be seen at the Green Eagle inn which was not as big as a splanuck (a very finely shaped animal of that country which was about six feet long) that looked in every way like a human being, which could speak several words and perform a hundred amusing tricks.

I was put on a table in the largest room of the inn, which was around three hundred feet square. My little nurse stood on a low stool close to the table, to protect me and tell me what to do. My master, to avoid crushing, only allowed thirty people in to see me at a time. I walked around the table as the girl ordered me; she asked me questions which she knew I could answer from my knowledge of the language and I answered them as loudly as I could. I turned round to the audience several times, bowed to them, told them they were welcome and made some other speeches I had been taught. I picked up a thimbleful of liquor, which Glumdalclitch had given me for a cup, and drank their health. I took out my sword and waved it like the fencers do in England. My nurse gave me a piece of straw with which I did pike exercises, having learnt the skill in my youth. I was shown to twelve different audiences that day, and had to perform the same foolishness each time, until I was half dead from exhaustion and annoyance. Those who had seen me gave such wonderful reports of me that people were ready to break down the doors to see me. My master, protecting his investment, would not let anyone touch me except my nurse, and to prevent any danger benches were put around the table at a distance which stopped anybody getting within arms' length. However, a naughty schoolboy threw a hazelnut at my head, which only just missed me. It was thrown so hard that it would undoubtedly have knocked my brains out, for it was almost as big as a small pumpkin, but I had the satisfaction of seeing the young rascal being given a good beating and thrown out of the room.

My master had it announced that he would show me again the next market day, and in the meantime he prepared a comfortable carriage for me, as well he might, for I was so tired with my first journey, and being exhibited for eight hours a day, that I could hardly stand or speak. It was at least three days before I got my strength back, and I got no rest at home as all the neighboring gentlemen from a hundred miles around, hearing about me, came to see me at my master's own house. There couldn't have been fewer than thirty people, with their wives and children (for the country is very populous), and my master demanded the same rate as for a full audience, even if it was only for a single family, so for some time I had hardly any rest all week (except on Wednesday, which is their Sabbath), even though I wasn't taken to town.

My master, discovering the great profits I was making for him, decided that he would show me in all the largest cities of the kingdom. So he got together all the things needed for a long journey, sorted out his business at home, said goodbye to his wife and on the 17th of August 1703, about two months after my arrival, we set out for the capital which is located in the middle of the empire, about three thousand miles from our house. My master ordered his daughter Glumdalclitch to ride with him. She carried me on her lap in a box tied to her waist. The girl had lined it on all sides with the softest cloth she could get, well folded over underneath, and she put the baby's bed in it, gave me bedclothes and other essentials, and made everything as comfortable as she could. We had nobody else with us apart from a serving boy from the house, who rode after us with the luggage. My master's plan was to show me in all the towns on the way and to go out of our way by fifty or a hundred miles to any village or nobleman's house where he thought he would get business. We travelled slowly, not going more than a hundred and forty or a hundred and sixty miles in a day, for Glumdalclitch, in order to spare me, often complained that the trotting of the horse had made her tired. She often took me out of the box, at my request, to give me some air and to show me the scenery, but she always held me on a rein. We passed over five or six rivers which were many times wider and deeper than the Nile or the Ganges, and there was hardly a stream as small as the Thames at London Bridge. The journey took us ten weeks, and I was exhibited in eighteen large towns as well as in many villages and private homes.

On October 26th we arrived in the capital, which in their language was called Lorbrulgrud, or Pride of the Universe. My master hired rooms on the main street of the city, not far from the royal palace, and put up posters in the normal way, with an exact description of my appearance and my accomplishments. He rented a large room which was between three and four hundred feet wide. He provided a table sixty feet in diameter for me to act on and put three foot high barricades all round three feet from the edge, to stop me falling off. I was shown ten times daily, to the amazement and pleasure of everyone. I could now speak their language quite well, and understood every word that was spoken to me. I had learnt their alphabet as well, and could understand a written sentence or two. Glumdalclitch had been my teacher while we were at home and during the quiet parts of our journey. She carried a little book in her pocket, not much bigger than Sanson's atlas; it was a common textbook for young girls which contained a short account of their religion: out of this she taught me the alphabet and read me the words.

Chapter III

[The author is summoned to court. The queen buys him from his master the farmer and gives him to the king. He debates with his majesty's great scholars. The author is given an apartment at court. He is much liked by the queen. He defends his own country. He quarrels with the queen's dwarf.]

The never ending efforts I had to make every day had, in a few weeks, a serious effect on my health, as the more my master earned through me the greedier he became. I had completely lost my appetite and became almost like a skeleton. The farmer noticed this, and thinking that I would soon be dead decided to make as much out of me as possible. While he was thinking and deciding this a Sadral, or gentleman-in-waiting, came from the court, ordering my master to take me there at once to amuse the queen and her ladies in waiting. Some of the ladies had already been to see me and told her amazing things about my beauty, behavior and intelligence. Her majesty, and those who waited on her, were enchanted with my appearance. I fell on my knees, and begged to have the honor of kissing the imperial foot, but the gracious princess held out her little finger to me when I was put on the table, and I hugged it with both arms and put the tip of it to my lips with the utmost respect.

She asked me some general questions about my country and my travels, which I answered as clearly and briefly as I could. She asked me if I would be happy to live at court. I bowed right down, and told her that I was the property of my master, but if it was up to me I would be glad to devote my life to her majesty's service. She then asked my master if he was willing to sell me for a good price. Knowing I could not live for more than a month he was willing enough to sell, and he asked for a thousand gold pieces, which were brought for him straight away; each piece was about the size of eight hundred large normal gold coins. However, considering the differences in proportion between Europe and that country, and the different values of gold, what he got was hardly equivalent to a thousand guineas in England. I then said to the queen that now I was her humble servant and property I must beg her to take Glumdalclitch, who had always looked after me so well, with such care and kindness, into her service, so that she could carry on as my nurse and teacher.

Her majesty agreed to my request, and the farmer quickly agreed as he was glad to have a daughter in favor at court; the poor girl herself was overjoyed. My former master withdrew, saying goodbye to me and that he had left me in a good position; I didn't say anything and made a very small bow.

The queen saw how cold I was, and when the farmer had left the room she asked me why. I was bold enough to say to her majesty that I owed my former master nothing, apart from the fact that he hadn't killed a poor creature which he had found in his fields, and he had got plenty of compensation for that by exhibiting me throughout the kingdom, as well as the price he had sold me for. I said that the life I had led had been hard enough to kill an animal ten times my strength, and that my health had been badly damaged through the drudgery of having to entertain the rabble all hours of the day. If my master hadn't thought I was going to die then her majesty wouldn't have got such a good bargain. But as I knew I would be well treated by such a great and good empress, who was the darling of all the world and a wonder of nature, loved by her subjects, the inspiration of creation, I hoped that he would be wrong, for I already felt better just to be in her mighty presence.

That was the substance of what I said, speaking with many mistakes and pauses. The last part was styled in the unique way of speaking of that people, which I had learned some phrases of from Glumdalclitch while she was carrying me to court.

The queen made many allowances for the defects in my speech, but she was surprised to find such intelligence and good sense in such a tiny creature. She took me in her hand and carried me to the king, who was resting in his room. His majesty, a very serious and stern faced prince, didn't see what I was at first, and asked the queen coldly how long she had been so fond of splacnucks, for it seems that is what he thought I was as I lay on my front in her majesty's hand. But the princess, who has a great amount of sense and humor, put me gently on my feet on the writing desk and told me to tell the king about myself, which I did in a few words. Glumdalclitch, who was waiting at the door of the room and couldn't stand me being out of her sight, was let in and confirmed my story of everything that had happened since I arrived at her father's house.

The king is as clever a man as anyone in his kingdom, having studied philosophy and particularly mathematics, but when he saw my shape and the way I walked, before I spoke, thought that I might be a clockwork toy (clockwork is very advanced in that country) made by some clever workman. But when he heard my voice and heard that what I said was normal and made sense he could not hide his amazement. He was not at all convinced by the tale I told him of the way I had arrived in his kingdom, thinking it was a story invented by Glumdalclitch and her father who had coached me in a speech to get a better price for me. Because of this idea he asked me several other questions, and still received intelligent answers, which were quite correct apart from my foreign accent, my imperfect knowledge of the language and some country phrases which I had picked up at the farmer's house which weren't suited to the polite style of the court.

His majesty sent for three great scholars, who were making their weekly visit as the custom of the country was. These gentlemen, after they had closely examined me, had different opinions about me. They all agreed that I could not have been made by regular natural processes, because I had no way of defending myself, either through speed, climbing trees or digging shelters in the earth. They saw from my teeth, which they looked at very closely, that I was a carnivorous animal, but as most quadrupeds were too big for me to tackle and the smaller ones like fieldmice and others were too quick they couldn't imagine how I kept myself alive, unless I lived on snails and other insects, which they claimed they had proof, through many learned arguments, I could not do. One of these geniuses thought that I might be an embryo or an abortion. But this opinion was rejected by the other two, who saw that my limbs were perfect and fully grown, and that I had lived for some years as they could see from my beard, the stubble of which they could clearly see through a magnifying glass. They said that I could not be a dwarf, as I was smaller than any that was ever known; the queen's favorite dwarf, the smallest that kingdom had ever seen, was nearly thirty feet high. After much debate they unanimously agreed that I was only "replum scalath", which literally means a freak of nature. This was a conclusion that fits in very well with the modern science of Europe, where the professors reject the old trick of blaming magic (which is how the followers of Aristotle tried vainly to cover up their ignorance) and have invented this wonderful way of getting round every problem, which has incomparably advanced human knowledge.

After this final conclusion I asked if I could say a word or two. I spoke to the king, and assured him that I came from a country where there were several million people of both sexes, and where the animals, trees and houses were all in proportion to me, and so I could find food and defend myself as any of his majesty's subjects might do here. I said that I thought that was a full answer to the learned gentlemen's arguments. They just smiled with contempt and said that the farmer had taught me what to say very well. The king, who had far more sense, dismissed the learned men and sent for the farmer, who luckily was still in town. He first questioned him in private, then confronted him with me and the young girl, and began to think that what we had told him could be true. He asked the queen to take very good care of me, and recommended that Glumdalclitch should carry on looking after me, as he could see the great affection we had for each other. A comfortable room was provided for her in the palace, and she had a sort of governess to take care of her education, a maid to dress her and two other servants for menial tasks, but she was given sole responsibility for my care. The queen commanded her own cabinet maker to run up a box to be used as a bedroom for me, to my and Glumdalclitch's design. This man was a very clever workman, and under my orders in three weeks he had made me a wooden room sixteen feet square, twelve high, with sash windows, a door and two wardrobes, like a London bedroom.

The board that made the ceiling lifted up on two hinges, to put in a bed furnished by her majesty's upholsterer. Glumdalclitch took the bed out every day to air, made it up with her own hands, then put it back at night and closed the roof over me. A clever workman, famous for miniature curios, agreed to make me two chairs, with backs and frames made of a substance rather like ivory, with two tables and a cabinet to put my things in. The room was padded on all walls as well as the floor and the ceiling, to stop any accidents if the people carrying me slipped, and to cushion the shaking when I went in a coach. I asked for a lock on my door, to stop mice and rats getting in. After several attempts the blacksmith managed to make the smallest lock ever seen in that country, and I have seen bigger on the gates of a gentleman's house in England. I made sure that I kept the key in my own pocket, as I was worried that Glumdalclitch might lose it. The queen also ordered the thinnest silk available to make me clothes, which were not much thicker than an English blanket and felt very clumsy until I got used to them. They were made in the fashion of the kingdom, partly in Persian style, partly Chinese, and they are a very sober and decent form of dress.

The queen became so fond of my company that she would not eat without me. I had a table and chair placed on her majesty's dining table, just by her left elbow. Glumdalclitch stood on a stool on the floor near my table, to help and care for me. I had a whole dinner service of silver dishes and plates and other things which were like the ones I have seen in a London toyshop for a doll's house, in comparison to those of the queen. My little nurse kept these in a silver box in her pocket and gave them to me when I needed them at mealtimes, always cleaning them herself. Nobody else dined with the queen except the two royal princesses, the older being sixteen years old and the younger at that time thirteen years and one month. Her majesty used to put a bit of meat on one of my plates which I would carve for myself, and she loved to see me eat in miniature. The queen herself had a small appetite but would pick up in one mouthful as much as a dozen English farmers would eat at one meal, which made me feel quite sick at first. She would crunch the wing of a lark, bones and all, between her teeth, even though it was nine times as large as a full grown turkey, and put a piece of bread in her mouth the size of two twelvepenny loaves. She drank out of a golden cup which could hold more than a hogshead. Her knives were twice as long as scythe blades set straight on a handle. The spoons, forks and other utensils were all the same. I remember when Glumdalclitch carried me, because I was curious, to see the court eating, and when I saw ten or twelve of those enormous knives and forks all being used at once I thought I had never seen such a terrible sight.

It is the custom that every Wednesday (which, as I have mentioned, is their Sabbath) the king and queen, with their children, all dine together in his majesty's rooms; I had now become a great favorite of his. At these times my little chair and table were placed on his left hand, in front of one of the salt cellars. The prince took great pleasure in talking to me and asking about the manners, religion, laws, government and learning in Europe, and I gave him the best account I could of it. He understood so well, and was so accurate in his judgements, that he made very good points about everything I told him. However, I must admit that one time when I had spoken a little too much about my own beloved country, about our trade and sea and land wars, the splits in our religion and our political parties, he couldn't help (through the prejudices of his own learning) lifting me up in his right hand, laughing heartily, and he stroked me gently and asked if I was a whig or a tory. Then he turned to his first minister, who was waiting behind him with his white staff of office which was almost as big as the main mast of the Royal Sovereign (one of our largest ships) and remarked what a pathetic thing human greatness was, when it could be copied by something as tiny as me. "And yet," he said, "I daresay these creatures have their titles and honors; they make little nests and burrows which they call houses and cities; they can dress up and wear armor; they love, fight, argue, cheat and betray!" And he carried on like this while I flushed and paled with indignation to hear our country, the leader in science and war, the defeater of France, the judge of Europe, the home of virtue, honor and truth, the pride and envy of the whole world, talked of with such contempt.

But I was in no position to hold a grudge, and thinking it over I began to wonder if I was really offended. Having got used to the sight and conversation of these people, and seen that everything was in proportion, the shock I had at first from seeing their size and looks had so far worn off that If I had then seen a group of English lords and ladies in their fine birthday clothes, playing their parts in the courtly way of strutting, bowing and gabbling, I must say that I would have been just as tempted to laugh at them in the same way the king and his courtiers laughed at me. And indeed I couldn't stop myself from smiling when the queen used to hold me on her hand and we would stand in front of a mirror, so they I could see us both together; the comparison did look ridiculous and I really did begin to imagine that I had shrunk many times smaller than my actual size.

Nothing angered and tortured me as much as the queen's dwarf, who, being the shortest person ever seen in that country (for I think he wasn't even thirty feet high), became so insolent at seeing a creature so much shorter than him that he would always strut and try to look bigger when he passed me in the queen's waiting room, when I was standing on a table chatting with the lords and ladies of the court, and he nearly always made some remark about my size. I could only get back at him by calling him my brother, and challenging him to wrestle, and making other such jokes that are usually made by the court servants. One day, at dinner, this malicious little shrimp was so annoyed by something I said to him that he climbed up on her majesty's chair and picked me up by the middle from where I was sitting, not imagining I was in danger, and dropped me into a silver bowl of cream and ran away as fast as he could. I plunged right in, and if I had not been a good swimmer I might have had a very hard time, because Glumdalclitch happened to be at the other end of the room and the queen was so shocked that she didn't have the sense to help me. But my little nurse ran to save me, and got me out after I had swallowed more than a quart of cream. I was put to bed; however I had suffered no ill effects apart from the fact that my suit of clothes was completely ruined. The dwarf was soundly whipped and, as a further punishment, made to drink up the bowl of cream he had thrown me into. He never got his position back either, for soon after the queen gave him away to a noblewoman and I didn't see him again, which was a great relief, for I couldn't tell what the little scoundrel might do to me out of resentment.

He had done me a bad turn before, which got the queen laughing, although she was very annoyed at the same time and would have sacked him on the spot if I hadn't intervened for him. Her majesty was eating a marrowbone, and after she had knocked out the marrow she had placed the bone upright on the dish as it had been before. The dwarf took his chance, when Glumdalclitch went to the sideboard, to climb on the stool she used to stand on to look after me at mealtimes, and grabbed me with both hands, squeezed my legs together and forced me into the marrowbone up to my waist, where I was stuck for some time, looking very ridiculous. I think it was almost a minute before anyone knew where I was, for I thought it would be undignified to call out. But princes rarely get their meat hot, so my legs were not scalded, though my stockings and breeches were in a sorry state. At my request the dwarf got no other punishment than a good whipping.

The queen frequently made fun of my anxieties, and she used to ask me if the people of my country were all as cowardly as me. What happened was, the kingdom has a lot of flies in the summer, and these horrible insects, each one the size of a lark, hardly gave me any peace during dinner with their continual buzzing and humming around my ears. Sometimes they would land on my food and leave their dung there, or their eggs, which I could see very clearly, though not to the natives whose large eyes were not as good at seeing small objects as mine. Sometimes they would land on my nose or forehead and give me very deep stings, and they smelt atrocious. I could easily see that sticky substance which, our naturalists tell us, they use to walk on ceilings. I had much work to defend myself against these horrid creatures, and I could not stop myself from jumping when they landed on my face. The dwarf often caught some of these creatures in his hand, as our schoolboys do, and then would let them out suddenly right under my nose to frighten me and amuse the queen. My answer to this was to chop them into pieces in the air with my knife, and my skill was much admired.

I remember one morning when Glumdalclitch had put me in a box on a windowsill, as she usually did on nice days so I could get some fresh air (for I didn't dare let the box be hung out of the window, tied to a nail, as we do with birdcages in England). After I had opened one of my windows and sat down to eat a piece of sweet cake for my breakfast over twenty wasps, drawn by the smell, came flying into the room, humming louder than bagpipes. Some of them grabbed my cake and carried it away in pieces, while others flew around my head and face, confusing me with their noise and making me very afraid of their stings. However, I had the courage to rise and draw my sword and attack them in the air. I killed four, but the rest escaped and I closed my window. These insects were as large as partridges; I took out their stings, which were an inch and a half long and as sharp as needles. I carefully saved them all, and I have since shown them, with other curiosities, in several parts of Europe. When I came back to England I gave three to the Royal Society and kept the fourth one for myself.

Chapter IV

[The country is described. The author proposes a way of correcting modern maps. The king's palace and the capital city described. The way the author travelled. The main temple.]

I shall now give the reader a short description of the country, at least what I saw of it, which was only the part less than two thousand miles round Lorbrulgrud, the metropolis. The queen, whom I was always with, never went farther when she accompanied the king on his journeys, and she would wait there until his majesty came back from visiting his frontiers. The prince's kingdom is about six thousand miles long and between three and five thousand wide, which makes me think that our geographers in Europe are very mistaken in thinking that there is nothing but sea between Japan and California. I have always thought that there must be a landmass to balance the great continent of Tartary, and so they ought to correct their maps and charts by adding this vast piece of land to the northwest parts of America; I would be happy to help them.

The kingdom is a peninsula, blocked at the northeast end by a range of mountains thirty miles high which are completely impassable because of the volcanoes on the tops. Not even the most learned men know what sort of people live on the other side of these mountains, or whether there is anyone there at all. On the other three sides it is surrounded by the ocean. There isn't a single seaport in the whole kingdom, and where the rivers run into the sea the coast is so full of pointed rocks, and the sea usually so rough, that it's impossible to sail, even in their smallest boats. This means that these people are completely cut off from the rest of the world. However, the large rivers are full of boats and have a very good stock of fish; they rarely take fish from the sea, because the sea fish are the same size as those of Europe, and so not worth catching. It is clear from this that the natural processes which produce such extraordinarily large animals and plants are confined to this continent; I leave it to the scientists to work out why this should be. However, sometimes they get a whale which has been washed up on the rocks, and the common people make a good meal of it. These whales can be so large that a man could hardly carry one on his shoulders; sometimes, as a novelty, they are brought in baskets to Lorbrulgrud. I saw one of them on a dish at the king's table, offered as a delicacy, but he didn't seem to like it, in fact I think he was disgusted by its size, although I have seen a rather larger one in Greenland.

The country is well populated, for it contains fifty-one cities, nearly a hundred major towns and a large number of villages. To satisfy the curious reader it should be enough to describe Lorbrulgrud. This city is made of two almost equal parts, standing on either side of the river which runs through it. It holds over eighty thousand houses and six hundred thousand inhabitants. It is three glomglungs in length (which is equal to about fifty-four English miles) and two and a half wide. I measured this myself on the royal map which the king ordered, which was a hundred feet long and was laid out on the ground for me. I walked round the diameter and circumference several times barefoot and by calculating the scale got the distances pretty exactly.

The king's palace is not a symmetrical construction but a heap of buildings about seven miles round. The main rooms are generally about two hundred and forty feet high and long and broad in proportion. Glumdalclitch and I were given a coach to use, and her governess often took her out in to see the town or visit the shops. I always went with them, carried in my box, although the girl would often, at my request, take me out and hold me in her hand, so that I could get a better view of the houses and the people as we went along the streets. I reckoned that our coach was about the length and width of Westminster Hall, but not quite as high; however, I can't do more than estimate. One day the governess ordered our coachman to stop at several different shops, and the beggars, seeing their chance, crowded round the coach and gave me the most horrible sight that a European ever saw. There was a woman with a tumor on her breast which was swollen to a terrible size and was covered in holes, two or three of which I could have easily crept into and covered my whole body. There was a fellow with a boil on his neck which was bigger than five woolsacks, and another who had two wooden legs, which were each over twenty feet high. But the most horrible thing of all was the lice crawling on their clothes. I could see the limbs of these vermin clearly with my naked eye, more clearly than one can see a European louse through a microscope, and I could see their snouts with which they dug around like pigs. They were the first I had ever seen, and I would have liked to dissect one if I had had my proper instruments with me, which unfortunately I had left behind on the ship – although I must say that the sight was so sickening it turned my stomach.

Apart from the large box I was usually carried in the queen ordered a smaller one, about ten feet by twelve, to be made for me for travelling, because the other one was rather too big for Glumdalclitch's lap and was awkward in the coach. It was made by the same workman, to my design. This travelling box was an exact square, with a window in the middle of three of the sides, each one barred with iron wire on the outside to prevent accidents on long journeys. On the fourth side, which had no window, there were two strong handles, and when I chose to go on horseback the person carrying me put a leather belt through these and then buckled it around his waist. This was always the job of some sensible servant whom I could trust, when I went with the king and queen on their journeys, or to see the gardens, or visit some great lady or minister of state at court, when Glumdalclitch was indisposed. I soon became known and liked among the highest people of the court, I think more because I was in favor with their majesties rather than through any merit of my own. When travelling, when I was tired of the coach, a servant on horseback would buckle on my box, and put it on a cushion in front of him. From there I had a good view of the country on three sides, through my three windows. In this box I had a camp bed and a hammock, hung from the ceiling, two chairs and a table, neatly screwed to the floor to prevent them being thrown around by the bumping of the horse or the coach. As I was used to long sea voyages these movements, although they were sometimes very violent, didn't much bother me.

Whenever I wanted to see the town I always went in my travelling box; Glumdalclitch put it on her lap as she sat in a kind of open sedan chair, as was the style in that country, carried by four men and followed by two others in the queen's uniforms. The people, who had heard a lot about me, often crowded around the sedan in curiosity. The girl was obliging enough to make the bearers stop and take me in her hand, so it was easier for the crowd to see me.

I was very keen to see the main temple, and particularly its tower, which is thought to be the highest in the kingdom. So my nurse took me there one day, though I must admit that I was disappointed; it is not more than three thousand feet high, measured from the ground to the top of the steeple. Allowing for the difference between the size of those people and us in Europe this is not particularly impressive, and if I remember rightly it is not as big, in proportion, as the steeple of Salisbury cathedral. But I don't want to criticize a nation to which I shall always owe a debt of gratitude, and I must admit that whatever the famous tower lacks in height it makes up for in beauty and strength. The walls are nearly a hundred feet thick and made of cut stone, each one being about forty feet square and decorated on all sides with statues of gods and emperors, sculpted from marble, larger than life size, each one in its own niche. I measured a little finger which had fallen off one of these statues and lay unnoticed amongst the rubbish and found it was exactly four feet and an inch in length. Glumdalclitch wrapped it up in her handkerchief and took it home in her pocket to keep with other little curios, which she was very fond of, as children of her age usually are.

The king's kitchen is an impressive building, with an arched roof about six hundred feet high. The great oven is ten paces shorter in width than the great dome of St.Paul's (I measured the latter to make the comparison when I returned). But if I described the kitchen fireplace, the huge pots and kettles, the joints of meat turning on the spits, and all the other details, I probably wouldn't be believed; at best a severe critic would suspect that I was exaggerating a little, as travellers are often accused of doing. To avoid this criticism I fear I have actually gone too far in the other direction, and if this work should be translated into the language of Brobdingnag (which is the name of that kingdom) and sent there the king and his people could justifiably complain that I had done them an injustice through making them smaller than they are.

His majesty does not usually keep more than six hundred horses in his stables; they are usually between fifty-four and sixty feet high. But when he goes out on ceremonial days he is accompanied, as part of his office, by a military guard of five hundred horsemen, which I thought was the most magnificent sight I had ever seen, until I saw part of his army in battle order, which I shall speak about elsewhere.

Chapter V

Several adventures that happened to the author. The execution of a criminal. The author shows his skill at sailing.]

I could have lived happily enough in that country if my size hadn't caused several ridiculous and annoying accidents, some of which I shall detail here. Glumdalclitch often carried me into the gardens of the court in my smaller box, and sometimes she would take me out and hold me in her hand or put me down to walk. I remember that the dwarf, before he left, followed us into those gardens one day and he and I were close together where my nurse had put me down near some dwarf apple trees. I had to show off my wit by making a silly comparison between him and the trees (the wordplay happened to work in their language as well as ours). At this the malicious scoundrel, watching for his chance, shook one of the trees as I was walking underneath it, and a dozen apples, each one as large as a big barrel, came tumbling down round my ears. One of them hit me on the back as I bent down and knocked me flat on my face. However, I was not otherwise harmed, and the dwarf was forgiven at my request, as I had provoked him.

Another time Glumdalclitch left me on a smooth lawn to amuse myself while she walked with her governess some way away. In the meantime there was sudden hail shower which smashed me to the ground. When I was down the hailstones battered me all over, as if I was being pelted with tennis balls. However, I managed to crawl and protect myself, lying face down on the sheltered side of a border of lemon thyme. But I was so bruised from head to foot that I could not go out for ten days. This is no surprise, as the hailstones in that country, in proportion as everything in nature is there, are almost eighteen hundred times as large as the ones in Europe, which I can say from experience, having been curious enough to weigh and measure them.

But a more dangerous accident happened to me in the same garden. My little nurse, thinking she had left me in a safe place (as I often asked her to do, so I could be alone with my thoughts), and having left my box at home, as she often did to save the bother of carrying it, went to another part of the garden with her governess and some ladies that she knew. While she was away and out of earshot a little white spaniel, that belonged to one of the chief gardeners, which had got into the garden by accident, happened to come by the place where I lay. The dog, following the scent, came right up to me, took me in his mouth and ran to his master wagging his tail and put me gently down on the ground. Luckily he was so well trained that I was carried in his teeth without taking the least harm or even tearing my clothes. But the poor gardener, who knew me well and was very fond of me, had a terrible fright: he gently picked me up with both hands and asked if I was alright, but I was so shocked and breathless that I could not speak a word. In a few minutes I pulled myself together and he carried me safely to my little nurse, who had by this time returned to the place where she had left me and was beside herself when I could not be seen and did not answer her calls. She severely scolded the gardener for not controlling his dog. But the matter was hushed up and was not known about at court, for the girl was afraid that the queen would be angry; and to be honest I didn't think it would do my reputation any good for the story to get around.

This accident made Glumdalclitch determined that in the future I would never be out of her sight when we went out. I had been afraid this might happen, and so I had kept some unlucky little mishaps, which had happened when I was left alone, to myself. Once a kite, hovering over the garden, made a dive at me, and if I had not drawn my sword and run under a thick plant he would certainly have carried me off in his talons. Another time, walking to the top of a fresh molehill, I fell in up to my neck in the hole that animal had made in the earth and I made up some lie, which is not worth remembering, to explain the dirtiness of my clothes. I also cut open my right shin when I stumbled over a snail shell when I was walking alone and thinking of poor England.

I didn't know whether to pleased or saddened to see, on those solitary walks, that the smaller birds did not seem to be in the least afraid of me, but would hop up a yard away, looking for worms and other food, as careless and safe as if there were no creature there at all. I remember a thrush felt safe enough to snatch out of my hand, with his beak, a bit of cake that Glumdalclitch had just given me for my breakfast. When I tried to catch any of these birds they would boldly turn on me and try to peck my fingers, which I didn't dare let within their reach. They would then hop back unconcerned to hunt for worms and snails as they had been doing before. But one day I took a thick club, and throwing it with all my strength at a linnet was lucky enough to knock him down, and I grabbed him by the neck with both hands and ran with him to my nurse in triumph. However the bird had only been stunned, and when he recovered he gave me so many blows with his wings all over my body, even though I held him at arm's length and was out of reach of his claws, that I thought twenty times of letting him go. But soon one of our servants rescued me, and wrung the bird's neck, and I had him the next day for dinner on the queen's orders. As far as I can remember this linnet was rather bigger than an English swan.

The maids of honor often invited Glumdalclitch to their rooms, and asked her to bring me along so they could have the pleasure of seeing and touching me. They would often strip me naked from top to toe and lay me on their chests at full length, which disgusted me very much, as to tell the truth their skin really stank. I am not saying this to insult these excellent ladies, for whom I have great respect, but I think that my senses were more acute than theirs in proportion to my size, and that those great people were no more disagreeable to their lovers, or to each other, than people of the same quality are to us in England. And I must say that I found I could cope better with their natural smell than the perfumes they used, which made me faint away at once. I cannot forget that a close friend of mine in Lilliput, on a warm day when I had had plenty of exercise, took the liberty of complaining that I smelt rather strongly, although I am no worse in that way than most of my sex. I guess that his sense of smell was as sharp regarding me as mine was with these people. Speaking of this I must be fair to my mistress the queen and my nurse Glumdalclitch, who smelt as nice as any lady in England.

What disturbed me most with these maids of honor (when my nurse carried me to visit them) was to see them treat me with no respect at all, like a completely unimportant creature. They would strip themselves to the skin and dress in my presence, while I sat on their washstand in full view of their naked bodies, which I can promise were not a pretty sight and gave me no other emotions apart from horror and disgust. Their skins were so coarse and lumpy, so multicolored, when I saw them close up, with a mole here and there as wide as a dinnerplate, and they had hairs hanging from them thicker than packthreads, to say nothing of the rest of their bodies. Nor did they have any hesitation, when I was around, in passing water, a least two hogshead's worth, into a vessel that held at least three tuns. The prettiest of these maids of honor, a pleasant, playful girl of sixteen, would sometimes sit me astride one of her nipples, and do other things, about which you'll excuse me if I don't go into in detail. I was so disgusted with this that I begged Glumdalclitch to make up an excuse for no longer going to see that young lady.

One day a young gentleman, a nephew of my nurse's governess, came and urged them both to go and see an execution. It was the execution of a man who had murdered one of that gentleman's intimate friends. Glumdalclitch was persuaded to join the party, which was very much against her inclinations as she was naturally tender hearted. As for myself, though I hated this kind of spectacle, I was tempted to go and see something which I thought must be quite extraordinary. The wrongdoer was tied to a chair on a scaffold which had been put up for the purpose and his head was cut off with one blow with a sword which was about forty feet long. The veins and arteries spurted out such a great quantity of blood, so high in the air, that while it lasted the great fountain at Versailles could not have matched it, and the head, when it fell to the floor of the scaffold, made such a thud that it made me jump, although I was at least half an English mile away.

The queen, who often heard me talking of my sea voyages, and always tried to cheer me up when I was depressed, asked me whether I knew how to sail or to row, and suggested a little rowing might be good exercise for me. I answered that I knew both very well, for although my real job had been ship's doctor or surgeon I was often, in an emergency, pressed into service as an ordinary sailor. But I could not see how it could be done in their country, where the smallest rowing boat was the equivalent of our largest warships, and any boat I could manage would never survive in any of their rivers. Her majesty said that if I would design a boat her own carpenter would make it and she would provide a place for me to sail in. This fellow was a clever workman, and under my instruction he had, in ten days, finished a pleasure boat with all its tackle which would have comfortably held eight Europeans. When it was finished the queen was so delighted that she ran with it to the king, who ordered it be put in a little tank to test it, but there was no room in it for me to try using my two sculls, or little oars. But the queen had already come up with another invention. She ordered the joiner to make a wooden trough three hundred feet long, fifty across and eight deep. It was well covered with tar to prevent leaks and was placed on the floor, along the wall, in an outer room of the palace. It had a tap at the bottom to let out the water when it got stale, and two servants could easily fill it in half an hour. I often used to row her for my own entertainment, as well as that of the queen and her ladies, who greatly enjoyed my skill and agility. Sometimes I would raise my sail, and then all I had to do was to steer while the ladies gave me a wind with their fans. When they were tired some of their servants would blow my sail forward and I would show my skill by steering left or right as I chose. When I had finished Glumdalclitch always took my boat back to her closet and hung it on a nail to dry.

I once had an accident taking this exercise which nearly cost me my life; one of the pages had put my boat in the trough and Glumdalclitch's governess very bossily lifted me up to put me in the boat. I happened to slip through her fingers and would undoubtedly have fallen forty feet to the floor if, by the greatest of luck, I had not been stopped by a large pin sticking out of that good woman's corset; the head of the pin passed through my shirt and the waistband of my breeches, and I was suspended by the middle in the air until Glumdalclitch ran to save me.

Another time one of the servants, whose job it was to fill my trough with fresh water every third day, was careless enough to let a large frog (which he hadn't noticed) slip out of his pail. The frog lay hidden until I was put in my boat, but then, seeing a place to rest, climbed up and made the boat lean over so much that I was forced to throw all my weight on the other side to stop it overturning. When the frog had got on board it hopped half the length of the boat and then over my head, to and fro, daubing my face and clothes with foul slime. The size of its features made it look like the most revolting animal imaginable. However, I asked Glumdalclitch to let me deal with it myself. I hit it with one of my oars for a long time and at last forced it to leap out of the boat.

But the greatest danger I ever faced in that kingdom was from a monkey which belonged to one of kitchen clerks. Glumdalclitch had locked me up in her room while she went to attend to some business or make a visit. The weather was very warm so the window of the room had been left open as had the windows and door of my larger box, which was where I usually lived due to its size and comfort. As I sat quietly thinking at my table I heard something hop in through the closet window and jump about the place. Although I was very alarmed I looked out the window, though I didn't leave my seat, and then I saw this playful animal jumping around until he came to my box, which he seemed to find very pleasing and intriguing, peeping in at the door and all the windows. I backed into the far corner of my room, or box, but the monkey looking in everywhere had put me in such a fright that I didn't think to hide under the bed as I might well have done. After some time spent peeping in, grinning and chattering he spotted me at last. He put a paw in through the door as a cat does when playing with a mouse; although I often moved around to escape him he eventually grabbed the lapel of my coat (which being made of the silk of that country was very thick and strong) and dragged me out. He picked me up in his right arm and held me as a nurse holds a child for breastfeeding. I have seen a monkey do the same with a kitten in Europe, and when I tried to struggle he squeezed me so hard that I thought it was safest to give in.

I have every reason to believe that he thought I was an infant of his own species, as he often stroked my face very gently with his other paw. He was interrupted in doing this by a noise at the closet door, as if someone was opening it, so he suddenly jumped up to the window he had come in at and from there got onto the slates and gutters, walking on three paws and carrying me in the fourth, until he had got to a roof next to ours. I heard Glumdalclitch shriek the moment he was carrying me out. The poor girl was almost driven mad; that whole part of the palace was in uproar; the servants ran for ladders; the monkey was seen by hundreds of the court sitting on the ridge of a building holding me like a baby in one of his arms and feeding me with the other, cramming food into my mouth which he had taken from some pouch in his cheeks, and he patted me on the head when I would not eat. Many of the rabble below couldn't help laughing at this, and I don't think they can be blamed, for, without question, the sight was hilarious for everyone but me. Some of the people threw stones to try and drive the monkey down but this was strictly forbidden because otherwise my brains would very probably have been beaten out.

The ladders were now raised and several men climbed up; the monkey saw this and, finding himself almost surrounded, he could not go quickly enough on his three legs so he dropped me on a ridge tile and made off. I sat there for some time, five hundred yards from the ground, expecting at any moment to be blown down by the wind or to fall through my own giddiness and come tumbling end over end from the roof to the gutters. But an honest lad, one of my nurse's footmen, climbed up, put me in his breeches pocket and brought me down safely. I was almost choking with the muck the monkey had crammed down my throat, but my dear little nurse picked it out with a needle, and then I started vomiting which made me feel much better. But I was so weak and bruised in the sides from the squeezes this horrid animal had given me that I was forced to stay in bed for a fortnight. The king, queen and all the court sent messages every day asking after my health, and her majesty visited me several times while I was ill. The monkey was killed and it was ordered that no animals like him could be kept in the palace.

When I went to see the king after my recovery, to thank him for his favors, he enjoyed making fun of me for this adventure. He asked me what I was thinking of, while I lay in the monkey's paw, how I enjoyed the food he gave me, how he fed me and whether the fresh air on the roof had given me an appetite. I told his majesty that in Europe we had no monkeys, except the ones that were brought as curiosities from other places, and they were so small that if they dared attack me I could deal with a dozen at once. As for that monstrous animal with which I had recently battled (for it was indeed as large as an elephant), if I had had the sense to use my sword (I looked very fierce and slapped my sword hilt as I spoke) when he poked his paw into my room then maybe I would have given him such a wound that he would have taken it out a good deal faster than he put it in. I said this in a stern voice, like somebody who thought his courage was being called into question. However, my speech caused nothing but loud laughter from all those around him, which even the respect due to his majesty couldn't control. This made me think how impossible it is for a man to be recognised for anything by those who are completely out of his sphere of equality or size. And I have seen much the same reaction to my behavior often in England since I came back, where a silly little rascal, with no pedigree, size, intelligence or common sense, will try to look important and put himself on a par with the greatest people in the kingdom.

I gave the court some new ridiculous story every day, and Glumdalclitch, though she loved me dearly, was cheeky enough to tell the queen whenever I did something stupid which she thought would amuse her majesty. The girl had been ill, and she was taken by her governess to get some country air about an hour's journey, or thirty miles, from the town. They got out of the coach near a small footpath in a field, and when Glumdalclitch put down my travelling box I got out of it to have a walk. There was a cowpat on the path, and I had to try and test my agility by leaping over it, but unfortunately I fell short and landed right in the middle up to my knees. I waded out with some difficulty, and one of the footmen wiped me down with his handkerchief, for I was covered in filth, and my nurse shut me in my box until we got home. She told the queen about it, and the footmen told all the court, so that for some days everyone had a good laugh at my expense.

Chapter VI

[Several inventions of the author which please the king and queen. He shows his skill in music. The king asks about the state of England, which the king tells him about. The king comments on this.]

I used to go to the king's morning reception once or twice a week, and had often seen him being shaved, which initially was very frightening to see, for the razor was almost twice as long as an ordinary scythe. His majesty, as was the custom in that country, was only shaved twice a week. I once asked the barber to give me some of the suds or lather, and I pulled thirty or forty of the strongest bristles out of it. I then took a thin piece of wood and cut into the back of it like a comb, making several holes at equal distances with the smallest needle I could get from Glumdalclitch. I fitted the stumps in so cunningly, sharpening them into points with my knife, that I made a very serviceable comb, which was a welcome item as my own had so many broken teeth that it was almost useless, and I didn't know any workman in the country who was precise enough to make me another.

And this reminds me of an entertainment with which I whiled away many of my leisure hours. I asked the queen's woman to save me the combings from her majesty's hair, and in time I got a good quantity of them. I asked my friend the cabinet maker, who had standing orders to do little jobs for me, to make two chair frames, no larger than the ones I had in my box, and to drill in holes with a fine point around the parts I had designed to be backs and seats; I wove the strongest hairs I had through the backs and seats, in the way we do with cane chairs in England. When they were finished I made a present of them to her majesty, and she kept them in her cabinet, and used to show them off as curios, and they amazed everyone who saw them. The queen wanted me to sit on one of the chairs but I absolutely refused, saying I would rather die than place such a rude part of my body on the precious hairs which were once on her majesty's head. As I always was good with my hands I also made a little purse from these hairs, about five feet long, with her majesty's name picked out in gold letters, which I gave to Glumdalclitch with her majesty's permission. To be honest it was more for show than use, as it couldn't hold the weight of the larger coins, so she just kept some little toys that young girls like in it.

The king loved music and often held concerts at court, and I was sometimes taken to them and put in my box on the table to listen, but the music was so loud I could hardly pick out the tunes. I am sure that all the drums and trumpets of a royal army, playing right next to your ear, couldn't match it. I used to have my box taken as far as possible from where the performers were in the room, then closed the doors and windows and drew the curtains, and after that I found their music tolerable.

When I was younger I had learned to play the spinet. Glumdalclitch had one in her room, and a master came twice a week to teach her. I call it a spinet as it looked something like one and was played in a similar way. I got the idea that I would entertain the king and queen by playing them an English tune on this instrument. This looked like it would be very difficult, for the spinet was nearly sixty feet long and each key was almost a foot wide, so that with my arms outstretched I could only reach five keys, and to push them down I had to give them a good thump with my fist, which would be too exhausting and would not work anyway. What I did was this: I made two round sticks, about the size of truncheons; they were thicker at one end than the other, and I covered the thicker ends with pieces of mouse skin, so that I wouldn't damage the keys, nor spoil the sound, when I tapped on them. A bench was put in front of the spinet, about four feet in front of the keys, and I was put on the bench. I ran up and down it, first this way and then that, as fast as I could, banging the right keys with my sticks, and I tried to play a jig, to the great enjoyment of their majesties. But it was the hardest exercise I ever had, and still I couldn't hit over sixteen keys, or play the bass and treble together, as other players do, which really held back my performance.

The king who, as I said before, was a very clever man, would often order that I should be brought in my box and put on the table in his bedroom. Then he would order me to bring out one of my chairs and sit down three yards from him on top of the table, which brought me almost level with his face. In this way I had several conversations with him. One day I took the liberty of telling his majesty that his contempt for Europe and the rest of the world didn't seem to fit with his excellent mind. I told him that the size of the body didn't show the size of the mind, and in fact we had often seen in our country that the tallest people were the stupidest, and amongst other animals bees and ants had a better reputation for hard work, skill and intelligence than many of the bigger ones, and that, insignificant as he thought I was, I hoped that some time in my life I might be able to do some important service for his majesty. The king listened to me carefully and began to form a far better opinion of me than he had previously. He asked me to give him as accurate an account of the government of England as I possibly could, because although princes usually think their own ways were the best (he thought this from listening to me speak about other monarchs) he would be glad to hear about anything that deserved to be copied.

You may imagine, dear reader, how much I wished I had the skills of Demosthenes or Cicero, that could have allowed me to praise my dear homeland in a style which its merits and beauty deserved.

I began my speech by telling his majesty that our lands consisted of two islands made up of three mighty kingdoms under one mighty ruler, leaving aside our American plantations. I spoke a lot about the fertility of our soil, and our climate. I then explained in detail the way an English parliament was made up; partly it was made of a fine body called the House of Peers, made up of people of the noblest descent who had the oldest and biggest estates. I told him how great care was always taken to give them the best education in science and war, to make sure they were skilled enough to be counsellors to the king and the kingdom, to have a part in making laws, to be members of the highest court in the judicial system, from which nobody can appeal, and to be champions always ready to defend their prince and their country with their bravery, behavior and loyalty. These were the delight and defence of the kingdom, worthy successors to their famous ancestors, who had been given their honors due to their virtues, and nobody in their descendants had ever disgraced them. They were joined in that assembly by several holy men, known as bishops, whose particular business is to take care of religion and those who teach the people about it. These were looked for and found through the whole country, by the prince and his wisest advisors, amongst those in the priesthood who were marked out by the sanctity of their lives and the depth of their learning. These bishops were indeed the spiritual fathers of the clergy and the people.

I told him the other part of the parliament was an assembly called the House of Commons, who were all great gentlemen, freely picked and called out by the people themselves due to their great ability and love of their country, to represent the wisdom of the whole nation. These two bodies made up the most distinguished assembly in all of Europe, and all law making powers are given to them, in partnership with the prince.

I then went down to the courts of justice, over which judges, those well respected wise men and interpreters of the law, ruled, to make decisions about disputes in rights and property, as well as punishing vice and protecting innocence. I mentioned the sensible way our treasury was managed, and the bravery and victories of our army and navy. I calculated the number of people in the country, and how many millions belonged to each religious sect or political party amongst us. I didn't even leave out our sports and pastimes, or any other detail which I thought might add to my country's honor. And I finished off with a brief description of the history of England for the last hundred years.

This conversation took five meetings, each of several hours, and the king listened very carefully to the whole thing, often taking notes of what I said as well as of questions he wanted to ask when I was finished.

When I had finished these long explanations, his majesty, at our sixth meeting, looked at his notes and put forward many doubts, queries and objections to everything I had said. He asked how we educated the minds and bodies of the young noblemen, and what kind of things did they do in the early parts of their lives when they were most open to teaching. He asked what was done to keep the assembly going if a noble family became extinct. He asked how somebody got to become a new lord; did the prince's whim, a payment to a lady at court, or a desire to strengthen a party which the public didn't want, ever play a part? What did these lords know about the law, and how did they learn it, which allowed them to be the final judges over all their fellow subjects? Were they always so free of bias, greed or poverty that they could never be bribed or swayed by other means? Were those holy lords I had spoken of always raised to that rank due to their knowledge of religion? Had there never been any who had swayed with the times when they were ordinary priests, or had been slavish prostitute chaplains to some nobleman, whose interests they carried on pushing once they got into the assembly?

Then he wanted to know how the ones I had called commoners were elected, and whether a stranger with a good bit of money might persuade the common people to vote for him rather than their landlord, or the best gentleman in the neighborhood? Why were people so desperate to get into this assembly, which I had admitted was hard work and very expensive and often bankrupted their families as they had no salary or pension? This seemed to his majesty such a high type of goodness and public spiritedness that he doubted it was always sincere.

He also wanted to know whether such keen gentlemen ever thought that they might get back the money and effort they spent back by sacrificing the public good to the schemes of a weak and vicious prince, along with his corrupt ministers? He asked many more questions, and quizzed me very thoroughly about all this, putting forward many inquiries and objections, which I don't think it would be sensible or wise to repeat.

His majesty wanted to know several things about our courts of justice, and I was well able to tell him about them, as I had in the past almost been ruined by a long lawsuit, which was eventually found against me, with costs. He asked me how long was usually spent deciding who was right and who wrong, and how much the costs should be? Were the advocates and orators allowed to speak for causes which they clearly knew were unjust, spiteful or bullying? Did one's party, political or religious, count for or against one in the courts? Did the lawyers know the universal laws of fairness, or did they just know about the local, regional and national laws? Had they or the judges had any part in writing the laws, which they took it upon themselves to interpret? Had they ever at different times pleaded for and against the same thing, and used the same examples to prove different things? Were they a rich or a poor body of men? Were they paid for pleading or giving their opinions? And particularly, did they ever become members of the lower house of parliament?

He asked next about the management of the treasury, and said he thought my memory must be wrong, as I had said that our taxes added up to five or six million a year, but when I mentioned expenditure he found that it sometimes came to more than twice that. The notes he had taken were very careful about this, because as he had said he hoped that what he learned about our conduct would be useful to him, and his calculations had to be right. But, if what I told him was right, he couldn't understand how a country could spend above its means like a private person. He asked me who our creditors were, and where did we find the money to pay them? He was amazed to hear me talk of expensive wars that could be charged for, and said we must be a very belligerent people, or have very bad neighbors, when our generals had to be paid more than our kings. He asked why we went to war outside our own islands, unless it was for trade, treaty obligations or to defend the coast with the navy. Above all he was astonished to be told about a paid for regular army being kept amongst a free people in times of peace. He said that if we were governed by ourselves, in the person of our representatives, he couldn't imagine whom we were afraid of or whom we thought we would fight. He wanted to know if a man, his children and family, might be better at defending his home than half a dozen rascals, taken off the streets at random, who might get a hundred times more than he offered by cutting their throats.

He laughed at my "odd kind of arithmetic", as it amused him to call it, in working out the whole population by adding up the different political and religious groups. He said he could not see why people who had opinions that went against the public good should not be forced to change them or to hide them. He said that as it would be tyrannous for any government to force people to change their minds, so it was weak not to force them to keep quiet: for anybody could be allowed to keep poisons at home, but not to sell them in the streets as drinks.

He said that he had noted that I had mentioned gambling amongst the entertainments of our nobility and gentry. He wanted to know at what age this entertainment was usually begun, and at what age they stopped; how much of their time it took up; whether they ever risked so much that it affected their fortunes; whether mean, vicious people, through their skill at cheating, might not get very rich and sometimes have a hold over our noblemen, and make them mix with low companions, stop them from improving their minds, and force them, because of their losses, to start trying to cheat others?

He was quite amazed at the history of the last century which I had told him, saying it was just a pile of conspiracies, rebellions, murders, massacres, revolutions, exiles, the very worst things that greed, party politics, hypocrisy, disloyalty, cruelty, rage, madness, envy, lust, malice and ambition could produce.

In another audience his majesty was keen to sum up everything I had said, comparing the questions he had asked with the answers I had given. He then took me into his hands and, stroking me gently, he said these words, which I shall never forget, nor the way he said them: "My little friend Grildrig, you have given a very good speech in praise of your country. You have clearly shown that ignorance, idleness and vice are the best qualifications for a lawmaker; that laws are best explained, interpreted and applied by those whose interests and abilities lie in perverting, defeating and avoiding them. I can see you have a system which might have been tolerable in its original form, but half the good things have been taken out and the rest has been totally ruined through corruption. From what you've said I can't see one post amongst you that needs any sort of perfection to get it: nowhere are men given titles because of their goodness; priests are not chosen for their piety or learning; soldiers are not chosen for their conduct or bravery; politicians are not chosen for their love of their country nor advisers for their wisdom. As for you," the king continued, "you have spent most of your life in travelling, and I hold out hopes that you may have escaped many of your country's vices. But from what I have gathered from your description, and the answers I have so painfully got from you, I can only conclude that most of your countrymen make up the most malicious race of nasty little vermin that nature has ever allowed to crawl on the surface of the earth."

Chapter VII

[The author's love of his country. He makes an offer which could be of great benefit to the king, but is rejected. The king's great ignorance of politics. The learning in the country is very imperfect and narrow-minded. The laws, military affairs and parties of the country.]

Only my extreme love of truth prevents me from hiding this part of my story. There was no point in showing my resentment, which always just led to ridicule; I was forced to sit patiently while my noble and beloved country was so shockingly spoken of. I am just as sorry as any of my readers that I gave the opportunity for this to happen, but this prince was so interested in everything that it would have been ungrateful and rude to refuse to answer his questions. In my own defence I will say that I cunningly dodged many of his questions, and gave every point a favourable spin, much more than strict truth would allow. I have always had that praiseworthy bias towards my own country which Dionysus Halicarnassensis, quite rightly, recommends in a historian: I like to hide the weaknesses and ugliness of my mother country, and show her goodness and beauty in the best light. This was what I was genuinely trying to do when I spoke with the king, although unfortunately I failed. But great allowances must be made for a king who lives completely cut off from the rest of the world, and so is completely ignorant of the most common manners and customs of other nations. A lack of knowledge will always produce many prejudices and a certain narrow mindedness, which we, and the politer nations of Europe, do not have. And it would be extremely wrong if such an isolated prince's ideas of virtue and vice were to be offered as a model for mankind.

To prove what I have just said, and to show more clearly the miserable effect of a narrow education, I'll put in a story which can hardly be believed. In the hope of ingratiating myself further with the king, I told him of, "an invention, discovered between three and four hundred years ago, of a certain powder which, if the smallest spark of fire falls on it, would catch fire in an instant, even if there was a heap of it as big as a mountain, and it would all fly up in the air at once, making a noise and shaking greater than thunder. A proper amount of this powder packed into a hollow tube of brass or iron, depending on its size, could drive a ball of iron or lead with such speed and force that nothing could resist it. The largest balls fired like this could not only cut down whole ranks of an army at once but batter the strongest walls to the ground, sink ships, with a thousand men in each, to the bottom of the sea, and when they were linked together with chains they could cut through masts and rigging, cut hundreds of bodies in half, and destroy everything in their path. We often put this powder into large hollow iron balls, and used a machine to throw them into a city we were besieging, where they would rip up pavements, tear the houses to pieces, burst and throw out splinters on every side and kill everyone nearby. I know the ingredients very well, which are cheap and easy to find; I know how to blend them, and I can tell your workmen how to make those tubes, of a size matching all other things in his majesty's kingdom, and the largest needn't be more than a hundred feet long. Twenty or thirty tubes like that, loaded with the right amount of powder and shot, could batter down the walls of the strongest towns in your kingdom within hours, or destroy the whole of the capital, if it ever tried to argue with your orders." I humbly offered to do this for his majesty, as payment for all the favors and protection I had received from him.

The king was horrified by my description of these terrible machines, and my proposal. He was amazed, that such a grovelling and powerless insect as me (those were his expressions) could entertain such inhuman ideas, and seem to take them so lightly that I was entirely unmoved by the killing and destruction that I had talked about as the usual effects of these destructive machines. He said that some evil genius who hated mankind must have invented them. As for himself, he said, though he loved nothing more than new discoveries in science or nature, he would rather lose half his kingdom than know the secret of them, and he ordered me, on pain of death, never to mention them again.

Here we see the odd notions caused by narrow principles and ideas! Here was a prince who had every quality which produces worship, love and respect; strong, wise, well educated, with many great talents, and greatly loved by his subjects; and he was going to pass up, through an unnecessary moral objection, which we wouldn't have in Europe, the offer of an opportunity to make him the absolute ruler of the lives, freedoms and fortunes of his people! I'm not saying this with the least intention of putting down the many virtues of that excellent king, who I know will be very much diminished, because of this, in the eyes of an English reader. I think this defect in them came from their ignorance, from not having reduced politics to a science as the sharper intelligence of Europeans has done. I can remember very well that I once told the king that we had several thousand books written about the art of government, and this made him think (which I didn't intend at all) that we must be very stupid. He claimed to hate and reject all secrecy, sophistication and plotting, on the part of either princes or ministers. He couldn't see why we had state secrets, if they weren't something being kept from an enemy or rival nation. He kept his ideas of governing within very narrow boundaries, of intelligence and common sense, justice and mercy, the speedy resolution of civil and criminal cases, and some other obvious ideas which are not worth talking about. And he said that he thought, "that whoever could make two ears of corn, or two blades of grass, grow in a place where only one had grown before, would be owed more by humanity, and do a greater service for his country, than all the politicians put together."

The education of these people is very flawed, being made up of only morality, history, poetry and mathematics, which it must be admitted they excel at. But that last subject is only used for practical purposes, to improve farming and machines, so we would think very little of it. As for ideas, abstract thoughts and meditation on things beyond the physical, I could never get the concept into their heads.

No law in that country is allowed to have a greater number of words in it than there are letters in their alphabet, which has only twenty-two letters. But in fact few of them even run to that length. They are written in the most plain and simple terms, which these people are not bright enough to interpret in more than one way. To write a commentary about any law is punishable by death. As for the resolution of criminal or civil cases, they have so few precedents to quote that they can hardly boast of their skill in this area.

They have been able to print as skilfully as the Chinese for as long as they can remember, but their libraries are not very large; the king's library, which is thought the largest, doesn't have more than a thousand volumes, in a gallery twelve hundred feet long, from which I was allowed to borrow any books I liked. The queen's carpenter built a wooden contraption in one of Glumdalclitch's rooms, twenty-five feet high and shaped like an upright ladder. The steps were each fifty feet long. In fact it was a moveable set of stairs, and the lowest end of it was placed ten feet from the wall of the room. The book I wanted to read was placed leaning up against the wall: I would climb up to the top of the ladder, face the book and begin at the top of the page, and walk about eight or ten paces to the right and the left, according to the length of the lines, until I had reached a point below my eye level, and then I would gradually climb down until I got to the bottom. After that I climbed up again and began the other page in the same way, and then turned over the page, which I could easily do with both hands, for it was as thick and stiff as cardboard, and even in the largest folios the pages were not more than eighteen or twenty feet long.

Their style is clear, manly and smooth, but not overblown, for they are careful to avoid using too many words unnecessarily or repeating themselves. I have read many of their books, especially the ones dealing with history and morality. Among the other books, I was most entertained by a little work which always lay in Glumdalclitch's bedroom, belonging to her governess, a serious elderly gentlewoman, which was full of essays on morality and religion. The book talks of the weakness of humanity, and is not highly rated except by women and common people. However, I was curious to see what an author of that country would have to say on the subject. The writer covered all the usual topics of European moralists, showing how small, insignificant and defenceless an animal man was, and how he couldn't defend himself against the weather or attacks of wild beasts; he detailed how one creature was stronger, another faster, a third had more foresight, a fourth was harder working.

He added that nature had degenerated in this late age of the world, and could now only produce tiny creatures, compared with those of ancient times. He said it was perfectly reasonable to think that not only were men larger then but also that there must have been giants, which history and tradition have always claimed, and it has been confirmed by the huge bones and skulls which had been accidentally dug up in the kingdom, which are far bigger than the shrunken race of men nowadays. He argued that the laws of nature dictated that we should have been larger in size, and stronger, at the beginning, so that we wouldn't be likely to be destroyed by every little mishap, by a tile falling from a house, or a stone thrown by a little boy, or drowning in a stream. From these thoughts the author drew several moral lessons, useful rules in life, but there's no need to repeat them here. For my own part, I couldn't help thinking how it seemed to be a universal thing to try and draw morals, and things that make us feel unhappy and fret, from our wars with nature. And I believe, from careful examination, that there is as little reason for those wars amongst us as there is with those people.

As for their military affairs, they boast that the king's army is made up of a hundred and seventy-six thousand foot soldiers and thirty-two thousand cavalrymen, if you can call it an army when it's drawn from tradesmen in the various cities and farmers in the country, with commanders just from the noblemen and gentlemen, who don't get wages or rewards. They are in fact perfect at their drill, and very well disciplined, but I didn't see much merit in that; what else would you expect, when every farmer was commanded by his own landlord, and every townsman was commanded by the principal men of his city, chosen, as they do in Venice, by voting?

I have often seen the Lorbrulgrud militia taken out to exercise, in a great twenty mile square field near the city. There were no more than twenty-five thousand infantry and six thousand cavalry, but it was impossible for me to accurately calculate them, seeing the amount of ground they took up. A cavalier, mounted on a large horse, might be about ninety feet high. I have seen this whole mass of cavalrymen, at a word of command, draw their swords at once, and wave them in the air. You cannot imagine anything so grand, so surprising, and so astonishing! It looked as if ten thousand lightning bolts were flashing from every part of the sky at the same time.

I was curious to know how this prince, whose country cannot be accessed by any others, came to think of having an army or teaching his people military discipline. But I soon found out why, both from conversation and reading histories: for, over the course of history, they have been troubled by the disease which affects every people: the nobility often fought for power, the people for freedom and the king for absolute rule. All of these groups have at various times tried to challenge the others, even though the others were nicely kept in check by the laws of the kingdom, and more than once there have been civil wars. The last one was happily brought to an end by the prince's grandfather, by a coalition of all three parties, and the militia was then established through general agreement, and has been kept up to the mark ever since.

Chapter VIII

[The king and queen make a journey to the frontiers. The author goes with them. The way in which he left the country is described in detail. He returns to England.]

I had always had a strong feeling that I would at some time be free again, though I couldn't guess how this would happen, or think of any project which would have any chance of succeeding. The ship I had sailed in was the first one ever seen off that coast, and the king had given strict orders that if any other appeared it should be brought ashore and brought on a cart to Lorbrulgrud. He was very keen on getting me a woman of my own size, so he could breed from me: but I think I would rather have died than left descendants who would have been kept in cages like canaries and perhaps, in time, sold around the kingdom to the upper classes as curiosities. I must say that I was treated with great kindness: I was a favorite of a great king and queen and loved by the whole court, but it was only on undignified terms. I could never forget the family I had left behind. I wanted to be with people I could talk to as equals, and to walk around the streets and fields without worrying about whether I would be trodden to death like a frog or tiny puppy. But my rescue came sooner than I imagined, and in a very unusual way; I shall tell the whole story and the background truthfully.

I had now been in this country for two years, and about the beginning of the third Glumdalclitch and I went with the king and queen on a visit to the south coast of the kingdom. I was carried as usual in my travelling box, which, as I have already described, was very comfortable, twelve feet square. I had ordered that a hammock should be fixed with silk ropes from each corner of the ceiling, to soften to the jolting when a servant carried me in front of him on horseback, as I sometimes asked him to do; and I would often sleep in my hammock when we were travelling. I ordered the carpenter to cut a hole a foot square in the roof of my closet, not directly above my hammock, so I could get some air as I slept in the hot weather. I could shut the hole when I pleased using a board that ran to and fro on a groove.

When we came to the end of our journey the king thought it would be right to spend a few days in a palace he has near Flanflasnic, a city within eighteen English miles of the coast. Glumdalclitch and I were very exhausted; I had a little cold, but the poor girl was so ill that she had to stay in bed. I was longing to see the ocean, which would be the only way I could escape, if I ever did. I pretended that I was feeling worse than I actually was, and asked permission to go and take the sea air with a page, of whom I was very fond and who had sometimes been trusted with looking after me. I shall never forget how unwillingly Glumdalclitch agreed, nor the strict orders she gave the page to take care of me, at the same time bursting into tears as if she had some premonition of what was going to happen to me. The boy took me out in my box towards the rocks on the seashore, about half an hour's walk from the palace. I ordered him to put me down, lifted one of my windows and gave many longing looks at the sea. I found that I was not feeling very well, and told the page I would take a nap in my hammock, which I hoped would make me feel better. I got in, and the boy shut the window tight to keep out the cold. I soon fell asleep, and all I can assume is that the page, thinking I was safe, went off to the rocks to look for birds' eggs, as I had seen him looking about before, and picking one or two out of clefts, when I watched him from my window.

Whatever happened, I was woken by a violent pull on the ring which was fixed to the top of my box to make it easier to carry. I felt my box lifted very high in the air, then rushed on at great speed. The first jolt nearly shook me out of my hammock, but the movement was smooth enough afterwards. I called out at the top of my voice, several times, but nothing happened. I looked through my windows, and could see nothing but the clouds and sky. I heard a noise just over my head like the beating of wings, and then I began to see the sorry state I was in. Some eagle had clearly got the ring of my box in his beak, meaning to drop it on to a rock, like a tortoise in its shell, and then take out my body and eat it, for the intelligence and sense of smell this bird has lets him discover his quarry at a great distance, even if it was better hidden than I was by two inch planks.

In a little while I noticed that the noise and flutter of the wings quickly got stringer, and my box was tossed up and down like a flag on a windy day. I heard several bangs or bumps, which I thought must have hit the eagle (for I am certain it must have been an eagle which had my box in his beak) and then, all of a sudden, I felt that I was falling straight down, for over a minute, but with such incredible speed that I almost lost my breath. My fall was stopped with a terrible splash, which sounded louder to me than Niagra Falls. After that I was quite in the dark for another minute, then my box began to rise up and I could see light from the tops of the windows. I now saw that I had fallen in the sea. My box, due to the weight of my body, the goods that I had inside, and the four pieces of iron that were fixed to the corners for strength, drew about five feet of water. I thought then, and still do, that the eagle which had my box was chased by two or three others, and was forced to let me drop while he defended himself against the others who wanted to have a share of his prey. The iron plates fastened to the bottom of the box (for they were the strongest and so heaviest) kept the box balanced as it fell and stopped it being broken when it hit the water. Every joint was well fitted, and the door did not swing on hinges but up and down like a sash window, so very little water got into my room. With great difficulty I got out of my hammock, having first drawn back the cover on the hole in the roof already mentioned, for I was almost suffocated for lack of air.

How often then did I wish I was with my dear Glumdalclitch, whom I had been driven so far away from in just an hour! And I can honestly say that in the middle of all my own troubles I couldn't help feeling sorry for my poor nurse, and how sad she would be to have lost me, how angry the queen would be, and how it would ruin her. Not many travellers have been in such difficulties and distress as I was at this point, expecting that at any moment my box would be broken into pieces, or at least overturned, by the first strong gust of wind or rising wave. A break in one pane of glass would have meant instant death, and nothing could have saved the windows if it hadn't been for the strong lattice of wires which were on the outside to protect against accidents when travelling. I saw water ooze in through several cracks, although the leaks weren't very big, and I stopped them up as well as I could. I wasn't able to lift up the roof of my room, because otherwise I certainly would have done and sat on the top of it, where I might save myself for at least a few more hours than I would by being shut up in the hold, as I might describe it. But if I escaped these dangers for a day or two what could I expect but a miserable death from cold and hunger? I spent four hours in these conditions, expecting, and indeed hoping, that every moment would be my last.

I have already mentioned that there were two strong staples fixed on that side of the box which had no window, and that when the servant carried me on horseback he would put a leather belt through them and buckle it around his waist. In my unhappy state I heard, or thought I heard, some kind of grating noise on the side of my box where the staples were fixed, and soon after I began to think that the box was being pulled or towed out to sea. Every now and then I felt a sort of tugging, which made the waves rise up almost to the tops of my windows, leaving me almost in the dark. This gave me some faint hope of being rescued, though I couldn't imagine how it would happen. I unscrewed one of my chairs, which were always screwed to the floor, and having worked hard to screw it down directly under the airhole I had recently opened I climbed up on it and, putting my mouth as close to the hole as I could, called for help in a loud voice, in all the languages I knew. I then attached my handkerchief to a stick I usually carried, and pushed it up through the hole and waved it several times in the air, so that if any boat or ship was nearby the seamen might guess that some unlucky man was locked up in the box.

Nothing I did had any effect, but I could tell that my room was being moved along; and in an hour or less the side of the box where the staples were, which had no windows, struck against something hard. I thought it was a rock, and was tossed around worse than ever. I clearly heard a noise on the lid of my box, like a cable, and it grated as it passed through the ring. I then found I was pulled up, gradually, at least three feet farther out of the water than I was before. Then I put up my stick and handkerchief again, calling for help until I was almost hoarse. I return I heard a great shout, repeated three times, which brought me such joy that cannot be imagined by those who have not experienced it. I now heard feet overhead, and somebody called through the hole, in English, that if there was anybody inside they should speak up. I answered that I was an Englishman, whose bad luck had landed him in the biggest disaster any creature ever endured, and I begged by everything holy that I should be freed from my dungeon. The voice told me that I was safe, as my box was fastened to their ship, and the carpenter would come at once and saw a hole in the lid, large enough to pull me out. I answered that that was unnecessary, and would take too much time, for all they had to do was for one of them to put a finger through the ring, and take the box out of the sea into the ship and into the captain's cabin. Some of them, hearing me talk like this, thought I was mad, and others laughed, for it never occurred to me that I was now amongst people of my own size and strength. The carpenter came, and in a few minutes had sawed an exit about four feet square, then let down a small ladder, which I climbed up and was taken onto the ship in a very poor state.

The sailors were all astonished, and asked me a thousand questions, which I didn't feel like answering. I was just as amazed at the sight of so many pygmies, which is what I thought they were, my eyes being so used to the enormous things I had left behind. But the captain. Mr.Thomas Wilcocks, an honest and good Shropshire man, seeing that I was ready to faint, took me into his cabin, gave me a drink to comfort me, and made me lie down on his own bed, telling me to get a little rest, which I very much needed. Before I went to sleep I told him that I had some valuable furniture in my box, too good to be lost: a fine hammock, a handsome camp bed, two chairs, a table and a cabinet. I also told him that the room was hung on all sides, or rather padded, with silk and cotton, and if he would ask one of the crew to bring it into his cabin I would open it up in front of him and show him what I had. The captain, hearing this nonsense, decided I had gone mad; however, (I guess to calm me down) he promised to do as I asked, and, going up onto the deck, he sent some of his men down into the box, from where (as I later discovered) they took out all my goods, and stripped the padding off the walls. But the chairs, cabinet and bedstead, being screwed to the floor, were very damaged by the crudeness of the sailors, who tore them up by force. Then they knocked out some of the boards to use on the ship, and when they had got all they wanted they let the main part drop into the sea, which sank to the bottom due to the many holes now in the bottom and sides. I must say I am glad I did not watch them being so destructive, as it would have brought past events to my mind which I would sooner have forgotten.

I slept for some hours, but very uneasily due to dreams about the place I had left and the dangers I had escaped. However, when I awoke I found I was feeling much better. It was now about eight o'clock at night and the captain ordered supper straight away, thinking I had already gone too long without food. He entertained me very kindly, seeing that I did not look mad or talk nonsense, and when we were alone he asked me to tell him about my travels, and how it was that I came to be set adrift in that monstrous wooden chest. He said that at about noon, as he was looking through his telescope, he had seen it at a distance, and thought it was a ship, and he decided to make for it, as it wasn't much out of his way, in the hope of buying some biscuit, as his own supplies were running low. When he came nearer and discovered his error he sent his longboat out to discover what it was, and they came back scared saying it was a swimming house. He laughed at their stupidity, and got into the boat himself, ordering his men to bring a strong cable.

The weather was calm, and he rowed round me several times, looking at my windows and the wire lattice which protected them. Then he found the two staples on the side which was all boards, without any holes for light. He ordered his men to row up to that side and fasten a cable to one of the staples, and then they began to tow my chest, as they called it, back to the ship. When they got there he gave instructions that another cable should be fastened to the ring in the lid and to pull the chest up with pulleys, but all of them together couldn't lift it more than two or three feet. Then they saw my stick and handkerchief pushed through the hole, and concluded that some unlucky man must be locked up inside. I asked whether he or the crew had seen any large birds in the air, about the time they first found me. He answered that talking it over with the crew while I was asleep one of them had said that he had seen three eagles flying northwards, but he hadn't said anything about their being an unusual size – which I suppose was due to the great height they were flying at, and he couldn't guess why I asked. I then asked the captain how far off we were from land, and he answered that by his best reckoning we were at least three hundred miles. I assured him that he must be mistaken by at least half, as I had not been out of the country I had come from for more than two hours before I was dropped in the sea.

At this he began again to suspect that my brain was disturbed, which he hinted at, and advised me to go to bed in a cabin he had allocated me. I assured him that I was well refreshed by his welcome and his company, and as sane as I had ever been in my life. He then became serious, and asked if he could enquire whether I didn't have some great crime pressing on my conscience, which I was being punished for by some prince by being sent out in that chest. This was how great criminals in other countries were forced to go to sea in leaky boats without provisions, and he would be unhappy to have picked up such a bad man, but he would give me his promise that he would put me safely ashore at the next port we came to. He added that his suspicions were confirmed by some ridiculous things I had said to his sailors, and afterwards to him, about my room or chest, and also by my odd looks and behavior at supper.

I begged him to indulge me and listen to my story, which I told him truthfully, from the last time I left England to the moment he first found me. As truth always finds its way into sensible minds, this honest and good gentleman, who had some education and very good sense was immediately convinced of my truthfulness and openness. But to back up what I had said I asked that my cabinet should be brought, which I had the key to in my pocket (he had already told me what the sailors had done with my room). I opened it in his presence, and showed him the little collection of curios I had brought from the country from which I had been rescued in such an unusual fashion. There was the comb I had made from his majesty's stubble, and another one of the same material but fixed into one of her majesty's thumbnail clippings, which served as the back. There was a collection of pins and needles, from a foot to half a yard long; four wasp stings, like carpenter's nails; some of the queen's hair; a gold ring which she had presented to me one day in a most amusing fashion, taking it from her little finger and throwing it over my head like a collar. I asked the captain to take the ring in return for his kindness, which he absolutely refused. I showed him a corn which I had cut off myself from the toe of a maid of honor; it was about the size of a Kentish apple, and had got so hard that when I got back to England I had it hollowed out into a cup and mounted in silver. Lastly, I asked him to look at the breeches I was wearing, which were made from mouse skin.

I could persuade him to take nothing other than a footman's tooth, which I noticed he examined with great interest and had taken a fancy to. He took it with great thanks, much more than such a small thing deserved. It had been taken from one of Glumdalclitch's men by mistake by a clumsy surgeon: the man had toothache but this one was as healthy as any in his head. I had it cleaned and put it in my cabinet. It was about a foot long and four inches round.

The captain was very interested in the story I told him and said that he hoped, when we got back to England, that I would do the world a favor by writing it down and publishing it. I said that we had too many travel books, and nothing was satisfactory now unless it was extraordinary. I doubted some authors drew as much from the truth as from their own vanity, self interest and the desire to entertain ignorant readers. My story would only contain normal events, without those florid descriptions of strange plants, trees, birds and other animals, or of the barbaric customs and idol worship of savage people, which most books are full of. However, I thanked him for the compliment and said I would bear it in mind.

He said one thing amazed him, and that was how loudly I was speaking. He asked if the king and queen of that country were hard of hearing. I told him that it was what I had become used to for the last two or three years, and I was just as amazed at the voices of him and his men, who seemed to me to be only whispering, although I could hear them well enough. But when I spoke in that country it was like a man talking in the street to another on top of a steeple, unless I was placed on a table, or held in someone's hand. I told him that I had also noticed another thing, that when I got onto the ship and all the sailors stood around me I thought that they were the most insignificant little creatures I had ever seen. For in fact it was true, that when I was in the prince's country I couldn't stand looking in a mirror, after my eyes had got used to such huge objects, because the comparison made me think of myself as so insignificant. The captain said that while we were having supper he had seen me looking at everything in amazement, which he couldn't work out, and he put it down to some confusion in my brain.

I answered that it was very true, and I couldn't stop myself, when I saw his dishes the size of a silver threepenny bit, a leg of pork that was hardly a mouthful and a cup smaller than a nutshell. I carried on, describing the rest of his household things and provisions in the same way. For, although the queen had ordered a little set of things I needed, while I was in her service, my imagination was completely full of the things I saw on all sides, and I ignored my own smallness, as people ignore their own faults. The captain completely understood the joke, and merrily replied with the old English proverb that he doubted my eyes were bigger than my stomach, as he couldn't see my stomach as well, although I had fasted all day. He continued joking, saying that he would gladly have given a hundred pounds to see my box in the eagle's beak, and afterwards see it falling from such a great height into the sea, which was surely a most astonishing sight which would have been worth telling future generations about. He also said that the comparison with Phaeton (who drove a carriage through the sky) was so obvious that he could not resist making it, although I didn't think much of the joke.

The captain had been in Vietnam, and on his return to England he was blown north-eastward to latitude 44, longitude 33. But we picked up a trade wind two days after I came on board and sailed southward for a long time, and rounding New Holland we kept our course west-south-west, then south-south-west until we came round the Cape of Good Hope. Our voyage was very successful, but I won't trouble the reader with the details. The captain called in at one or two ports, and sent his longboat in to collect provisions and water, but I never left the boat until we got to the English Channel, which was on the third of June, 1706, about nine months after I escaped. I offered to leave my goods as a promise that I would pay for my passage, but the captain protested that he would not accept a farthing. We parted on excellent terms, and I made him promise that he would come and visit me at my house in Redriff. I hired a horse and guide for five shillings, which I borrowed from the captain.

As I journeyed I saw how small the houses, the trees, the cattle and the people were, and I began to think I was back in Lilliput. I was afraid of trampling on every traveller I met, and I often shouted for them to get out of my way, so I could have received a couple of good beatings for my rudeness.

When I came to my own house, which I was forced to ask directions for, when one of the servants opened the door I bent down to go in, like a goose going under a gate, for fear of banging my head. My wife ran out to embrace me, but I bent down lower than her knees, thinking that otherwise she would never be able to reach my mouth. My daughter kneeled to ask for my blessing, but I could not see her until she got up, having been used for so long to stand with my head and eyes looking sixty feet skywards, and then I tried to pick her up by the waist with one hand. I looked down on the servants, and one or two friends who were there, as if they were pygmies and I was a giant. I told my wife that she had been too thrifty, as it looked to me as if she had starved herself and my daughter down to nothing. To sum up, I behaved so oddly that they thought the same as the captain when he first saw me, and thought I had lost my mind. I mention this as an example of how powerful habits and prejudice are.

In a little while my family, friends and I came to understand each other, but my wife insisted that I was not to go to sea again. However, my evil fortune arranged things so that she did not have the power to stop me, as the reader may learn later. In the mean time, this is where I end the account of the second part of my unfortunate voyages.

Part III: A Voyage to Laputa, Balnibarbi, Luggnagg, Glubbubdrib, and Japan

Chapter I

[The author sets out on his third voyage. He is captured by pirates.
The spite of a Dutchman. He arrives at an island. He is welcomed
to Laputa.]

I had not been home for more than ten days when Captain William
Robinson, a Cornishman and commander of the Hopewell, a good
boat of three hundred tons, came to my house. I had before been the
surgeon on another ship of which he was master and quarter owner
in a voyage to the eastern Mediterranean. He had always treated me
more like a brother than a lower ranked officer. Hearing of my
homecoming he paid me a visit, which I assumed was only out of
friendship, for we spoke of nothing but the usual things one does
after long absences. But he came back often, saying how pleased he
was that I was in good health and asking if I had decided to settle
down for life. He said that he was planning to make a voyage to the
East Indies in two months, and eventually he openly invited me,
though somewhat apologetically, to be the surgeon on his ship. He
said that I would have another surgeon under me, in addition to the
two mates, that my salary would be twice the normal rate, and that as
he knew my experience in nautical matters was at least as good as
his he would make any promise I liked that he would follow my
advice as if I shared his command. He said so many other flattering
things, and I knew he was such an honest man, that I could not turn
down his offer. My thirst to see the world was still as strong as ever,
despite my past misfortunes. The only remaining problem was to
persuade my wife to allow me to go, but she eventually agreed,
thinking of the money it could bring in for the children.

We set out on the 5th day of August 1706 and arrived at Fort St.George on the 11th of April 1707. We stayed there three weeks to give our crew a rest, as many of them were sick. From there we went on to Vietnam, where the captain decided to wait for some time, because many of the things he intended to buy were not ready, and they would not be ready for several months. So, in order to offset some of the expenses of this, he bought a sloop, stocked it with several types of goods of the type the Vietnamese usually trade with other islands, and put fourteen men on it, including three natives. He made me captain of the sloop and gave me authority to trade while he conducted his business at Vietnam.

We had not been sailing for three days when a great storm broke, which drove us north-north-east for five days, and then we were driven east. After that the weather was better, though there was still a strong westerly wind. On the tenth day we were chased by two pirate ships, who soon caught us, because my sloop had such a heavy load that she was very slow, and we were in no state to defend ourselves.

Both pirate captains boarded us about the same time, exploding onto the boat with their men, but they found us all lying face down on the deck (as I had ordered) so they tied us up with strong ropes and, putting a guard on us, they went to search the boat.

I saw that one of them was a Dutchman, who seemed to have some authority, though he was not captain of either ship. He knew from our appearance that we were English men, and jabbering at us in his own language he swore that we would be tied back to back and thrown into the sea. I spoke Dutch quite well, so I told him who we were and begged him, as we were Christians and Protestants as well as from a neighboring country with which Holland had a strong alliance, that he would ask the captains to have pity on us. This made him more angry; he carried on with his threats and turned to his companions and spoke very angrily in what I assume was Japanese, often using the word "Chrsitianos."

The largest of the two pirate ships was commanded by a Japanese captain who spoke a little Dutch, though very poorly. He came up to me, and after asking several questions, which I answered very meekly, he said that we would not be killed. I made a very low bow to the captain and then, turning to the Dutchman, I said that I was sorry to see that I could get more mercy from a heathen than a fellow Christian. But I soon had reason to regret these foolhardy words; that spiteful scoundrel, after having tried in vain to persuade both captains that I should be thrown in the sea (which they would not agree to, after promising I would not die), managed to get his own way to the extent that he persuaded them to give me a punishment which seemed, as far as I could see, worse than death. My men were spilt up equally between the pirate ships, and the sloop was given a new crew. For me, it was decided that I would be set adrift in a small canoe, with paddles and a sail, and four days' provisions. The Japanese captain was kind enough to double the provisions from his own stores, and would not let any man search me. I climbed down into the canoe while the Dutchman, from the deck, threw all the curses and insults at me his language could provide.

About an hour before we saw the pirates I had made a measurement of our position and found that we were at latitude 46N and longitude 183. When I was some way from the pirates I saw through my pocket telescope some islands to the south-east. I set up my sail, as the wind was in the right direction, meaning to get to the nearest of these islands, which I managed in about three hours. It was very rocky, however I got many birds' eggs, and, striking a spark, I burned some bracken and dry seaweed, which I used to roast my eggs. I ate nothing else, being determined to make my provisions last as long as possible. I spent the night sheltered under a rock, with some bracken for a bed, and slept pretty well. The next day I sailed on to another island, and from there to a third and fourth, sometimes using my sail and sometimes my paddles. But without bothering the reader with a detailed account of my troubles it's enough to say that on the fifth day I arrived at the last island I could see, which was south-south-east of the others.

This island was farther away than I had thought, and it took me more than five hours to reach it. I sailed almost all round it before I could find a good landing spot in a small creek, about three times as wide as my canoe. I found the island was very rocky, with just some tufty grass and sweet smelling herbs. I took out my small stock of provisions and after I had refreshed myself I hid the rest in a cave, of which there were great numbers. I gathered up plenty of eggs from the rocks, and got some dry seaweed and dead grass, which I intended to make a fire with the next day and roast my eggs as well as I could, for I had on me my flint, steel, matches and a magnifying glass for burning. I lay all night in the cave where I had put my provisions. My bed was the same dry grass and seaweed which I meant to use as fuel. I slept very little, as my worries won over my tiredness and kept me awake. I thought how impossible it was going to be to stay alive in such a barren place, and how miserable my death was going to be. I found that I was so listless and depressed that I did not have the heart to get up, and the day was well advanced before I could get the energy to walk out of my cave. I walked amongst the rocks for a while: there was a cloudless sky and the sun was so hot that I was forced to turn my face away from it. All of a sudden the sun disappeared, and it seemed to me in a very different way to the way it did when covered by a cloud. I turned round, and saw a vast solid object between me and the sun, moving towards the island. It seemed to be about two miles high, and hid the sun for six or seven minutes, though the air wasn't much colder, or the sky darker, than if I had been in the shade of a mountain.

As it came nearer to me I saw that it seemed to be a firm substance, with the bottom flat, smooth, and shining very brightly from the reflection off the sea below. I stood on a high spot about two hundred yards from the shore and saw this great body coming down almost parallel to me, less than an English mile away. I took out my pocket telescope and could clearly see a number of people moving up and down its sides, which seemed to slope, but I couldn't see what these people were doing.

My natural instinct for life gave me a thrill of joy, and I started to hope that this strange event might in some way or other help to rescue me from the barren place and sad state I was in. But at the same time the reader can hardly imagine my amazement at seeing an island in the air, inhabited by men, who were able, it seemed, to rise and sink, or move forward, as they wished. But at that time I didn't feel like working out how it worked, and was more concerned with observing which way the island would go, as it seemed to be standing still. However it soon came nearer, and I could see that the sides of it had several levels of galleries, with stairs at intervals to go from one to the other. On the lowest gallery I saw some people with long fishing rods and others looking on. I waved my cap (for my hat had long ago worn out) and my handkerchief at the island, and as it got closer I shouted at the top of my voice. Looking carefully I could see that a crowd had gathered on the side I could see. I saw by the way they were pointing at me and each other that they had obviously seen me, although they didn't return my shouts. But I could see four or five men hurrying up the stairs to the top of the island; they then disappeared. I guessed, correctly as it turned out, that they had been sent to get orders from some person in authority.

The crowd increased, and in less than half an hour the island was raised and moved in such a way that the lowest gallery appeared level with me, less that a hundred yards from the high point where I stood. I then put myself in a very begging stance, and spoke in the meekest way, but I got no answer. Those who stood nearest to me seemed, as I guessed from their clothes, to be of a high rank. They talked seriously amongst themselves, often looking over at me. Eventually one of them called over in a clear, polite, smooth tone, which sounded not unlike Italian. I therefore answered in the Italian, hoping at least that the rhythm would sound pleasant to him. Although neither of us understood the other my meaning was clear, as they could see the distress as I was in.

They signalled that I should come down from my rock and go towards the shore, which I did. The flying island was lifted to a convenient height, with the edge directly over my head; a chain was lowered from the bottom gallery, with a seat fastened to the end of it. I sat in this and was pulled up with pulleys.

Chapter II

[The moods and characters of the Laputians are described. Their learning is detailed. About the king and his court. The author's reception at court. The fears and anxieties the inhabitants suffer. The women described.]

When I boarded, I was surrounded by a crowd of people, but those who stood nearest seemed to be of the higher ranks. They looked at me with every sign of utter astonishment, and I did much the same, for I had never before seen a race of men so unusual in their shapes, clothes and faces. Their heads all leaned to one side, right or left; one of their eyes looked inwards and the other straight up at the sky. Their clothes were decorated with pictures of suns, moons and stars, mixed in with fiddles, flutes, harps, trumpets, guitars, harpsichords and many other musical instruments unknown in Europe. I saw, here and there, many who were dressed like servants, with a balloon, fastened like a fly swat on the end of a stick, which they carried in their hands. In each balloon there was, as I learnt afterwards, a little quantity of dried peas or little pebbles. With these bladders they now and then flapped at the mouths and ears of those standing near them; I couldn't at that point work out why they did this.

It seems that these people's minds are so involved with intense thoughts that they cannot speak, nor listen to others, unless some external stimulation on their ears and mouths is provided. For this reason, the people who can afford it always keep a flapper (their word is "climenole") on hand, as one of their servants, and they never go out or make visits without him. The business of this person is, when two, three or more persons are together, to gently strike with his balloon the mouth of the person who should be speaking, and the ears of the person addressed. The flapper is also used when his master goes on walks, to occasionally give him a soft flap on the eyes, because he is always so wrapped up in thought that he is in continual danger of falling over every ledge, and walking into every post, and in the streets he will bump into others, or be bumped into the gutter himself.

I have to tell the reader this, or he would be as confused as me about the way these people carried on as they conducted me up the stairs to the top of the island, and from there to the royal palace. While we were climbing they forgot several times what they were doing, and left me alone, until they were brought to attention by their flappers. They didn't seem to think anything at all about my unusual clothes or appearance, nor the shouts of the common people, whose thoughts and minds weren't so intensely focussed.

At last we entered the palace, and went into the audience chamber, where I saw the king sitting on his throne attended on each side by people of the highest nobility. There was a large table in front of the throne filled with globes and spheres, and mathematical instruments of all sorts. His majesty completely ignored us, even though our entrance caused a good deal of commotion amongst all the people connected to the court. But he was deeply involved with a problem, and we waited at least an hour for him to solve it. On each side of him there stood a young page with flaps in their hands, and when they saw he was free one of them gently struck his right ear and the other his mouth, at which he started like someone suddenly awoken, and looking at me and my attendants he remembered that we had come, which he had been notified of previously. He said something, and a young man with a flap immediately came up to my side and flapped me gently on the right ear; but I indicated, as well as I could, that I did not need this help. I found out afterwards that this gave his majesty and the whole court a very poor opinion of my intelligence.

The king, as far as I could work out, asked me several questions, and I spoke to him in all the languages I knew. When it was realised that I could neither understand nor be understood I was taken by his order to an apartment in his palace (this prince is the greatest of all his line in terms of his hospitality towards strangers), where two servants were appointed to look after me. My dinner was brought, and four very noble people, whom I remembered had been standing very near the king, did me the honor of dining with me. We had two courses of three dishes each. For the first course there was a shoulder of mutton cut into an equilateral triangle, a piece of beef cut into rhomboids, and a pudding in the shape of a cycloid. The second course was two ducks tied up to look like violins, with sausages and puddings resembling flutes and oboes and a breast of veal in the shape of a harp. The servants cut our bread into cones, cylinders, parallelograms and several other mathematical shapes.

While we ate I ventured to ask the names of several things in their language, and those noble people, with the help of their flappers, were delighted to answer me, hoping that if I could talk with them I would be able to admire their great abilities. I was soon able to ask for bread and drink, or whatever else I wanted.

After dinner my companions left, and a person was sent to me by order of the king, accompanied by a flapper. He brought a pen, ink, paper, and three or four books, and he indicated with signs that he had been sent to teach me the language. We sat together for four hours, in which time I wrote down many words in columns, with their meaning next to them. I also learnt several short sentences, demonstrated by my tutor ordering a servant to fetch something, turn around, make a bow, stand, sit, walk and so on. Then I would write down the sentence. He also showed me, in one of his books, pictures of the sun, moon, and stars, the zodiac, the tropics, the polar circles, along with the names of many angles and shapes. He gave me the names and descriptions of all the musical instruments, and the general terms associated with the skill of playing them. After he left I placed all the words, and their translations, in alphabetical order. And so, in a few days, helped by my very good memory, I got some insight into their language. The word which means the flying or floating island is "Laputa," and I was never able to get the true derivation of this. "Lap," in their old, obsolete language, means high, and "unuth" means a governor, which they say developed into "Laputa," from "Lapuntuh." But I don't believe this derivation, which seems a bit forced to me. I offered their learned men a suggestion of my own, which was that Laputa came from "Lap outed", "Lap" meaning the dancing of sunbeams on the sea and "outed" meaning a wing. However, I shall not push my idea, but leave it to the discerning reader to decide if I am right.

Those whom the king had put me in the care of, seeing how poorly I was dressed, ordered a tailor to come the next morning and measure me for a suit of clothes. This craftsman did this in a different way from his counterparts in Europe. He first measured my height by using angles, and then he drew out all the outlines and dimensions of my body with a ruler and compasses. In six days he brought me my clothes, very badly made and completely ill-fitting, as he had made an error in his calculations. I wasn't too bothered as I noticed that such mistakes were very frequent, and nobody seemed to notice them.

During my isolation due to not having clothes, and then some more days due to an illness, I greatly expanded my dictionary, and when I next went to the court I was able to understand many of the things his majesty said and give him some sort of answers. His majesty had given orders that the island should travel north-east by east until it was directly over Lagado, the capital city of the whole kingdom below on solid ground. It was about two hundred and fifty miles away, and our journey took four and a half days. I didn't feel the movement of the island in the air in any way. On the second morning, about eleven o'clock, the king in person, attended by his noblemen, courtiers and officers, got out all their musical instruments and played them for three hours without a break, so that I was quite stunned by the noise. I could not guess why they did this, until my tutor told me. He said that the people of the island were able to hear the music of the universe, which played at certain times, and the court was accustomed to joining in on whatever instrument they were best at.

In our journey towards Lagado, the capital city, his majesty ordered that the island should stop over certain towns and villages, so he could hear the requests of his subjects. For this purpose several packthreads were lowered, with weights on the end of them. People tied their petitions to these packthreads, which went up the string like the scraps of paper schoolboys fasten to their kite strings. Sometimes we got wine and food from the ground, which was pulled up with pulleys.

My knowledge of mathematics helped me very much in acquiring their language, which was very much based on that science, and also on music, which I had some skill at. When they talk it is always in terms of lines and shapes. If they describe, for example, the beauty of a woman, or any other animal, they do it through rhomboids, circles, parallelograms, ellipses and other geometrical terms, or through words drawn from the art of music which I need not repeat here. I saw that in the king's kitchen there were all sorts of mathematical and musical instruments, which they used as models to cut the shapes of the joints served at the king's table.

Their houses are very poorly made, all the walls lean at angles, without one right angle in any apartment; these faults come from their contempt for practical geometry, which they think is vulgar and mechanical. The plans they make are too complex for the intellects of their workmen, which means there are always mistakes. Although they are very skilful with a piece of paper in their use of rulers, pencils and compasses, I have never seen a more awkward, clumsy and impractical people in everyday life, nor any who are so slow and confused in their understanding of every subject except for music and mathematics. They are very bad thinkers, and love to argue against things, except when they are right, which is not very often. They are completely unable to use imagination, fantasy or invention, and there are no words in their language to express these things. Their entire minds are taken up with the two sciences I have mentioned.

Most of them, especially the astronomers, are great believers in astrology, although they are too ashamed to admit it in public. But what I really noticed, and could not understand, was that they were obsessed with news and politics, always asking about public affairs, giving their judgements in matters of government, and arguing over every tiny detail of party politics. I have often noticed the same thing with the mathematicians I have known in Europe, although I could never understand how the two sciences were in any way related, unless it is that people think that because the smallest circle has the same number of angles as the largest then the ruling and management of the whole world is as easy as turning a globe in one's hands. But I think this quality comes from a very common weakness of human nature, which makes us most curious and arrogant about matters which concern us least, and for which nature and education has given us no talent.

These people suffer from continual anxiety, never having a minute's peace of mind; their worries come from ideas which most other people don't think about. They worry about the changes which they think will occur in relation to the planets; they think, for example, that the earth, as the sun is always approaching it, must eventually be swallowed up by the sun; that the face of the sun will gradually become encrusted with its own lava, and stop giving light to the earth; that the earth only just missed being brushed by the tail of the last comet which passed, which would have burnt it to cinder, and that the next, which they have calculated is coming in thirty-one years, will probably destroy us. For if on its orbit it should come within a certain distance from the sun (as they have calculated it will) it will be heated to a temperature ten thousand times hotter than a red hot iron, and as it leaves the sun it will drag a blazing tail a million and fourteen miles long. If the earth should pass through this tail at a distance of one hundred thousand miles from the nucleus, or main body, of the comet, it must be set on fire and be reduced to ashes. They also fear that the sun, daily burning its rays without any new fuel being added, must at last burn up and disappear, which would mean the destruction of the earth and all the planets which receive their light from it.

They are so permanently anxious about this and similar threats that they can never rest easy in their beds, nor can they enjoy any of the ordinary pleasures and amusements of life. When they meet an acquaintance in the morning the first thing they ask is about the state of the sun, how it looked when it rose and set, and what hope they have of avoiding the blow from the approaching comet. In their conversations about this they are just like boys who love to hear terrible stories about ghosts and hobgoblins, which they devour, and then can't go to sleep because they are frightened.

The women of the island are very jolly; they have contempt for their husbands and are very fond of strangers, of which there are always a large number at court from the continent below, either dealing with the business of the towns and their councils or for their own special reasons, but they are much despised by the men as they are not as accomplished as them. The ladies choose their special favorites from them, and the terrible thing is that they can carry on far too easily and safely, because the husband is always so wrapped up in his thoughts that the mistress and her lover may do what they like right in front of his face, as long as he has paper and pencil and does not have his flapper at his side.

The wives and daughters complain about being kept on the island, although I think it's the most delightful spot in the world. Although they live in great wealth and magnificence, and can do just as they please, they long to see the world and enjoy the entertainments in the capital city, which they are not allowed to do without the special permission of the king, and this is not easy to get, because the noblemen have found, through many experiences, how difficult it is to get their women to come back from below. I was told that a very great lady of the court – married to the prime minister, the richest subject in the kingdom, a very good man who is extremely fond of her and lives in the finest palace on the island – went down to Lagado pretending she was going for her health and disappeared for several months, until the king sent orders to search for her. She was found in a low inn dressed in rags, having pawned her clothes to support an old crippled footman who beat her every day and who was there when she was captured, very much against her wishes. Although her husband welcomed her back with all possible kindness, and without any reproach, she soon managed to sneak down again, with all her jewellery, to the same lover, and she hasn't been heard of since.

The reader might think that this was a story from Europe or England, rather than from such a remote country. But he should remember that the changeability of women isn't confined to any one region or nation, and that they are much more similar than we think. In about a month I had become reasonably fluent in their language, and was able to answer most of the king's questions, when I had the honor to visit him. His majesty did not show the least curiosity about the laws, government, history, religion or customs of the countries I had visited; all he asked about was the state of mathematics in them, and he received my answers with great contempt and indifference, even though his flappers on each side kept waking him.

Chapter III

[A problem is solved with modern philosophy and astronomy. How the Laputians have made great improvements in astronomy. How the king puts down rebellions.]

I asked the prince's permission to see some of the curiosities of the island, which he was kind enough to give, and he ordered that my tutor should go with me. The main thing I wanted to know was how, through art or nature, the island moved, and I will now give the reader a scientific account of this. The flying or floating island is perfectly round, with a diameter of 7837 yards, or about four and a half miles, and so it has an area of ten thousand acres. It is three hundred yards thick. The bottom, or underside, which is what those below see, is one even smooth plate of diamond, about two hundred yards thick. Above it there are several veins of minerals in their usual order, and over everything there is a coating of rich earth, ten or twelve feet deep. The saucer shape of the upper surface, going down from the edge to the center, is the reason why all the dew and rain which falls on the island runs down in little streams towards the middle, where they empty into four large basins, each about half a mile round and two hundred yards from the center. During the daytime the water in these basins continually evaporates in the sun, which stops them from overflowing. In any case, the king has the power to lift the island above the clouds and fogs, so he can stop dew and rain whenever he wishes. For as naturalists agree, the highest clouds cannot rise more than two miles, at least they never did in that country.

In the middle of the island there is a hole about fifty yards across, which the astronomers go down into in a large dome which is called "Flandona Gagnole," or the astronomer's cave, which is placed a hundred yards below the top of the diamond layer. In this cave there are always twenty lamps burning which, from the reflection off the diamond, shine a strong light everywhere. The place is equipped with a great quantity of sextants, quadrants, telescopes, astrolabes and other astronomical instruments. But the strangest thing, which the survival of the island depends on, is a huge magnet, shaped like a weaver's shuttle. It is six yards long, and more than three yards thick at its thickest part. This magnet is supported by a very strong diamond axle passing through its center, which it spins on, and it is so perfectly balanced that the weakest person can turn it. It is surrounded by a hollow cylinder of diamond, four yards across, placed horizontally and supported by eight diamond feet, each one six yards high. In the middle of the concave side there is a groove twelve inches deep, in which the ends of the axle are placed, and turned as needed.

The stone cannot be taken from its place by any force, because the hoop and its feet are carved out of the solid diamond which makes up the base of the island. By the use of this loadstone the island is made to rise and fall, and move from one place to another. In relation to the part of the earth that king rules over, the stone has at one end a power which draws it in, and at the other a power which pushes it away. When the magnet is turned upright, with its attracting end pointing downwards, the island descends, but when the repelling end points downwards the island rises straight up. When the stone lies diagonally this is the direction the island takes as well, for in this magnet, the forces always act in lines which run parallel to its direction. By this diagonal motion, the island is carried to different parts of the kingdom.

To explain how this works, imagine AB as a line drawn over the region of Balnibarbi, let the line CD represent the loadstone, with D being the repelling end and C the attracting end, with the island being over C. Let the stone be placed in the position CD, with its repelling end pointing down, then the island will be driven upwards diagonally towards D. When it gets to D, let the stone be turned on its axle until its attracting end points toward E, then the island will be carried diagonally to E, where, if the stone is turned again on its axle, until it stands in the position EF, with the repelling end pointing downwards, the island will rise diagonally towards F, where by turning the attracting end towards G the island may be carried towards G and from G to H by turning the stone so that its repelling end points directly downwards. And so, by changing the position of the stone as often as necessary, the island is made to rise and fall in a diagonal manner, and by these alternate risings and fallings (the diagonal not being very steep) it is conveyed from one part of the kingdom to another.

But it should be noted that the island cannot go beyond the boundaries of the kingdom below it, nor can it rise higher than four miles. The astronomers (who have written many theories about the stone) deduce this reason for it: that the power of the magnet does not work beyond a distance of four miles, and that the mineral in the earth, and about twenty miles out to sea, which works with the stone is not present everywhere on earth but stops at the borders of the kingdom. It was easy, with the great advantage of such a lofty position, for the king to make anywhere where the magnet worked obey him.

When the stone is put parallel to the horizon, the island stands still, for when that happens the two ends, being the same distance from the earth, act with equal force, one pulling down and the other pushing up, and consequently no movement takes place.

The loadstone is in the hands of certain astronomers who, from time to time, adjust it as the king directs.

They spend most of their lives observing the stars and planets, which they do with the help of lenses which are far better than ours. For, although their largest telescopes are not bigger than three feet long, they have a far greater magnification than those a hundred feet long do with us, and they show the stars more clearly. This advantage has allowed them to make far greater discoveries than our astronomers in Europe; they have made a list of ten thousand stars, while the largest of our lists don't have more than a third of that. They have also discovered two smaller stars, or satellites, which orbit Mars. The nearer one is exactly three times the planet's diameter away, the outer one five times. The former orbits every ten hours, the outer one every twenty-one and a half. This means the square of the time of their orbits are almost equal to the cube of their distances from the center of Mars, which proves that they are governed by the same laws of gravity that work on other planets.

They have observed ninety-three different comets, and worked out when they will appear very precisely. If this is true (and they are very confident it is) then it would be a very good thing if their observations were made public, and then the theory of comets, which at the moment is very poor and flawed, could be brought to the same level of perfection as the other branches of astronomy.

The king would be the most powerful ruler in the universe, if he could only persuade his powerful nobles to join with him in an administration, but they have their estates down on the continent, and as they think that the position of favorite is a very shaky one they would never agree to their country being enslaved. If any town starts a rebellion or mutiny, starts fighting internally or refuses to pay its taxes, the king has two ways to bring them into line. The first and most peaceful method is to hover the island over the town, and the land around it, so that they do not get sun or rain, and so the inhabitants suffer from famine and disease. If their crime deserves it they are pelted from above with great stones, which they have no defence against apart from creeping into cellars and caves, while the roofs of their houses are smashed to pieces. But if they still won't behave, or try to fight back, he goes on to his last resort, which is to drop the island directly onto their heads, wiping out both the houses and the people. However, situations rarely get bad enough to consider doing this, and the king does not want to do it, and his ministers do not advise him to do such a thing as it would make the people hate them, which consequently would do great damage to their own estates, which are all below, for the island belongs to the king.

But there is another even more important reason why the kings of this country have always been against performing such a terrible action, unless they absolutely had to. If the town they were going destroy had any rocky hills in it, as there generally are in the bigger cities, or high towers, or pillars of stone, a sudden drop might risk the bottom of the island. Although, as I have said, it is made of one huge diamond, two hundred yards thick, it might crack from such a great shock, or burst from getting too near the fires from the houses below, just as the backs of our chimneys, iron and stone, often do. The people know all about this, and know how far they can push their disobedience, where their freedom or property is concerned. And the king, when he has been pushed too far, and wants to crush a city to rubble, orders the island be let down very softly. He pretends that this is out of kindness for his people, but in fact it is so the diamond bottom doesn't break, because if it did all their philosophers agree that the loadstone could no longer support it and the whole island would fall to the ground. One of the most important laws of the land is that neither the king nor his two eldest sons can leave the island; nor can the queen, until she is past the age when she can have children.

Chapter IV

[The author leaves Laputa; is taken to Balnibari and arrives at the city. There is a description of the city, and the adjoining country. The author gets a warm welcome from a great lord. His conversation with him is described.]

Although I can't say that I was badly treated on this island, I must admit that I felt that I was rather ignored and not respected. Neither the prince nor his people appeared to be interested in anything apart from mathematics and music, which I was far worse at than them, and so they didn't think much of me.

For myself, after seeing all the curiosities of the island, I was very keen to leave it, for I was thoroughly fed up with these people. I must admit that they were excellent in two sciences for which I have great respect, which I have some expertise in, but at the same time they are so distant and wrapped up in their thoughts that I never met any people whose company I liked less. I only talked with women, tradesmen, flappers and court servants during the two months I was there; this caused the others to have utter contempt for me, but these were the only people I could have a sensible conversation with.

Through hard work I had got a good knowledge of their language: I was tired of being kept on an island where I got such little respect, and decided to leave it as soon as I could.

There was a great lord in the court, closely related to the king, and that was the only reason he got any respect. Everyone thought he was the most ignorant and stupid person among them. He had done many great services for the king, had many great virtues, both natural and learned, and he also had integrity and honor. But he had such a bad ear for music that, his critics said, he had often been known to clap time off the beat, and his tutors couldn't get him, without great effort, to understand the simplest mathematical problems. He was kind enough to show me much respect, often did me the honor of visiting, and wanted to know about Europe and the laws and customs, manners and learning of the different countries I had visited. He listened to me carefully, and made very intelligent observations about everything I said. He had two flappers attending him for show, but he never used them, except at court and on ceremonial visits, and he would always send them away when we were alone together. I asked this noble person to speak on my behalf with his majesty and ask permission for me to leave. He did so, with regret, as he was kind enough to tell me, and he made me several good offers to stay; however I refused them, though with much thanks.

On the 16th of February I said goodbye to his majesty and his court. The king made me a gift that was equivalent to about two hundred English pounds, and my patron, his relative, gave me the same, as well as a letter of recommendation to a friend of his in Lagado, the capital. The island was then hovering over a mountain about two miles from it, so I was lowered from the bottom gallery in the same way I had been taken on board.

The continent, or the parts of it that make up the kingdom of the monarch of the flying island, goes under the general name of Blanibarbi, and the capital, as I said before, is called Lagado. It felt good to back on solid ground again. I was not worried about the walk to the city, as I was dressed like a native and knew enough of their language to talk with them. I soon found the house of the person to whom I was recommended, gave him the letter from his noble friend on the island, and was warmly welcomed. This great lord, whose name was Munodi, set me up with rooms in his own house, which I used throughout my stay, and he entertained me very hospitably.

The morning after my arrival he took me in his chariot to see the town, which is about half the size of London. The houses are built in a very strange way, and most of them were in a poor state. The people in the streets walked fast, looked disturbed, staring ahead, and most of them were dressed in rags. We went out of one of the town gates and about three miles into the country, where I saw many laborers working the ground with several different implements, but I could not see what they were doing, and I could see no signs that there was either corn or grass growing, although the soil seemed to be excellent. I could not help staring at these odd sights, both in town and country, and I asked my guide if he would kindly explain to me why everybody seemed to be so incredibly busy, both in the streets and the fields, because I could not see any good results from it; on the contrary, I never saw land so badly farmed, houses so badly built and in such poor repair, or a people whose faces and clothes showed such misery and poverty.

This lord Munodi was a person of the highest rank, and for some years had been governor of Lagado, but he had been dismissed for incompetence by a group of ministers. However, the king treated him kindly, thinking that he was well meaning but stupid.

When I freely criticized the country and its inhabitants all he answered was that I had not been there long enough to pass judgement, and different nations had different customs, and he answered other questions in the same way. But when we got back to his palace he asked me what I thought of the building; what faults could I find with it, or the clothes of looks of his servants. He could safely do this, because everything about him was magnificent, normal and polite. I answered that his excellency had common sense, nobility and money which had saved him from those flaws which stupidity and waste had given to others. He said that if we went to his country house, about twenty miles away, where he had his estate, we would have more time for this sort of conversation. I said that I was entirely at his disposal, and so we set out next morning.

During our journey he told me to look at the different ways farmers managed their land, which was incomprehensible to me, because except in a very few places, I could not see one ear of corn or one blade of grass. But after three hours' travel the scene completely changed; we came to a very beautiful country; there were farmers' houses, quite close together, nicely built; the fields were fenced in, containing vineyards, cornfields and meadows. I can never remember seeing such a lovely scene. His excellency saw my face brighten. He sighed and told me that this was the beginning of his estate, and it would all be the same until we got to his house. His countrymen, he said, despised and mocked him for his poor management of his land and for setting such a bad example for the kingdom; however, there were a few who copied him, people who were old, obstinate and weak like him.

We came at last to his house, which certainly was a noble building, built in accordance with the best rules of classical architecture. The fountains, gardens, paths, avenues and groves were all laid out with perfect judgement and taste. I complimented everything I saw, but his excellency ignored my words until after supper. As we were alone he told me, very sadly, that he thought he was going to have to demolish his houses in the town and the country, to rebuild them in the current style; he would have to destroy his plantations and make them as the modern custom dictated and give directions to all his tenants to do the same. If he didn't he would be criticized for pride, individuality, affectation, ignorance, wilfulness and perhaps turn his majesty even more against him. He said that my admiration would lessen or disappear when he had told me about some things which I had probably never heard of at court, as the people up there were too wrapped up in their thoughts to take any notice of what happened on the ground.

This was the essence of his talk: that forty years ago, some people went up to Laputa, either for business or entertainment, and after they had stayed there five months they came back with a very basic knowledge of mathematics but full of the changeable spirits of that high place. When these people returned they did not like the way things below were managed, and they started schemes to make things different in all the arts, sciences, languages and mechanics. To achieve this they obtained permission to establish an academy of projectors in Lagado, and the idea caught on so well with the people that there is no important town in the kingdom which does not have such an academy. In these colleges the professors invent new rules and methods for farming and building, and new implements and tools for all trades and crafts. They promise that with these, one man shall do the work of ten, a palace can be built in a week, of materials so strong that they will last forever without needing repair. All the crops shall become ripe whenever we choose, and they will be a hundred times what they are now. They made many other fine sounding proposals like this.

The only problem was that none of these projects had been perfected yet, and in the meantime the whole country is devastated, the houses are in ruins and the people lack food and clothes. Rather than discourage them they are fifty times more keen on following their plans, driven on by hope and despair equally. For himself, as he was not a very go-ahead sort of person, he was happy to carry on with the old ways, to live in the houses his ancestors had built and act as they did in every way, with nothing new. A few other nobles and gentlemen did the same but they were regarded with contempt and hatred as enemies of science, stupid, and poor patriots, preferring their own comfort and laziness ahead of the improvement of their country.

His lordship added that he would not give further details which would detract from my pleasure at seeing the grand academy, which he thought I should visit. He just wanted me to look at a ruined building on the side of a hill about three miles away. He told me that he had had a very useful mill within half a mile of his house, turned by the current of a large river, and big enough to serve his own family as well as many of his tenants. About seven years ago a group of these projectors came to him with proposals that they should destroy this mill and build another on the mountainside. They were going to cut a long canal on the mountain ridge, to hold water which would be carried up by pipes and machines to supply the mill, because the wind and air up there would agitate the water and make it stronger, and also the water running down a slope would turn the mill with half the amount needed by a river on the level. He said that as he was not much in favor at court, and as many of his friends urged him on, he agreed; and after employing a hundred men for two years the project failed and the projectors left, laying the blame completely upon him, criticizing him ever since and getting others to try the same thing, with the same promises of success, as well as the same failures.

In a few days we returned to town, and his excellency, thinking of the bad reputation he had in the academy, would not go in with me himself, but asked a friend of his to accompany me. My lord told him that I was a great admirer of projects, and that I was very curious and ready to believe – this in fact was true in a way, as when I was younger I had been a sort of projector myself.

Chapter V

[The author is allowed to see the grand academy of Lagado. The academy is generally described. What the professors do.]

This academy is not one whole building, but a collection of several houses on both sides of a street which became derelict and were purchased and put to this use.

I was given a very friendly welcome by the warden, and went to the academy for many days. Every room has one or more projectors, and I believe that there cannot be fewer than five hundred rooms. The first man I met looked rather starved, with sooty hands and face, long hair and beard, ragged and singed in several places. His clothes, shirt and skin were all of the same color. He has spent eight years on a project to get sunbeams out of cucumbers, which were to be put in sealed tubes and would let out warm air in cold summers. He told me that in eight years more he would be able to supply the governor's garden with sunshine, at a very reasonable rate; but he complained that his stock was low, and asked me to give him something to encourage invention, especially as cucumbers were very expensive this year. I gave him a small present, for my lord had given me money for this purpose, knowing that they always begged from visitors.

I went into another room, but was ready to jump back, being almost overpowered with a horrible stink. My guide pushed me forward, telling me in a whisper not to show any distaste, which would be very much resented, and so I did not dare even hold my nose. The projector in this room was the oldest student in the academy; his face and beard were pale yellow, and his hands and clothes were covered in filth. When I was introduced he gave me a close embrace, which I could well have dome without. His work, since he first came to the academy, was an experiment to try and separate human excrement into its original food by dividing it into its parts, removing the taint it gets from stomach acid, letting the smell evaporate and skimming off the saliva. He had a weekly allowance from the society of a very large barrel of excrement.

I saw another at work to turn ice into gunpowder, and he also showed me a treatise he had written about how to mould fire, which he meant to publish.

There was a very ingenious architect, who had invented a new way of building houses by beginning at the roof and working downwards to the foundations; he explained that he was copying the methods of two very clever insects, the bee and the spider.

There was a man who was born blind, who had several assistants who were the same: their job was to mix colors for painters, which their master taught them to distinguish between by touch and smell. It was unfortunate that I found that at that time they were not very good at their lessons, and the professor himself was almost always wrong. This artist is much admired and encouraged by everyone in the academy.

In another room I was very impressed with a projector who had found a way to plough the ground with pigs, to save the expense of ploughs, cattle and workmen. This is what you do: in an acre of ground you bury, six inches apart and eight deep, acorns, dates, chestnuts and other fruit and vegetables which these animals like, then you drive six hundred or more of them into the field, and in a few days they will have dug up the whole place looking for their food and made it ready for seeds, and at the same time they will have manured it with their dung. It is true that when they tried this it was very difficult and expensive, and they got little or no crops, but everyone agrees that many improvements could be made.

I went into another room where the walls and ceiling were all hung with cobwebs, except for a narrow passage to let the artist in or out. When I came in he shouted to me not to disturb the webs. He said what a terrible mistake the world had made for so long, using silkworms, when we had plenty of domestic insects that were far better, as they knew how to weave as well as spin. And he also said that by using spiders the whole cost of dyeing silk could be saved, and I completely believed him when he showed me a huge number of beautifully colored flies which he fed to his spiders, assuring us that the webs would soon take on their color, and as he had them in all colors he hoped that soon he could suit everybody's taste, as soon as he could find the right food for the flies, made of gum, oil or other sticky substances which would give strength and density to the threads.

There was an astronomer who had promised he could put a sundial on top of the great weathervane on the town hall which would adjust itself to always point the right way, whichever direction the wind turned it.

I mentioned that I had a slight stomach ache, and my guide led me to a room where there was a great doctor who specialised in curing that illness by using the same instrument in different ways. He had a large pair of bellows with a slender ivory nozzle. He pushed this eight inches up the anus and he said that he could suck out the wind, which would make the stomach as limp as a dried bladder. But when the disease was more stubborn and strong he pushed the nozzle in when the bellows were full, and blew all the air into the patient's stomach, then he would take the instrument out to refill it, keeping his thumb firmly over the hole. Once he had done this three or four times the added wind would rush out, bringing the poison out with it, like water out of a pump, and the patient recovered. I saw him try both these experiments on a dog, and didn't see any change with the first method. After the second one the animal was ready to burst, and made a violent explosion that disgusted me and my companion.

The dog died on the spot, and we left the doctor trying to bring him back to life by the same method.

I visited many other rooms, but I will not trouble the reader with all the strange things I saw, as I wish to be concise.

So far I had only seen one side of the academy, the other being given over to the philosophers, whom I shall speak of when I have mentioned one more great man, whom they call "the universal artist." He told us that he had spent thirty years thinking about the ways he could improve human life. He had two large rooms full of wonderful curiosities, and fifty men at work. Some were condensing air into a dry touchable matter, by taking out the nitre, and boiling off the fluid particles; others were making marble soft, to be used as pillows and pincushions; others were turning the hoofs of a living horse to stone, to stop them breaking. The artist himself was busy with two great plans; the first was to sow land with wheat stalks, which he said contained the true seeding powers, as he demonstrated with several experiments which I was not skilled enough to understand. The other plan was to stop wool growing on a pair of young lambs by applying a mixture of gums, minerals and vegetables, and he hoped in good time to have a breed of naked sheep all over the kingdom.

We crossed the road to the other part of the academy where, as I have already said, the philosophers lived.

The first professor I saw was in a very large room, with forty pupils around him. After greeting us he saw me looking very closely at a machine which took up the largest part of the length and breadth of the room. He said that he thought I might be surprised to see him employed in a project to improve philosophy by practical and mechanical means. But the world would soon see how useful it was, and he flattered himself that nobody had ever thought of such a noble and exalted thing. Everyone knew what hard work it usually is to learn the arts and sciences, but with his machine the most ignorant person, for a reasonable price and a little physical effort, might write books about philosophy, poetry, politics, laws, mathematics and theology, with no need of intelligence or study.

He then took me to the machine, round which all his pupils were standing. The surface was made up of several bits of wood, about the size of dice, though some were larger than others. They were all linked with slender wires. These bits of wood were covered, on every face, with paper pasted on them; and on the papers were all the words of their language in their different forms, plurals and tenses, but in no order. The professor then told me to watch as he was going to set his machine to work. The pupils, at his command, each took hold of an iron handle, of which there were forty fixed around the edges of the frame, and when they were all suddenly turned, all the words moved around. He then ordered thirty-six of the lads to read the lines quietly, as they appeared, and when they found three or four words together that might make up part of a sentence they dictated them to the other four, who were scribes. This was done three or four times, and the machine was designed so that each time all the words went to new places as the squares of wood moved up and down.

The young students worked like this for six hours a day, and the professor showed me several large books of broken sentences, which he intended to piece together and out of those rich materials he was going to give the world a complete work of arts and sciences. However, it could be improved, and greatly speeded up, if the public could pay for making and using five hundred machines like this in Lagado, from which all the results could be pooled.

He told me that the invention had been in his head since childhood, and that he had put the whole language into the machine, based on a strict calculation of the proportions of all parts of speech in books.

I gave this person a very low bow, for his great kindness in telling me, and promised him that if I ever had the luck to return to my home country I would certainly acknowledge him as the sole inventor of this great machine, the shape and machinery of I asked if I could sketch, as in the attached figure. I told him that although it was the custom of educated men in Europe to steal inventions from each other, so that at least it became unclear as to who the owner was, I would take great care that he should get all the credit for this one.

Next we went to the school of languages, where three professors sat in debate as to how to improve their own.

The first plan was to make multisyllabic words singular and leave out verbs and participles because, in reality, one only needs something to provoke the imagination.

The other project was a scheme to abolish words completely, and this was put forward as a great thing for health, as well as timesaving. For it is obvious that every word we say will, to some extent, erode our lungs, and so make our lives shorter. It was therefore suggested that since words only represent things men should carry around the things they needed to demonstrate what they were discussing. And this invention would certainly have been used, if women, along with the common and illiterate, had not threatened a rebellion if they were not allowed the freedom to speak with their tongues, in the way their ancestors had; this shows what terrible opponents of science the common people are.

However, many of the most learned and wise stick to this new plan of expressing themselves with objects, which only has this disadvantage, that if a man has a lot to say about various things then he is obliged to carry a great bundle of objects around on his back, unless he can afford a servant or two to carry them. I have often seen two of these wise men bent double under the weight of their sacks, and when they met in the street they would put down their loads, open their sacks and chat for an hour, then they would pack up their objects, help each other pick up their sacks, and leave. But for short conversations a man can carry enough things in his pockets or under his arms, and in his house he cannot be caught out. So the room where those who practise this art meet is full of all objects, ready to hand, that are needed to provide for this sort of artificial conversation.

Another great advantage put forward in favor of this plan was that it would work as a universal language, understood in all civilised nations where goods and tools are generally the same, or nearly the same, so that their uses could easily be understood. And so ambassadors could negotiate with foreign princes or ministers without any knowledge of their language.

I visited the mathematical school, where the master taught his pupils in a way we could hardly imagine in Europe. The question, and the answer, were neatly written on a thin wafer with an ink made from brains. The student was supposed to swallow this on an empty stomach and eat nothing but bread and water for the next three days. But success has not yet been achieved, partly due to some mistake in the quantities or mixture and partly from the awkwardness of the lads, who find this pill so sickening that they generally sneak away and vomit it up before it can work, and they haven't yet been persuaded to starve themselves to make it work as the prescription demands.

Chapter VI

[More details about the academy. The author suggests some improvements, which are welcomed.]

In the school of political projectors I did not enjoy myself much; the professors seemed, to me, to be completely mad, and seeing this always makes me sad. These unfortunate people were proposing ways to persuade kings to choose their favorites on the grounds of wisdom, capability and goodness; to teach ministers to think of what was good for the public; to reward merit, ability and good service; to teach princes that their interests and those of the people should be the same; to make state jobs be given to the people who suited them best, and many other crazy ideas which nobody had ever thought of before. This proved the truth of the old proverb, that there is nothing so strange and wild that some philosophers won't say it's true.

However, to be fair to this part of the Academy I must acknowledge that not all of them were so impractical. There was a very clever doctor, who seemed to know all about the system and nature of government. This illustrious man had done some very useful investigations, finding out the best remedies for all the diseases and corruptions from which different kinds of government suffer, from the vice and weakness of the governors or the disobedience of those who should obey. For instance, as all writers and thinkers have agreed that there is a very exact resemblance between the human body and the body politic, could anything be more obvious than that they should be cared for, and cured with, the same prescriptions? It is agreed that senates and great councils are often troubled with depression, mania, and other peculiar moods; they have many diseases of the head, and more of the heart; they have strong convulsions, with painful contractions of the nerves and muscles in both hands, but especially the right; they have stomach disorders, flatulence, vertigo and madness, scrofulous tumors, full of foul rotting matter; the appetites of dogs, poor digestions and many others which needn't be named.

So this doctor proposed that when the senate met, doctors should attend the first three days of their meeting, and at the end of each day's debate they should take the pulse of each senator. They should then consult and reflect on the nature of their illnesses, and what the cure should be, then go back to senate house on the fourth day with their chemists carrying the right medicine, and before the members sat down they should give each of them lenitives, aperitives, abstersives, corrosives, restringents, palliatives, laxatives, cephalalgics, icterics, apophlegmatics, acoustics as required, and depending how the prescriptions worked they should use, repeat, change or omit them at the next meeting. This project would not cost the public much, and in my opinion it might be very effective to speed up the process in the countries where senates have any share of power. It would cause agreement, shorten debates, open a few mouths which are now closed and close many more which are now open, restrain the petulance of the young and calm down the certainties of the old, it would wake up the dull, and restrain the over-energetic.

Also, as it is often complained that the favorites of princes seem to only have short, poor memories, the same doctor proposed that anyone who goes to see a first minister should tell him his business as quickly and clearly as possible, and then when leaving he should twist the minister's nose, or kick him in the belly, or tread on his corns, or tug both his ears three times, or stick a pin in his backside, or pinch his arm until it bruises, to make him remember, and every time they had a meeting he should do it again until the business was settled or completely rejected. He also suggested that every senator in the great council of a nation, after he had given his opinion, and argued in defence of it, should be obliged to vote against what he had said, because if that were done it would unquestionably be of benefit to the public.

When different parties are clashing with each other, he offered a wonderful plan to get them to agree. His method was this: you take a hundred leaders of each party, and divide them into couples whose heads are the same size, then let two precise surgeons cut the heads off each couple at the same time, in such a way that their brains are split exactly in two. Let those heads, cut off like that, be swapped over, putting each one on the head of his opponent. It does look as if that would be very difficult work, but the professor assured us that if it was skilfully done then the cure was certain to happen. He argued that with the two half brains left to debate with each other inside one skull they would soon come to an agreement, and produce the moderation and sensible thought that is so desirable in the heads of those who think that they were put on earth to govern everything; as for the difference in brains, in size and quality, between the leaders of different parties, the doctor assured us that it was minimal.

I heard a very heated debate between two professors about the best ways to raise money without upsetting the subjects. The first said that the fairest way would be to out a tax on vice and stupidity, and the amount to be paid by every man would be decided in the fairest manner by a jury of his neighbors. The second had an entirely opposite opinion, wanting to tax the qualities of body and mind which men think are the best. The rate should be higher or lower, depending on how excellent they were, the decision should be left entirely up to them. The highest tax would be put on the men who were most liked by the opposite sex, and this would be assessed according to the number and quality of kisses they had got – their word would be accepted for the total. Wit, bravery, and good manners would also be heavily taxed, and collected in the same way, with every person giving his word about the amount he possessed. But honor, justice, wisdom and learning should not be taxed at all, because they are so unusual that no man will admit his neighbor has them nor will he value them in himself.

Women were to be taxed according to their beauty and skill in dressing, and they would be given the same privilege as men in that they would rate themselves. But faithfulness, good sense and good nature would not be taxed, as such a small sum wouldn't be worth collecting.

To keep senators voting for the king, it was proposed that members of the senate should draw lots for jobs, with every man first taking an oath, and giving a deposit as security, that he would vote for the court, whether he won or not. After that the losers would have the chance to draw lots again the next time there was a vacancy. This way everyone's hopes of preferment would be kept alive; nobody could complain about broken promises and they would blame their disappointments on the luck of the draw, which is a more powerful thing than any ministry.

Another professor showed me a large sheet of instructions for revealing plots and conspiracies against the government. He advised great statesmen that they should look into the diet of any suspects; what time they ate, which side they lay on in bed, which hand they wiped their backsides with; he should closely examine their excrement and from the color, smell, taste, consistency, the goodness or badness of digestion, form an opinion on their thoughts and plans, because men are never so serious, thoughtful and concentrated as when they are on the lavatory, as he had discovered through many experiments. Just as an experiment he had, when in this position himself, though about the best way to murder a king, and his excrement would turn green, but it would be quite different if he was just thinking about starting a rebellion, or burning down a city.

The whole argument was written with great perception, containing many observations both strange and useful for politicians, but, as I saw it, not altogether finished. I took it on myself to tell the author this and offer him some additions. He welcomed my proposal with more agreement than writers usually do, especially those who are projectors, and he said he would be glad to have further information.

I told him that in the kingdom of Tribnia, which the natives called Langdon, where I had rested at one point in my travels, most of the people are exposers, witnesses, informants, prosecutors, evidence givers, swearers, together with their helpers, who were all servants paid for by the ministers of state and their deputies. In that kingdom the plots are usually started by people who want to make themselves look good as politicians, to give new strength to a confused administration, to suppress or turn away general dissatisfaction, to fill their pockets with forfeited goods, and raise or lower the strength of public credit, depending on how it suited their private plans. It is first agreed and settled which suspects will be accused; then good care is taken to seize all their letters and papers and put the owners in chains. These papers are delivered to a set of craftsmen who are very skilled at discovering the mysterious meanings of words, syllables and letters. For example, they can show that a close stool meant a privy council, a flock of geese, a senate; a lame dog, an invader; the plague, a standing army; a buzzard, a prime minister; the gout, a high priest; a gibbet, a secretary of state; a chamber pot, a committee of noblemen; a sieve, a court lady; a broom, a revolution; a mouse-trap, a state job; a bottomless pit, a treasury; a sink, a court; a cap and bells, a favourite; a broken reed, a court of justice; an empty barrel, a general; a running sore, the administration.

When this method fails they have two other better ones, which the educated ones of them call acrostics and anagrams. Firstly they give all first letters political meaning. So N means a plot, B a cavalry regiment, L a fleet at sea; or, the second method is that by swapping the letters of the alphabet in any suspect message they can reveal the deepest plans of the plotters. So for example, if I wrote to a friend, "Our bother Tom has just got the piles," a skilful decipherer could show that the same letters which make up that sentence can be moved to make the following: "Resist – a plot is brought home – the tour." And this is the anagrammatic method.

The professor gave me many thanks for telling him all this, and promised that he would give me an honorable mention when his work was published.

I saw nothing in that country that would make me want to stay, and began to think of returning home to England.

Chapter VII

[The author leaves Lagado and arrives at Maldonada. There is no ship ready. He takes a short voyage to Glubbdubdrib. How he is welcomed by the governor.]

The continent which this kingdom is part of extends, I have reason to believe, east towards that unknown part of America to the west of California, and north to the Pacific Ocean, which is less than a hundred and fifty miles from Lagado. There is a good port there, which does much business with the great island of Luggnagg, which is to the north-west, about 29 degrees north latitude and 140 longitude. The island of Luggnagg stands to the south-east of Japan which is about three hundred miles away. There is a strong alliance between the emperor of Japan and the king of Luggnagg, which means that there are frequent boats going in both directions. So I decided that I would journey there to begin my return to Europe. I hired two mules to carry my small possessions and a guide to show me the way. I said goodbye to my noble patron who had shown me such kindness and gave me a generous present when I left.

My journey had no mishaps or adventures worth telling. When I arrived at the port of Maldonada (as it is called) there was no ship in the harbor sailing for Luggnagg, nor was there likely to be one for some time. The town is about the size of Portsmouth. I soon met some people and they gave me a very hospitable welcome. A distinguished gentleman advised me that as there would be no ships bound for Luggnagg in less than a month I might enjoy a trip to the little island of Glubbdubdrib, about fifteen miles off to the south-west. He offered to come with me, bring a friend, and provide me with a comfortable small ship for the journey.

Glubbdubdrib, as far as I can discover, means "island of sorcerers or magicians". It is about a third of the size of the Isle of Wight, and is extremely fertile. It is ruled by the head of a certain tribe, all of whom are magicians. This tribe only marries their own kind, and the oldest in line is prince or governor. He has a fine palace, and a park of about three thousand acres, surrounded by a wall of cut stone twenty feet high. In this park there are several small enclosed areas for cattle, corn and gardening.

The governor and his family are looked after and waited on by rather unusual servants. Through his skill in magic he has the power of calling anyone he pleases up from the dead, and making them serve him for twenty-four hours, but not longer, and he cannot call on the same person again for three months, unless there is a very special occasion.

When we arrived at the island, which was about eleven in the morning, one of the gentlemen who accompanied me went to the governor and asked permission for a stranger to land, who had come to have the honor of seeing his highness. This permission was given at once, and all three of us entered the gate of the palace between two rows of guards who were armed and dressed in a very old-fashioned way, and there was something in their faces that made my flesh creep with a horror I cannot describe. We passed through several rooms with servants of the same sort, lined up on each side as before, until we came to the audience chamber. After three great bows, and a few general questions, we were allowed to sit down on three stools near the lowest step of his majesty's throne. He understood the language of Balnibari, though it is different to that of the island. He asked me to tell him about his travels, and to let me see that everything was quite informal he dismissed all his servants with a snap of his fingers; when he did this, to my astonishment they vanished in an instant, like figures in a dream when we suddenly awake. I could not compose myself for some time, until the governor assured me that I would not be hurt. Observing that my companions were not worried, as they had seen it all before, I began to take heart, and told his highness briefly about my adventures, though I did so rather haltingly and I often looked behind me to the place where I had seen those ghostly servants.

I had the honor of dining with the governor, and a new set of ghosts served the meat and waited at the table. I noticed that I felt less terrified than I had in the morning. I stayed until sunset, but I politely asked his highness to excuse my not accepting his invitation to stay at the palace. My friends and I stayed at a private house in the adjacent town, and we went back the next morning to pay our respects to the governor as he had told us to.

We stayed ten days on the island in this fashion, spending most of the day with the governor and the night in our lodgings. I soon grew so accustomed to the sight of spirits that after the third or fourth time they didn't cause any feelings in me at all, or if I did have any fears left my curiosity triumphed over them. His highness the governor ordered me to call up any people I cared to name, in whatever numbers, from everyone who had died from the beginning of time to the present day, and ask them any questions I liked, on condition that I stuck to questions about their own times. And one thing I could depend on was that they would definitely tell me the truth, for lying was a skill that was useless in the afterlife.

I humbly thanked his highness for such a great favor. We were in a room which gave a nice view into the park, and because my first thought was to see scenes of pomp and magnificence I asked to see Alexander the Great at the head of his army, just after the battle of Arbella. At a sign from the governor they appeared in a large field below our window. Alexander was called up to the room; I had much difficulty understanding his Greek, and I could not speak much myself. He promised me that he had not been poisoned but had died of a fever caused by excessive drinking.

Next I saw Hannibal crossing the Alps, who told me that he had not had a drop of vinegar in his camp.

I saw Caesar and Pompey at the head of their troops, just about to fight. I saw Caesar in his last great triumph. I asked to see the senate of Rome in front of me in one large room, and at the same time see the assembly of a rather later time in another, to balance them against each other. The Romans seemed an assembly of heroes and demigods; the others, a pack of pedlars, pickpockets, highwaymen and bullies.

At my request the governor signed for Caesar and Brutus to come towards us. I was struck with a feeling of great worship at the sight of Brutus, and could easily make out great goodness, bravery and firm-mindedness, patriotism and general love for mankind in every line of his face. I observed, with great pleasure, that these two people were on good terms, and Caesar freely admitted to me that the greatest things he had done in his life were far below, in terms of glory, the act of taking it away. I had the honor of a long talk with Brutus, and he told me that his ancestor Junius, Socrates, Epaminondas, Cato the younger, Sir Thomas More and himself were always together; a group of six that the whole history of the world wouldn't be able to find a worthy seventh for.

It would be boring to bother the reader by telling him about the great number of notable people I had called up to gratify my insatiable desire to see the world at every point of history in front of me. I mainly looked at the destroyers of tyrants and rebels, and the ones who gave liberty back to oppressed and injured nations. But I can't express the pleasure it gave me in way which will entertain the reader.

Chapter VIII

[More about Glubbdubdrib. Ancient and modern history is corrected.]

Wanting to see those of olden days who were most famous for their intelligence and learning, I set aside a whole day for this. I asked that Homer and Aristotle should appear with all the people who had written about them, but there were so many that hundreds had to wait in the courtyard and the outer rooms. I recognized the two great men at once and could not only tell them apart from the rest of the crowd but from each other. Homer was the taller and more handsome of the two, standing very straight for someone his age, and his eyes were the brightest and most piercing I ever saw. Aristotle was very bent, and used a walking stick. His face was worn, his hair was lank and thin and his voice was weary. I soon discovered that both of them were complete strangers to all the others, and had never seen or heard of them before. A ghost, whom I won't name, whispered to me that these critics, in the underworld, always kept as far away as they could from their subjects, as they felt ashamed and guilty about the way they had misrepresented their works to future ages. I introduced Didymus and Eustathius to Homer, and persuaded him to treat them better than they maybe deserved, for he soon discovered that they weren't intelligent enough to really understand a poet. But Aristotle couldn't stand the account I gave him of Scotus and Ramus, when I introduced them, and he asked them if all the others were as stupid as they were.

I then asked the governor to call up Descartes and Gassendi, whom I asked to explain their ideas to Aristotle. This great philosopher freely acknowledged his own errors in science, because he had had to make many guesses, as all men must, and he said that Gassendi, who had made Epicurus' ideas as sensible as they could be, and Descartes' planetary theories, would both have their mistakes revealed in time. He said that the same thing would happen to attraction, the theory learned men are currently so fond of. He said that new systems of science were just new fashions, which changed over time, and even the ones that pretended to be mathematically perfect would only be popular for a short time, and would fall out of fashion when that time was over.

I spent five days talking with many other learned men of ancient times. I saw most of the early Roman emperors. I asked the governor to call up Heliogabalus' cooks to make dinner for us, but they couldn't show us much of their skill as we lacked the ingredients. A servant of Agesilaus made us some Spartan soup, but I stopped eating after one taste.

The two gentlemen who came with me to the island had to go back to attend to their business for three days, and I spent this time seeing some of the recent dead, the most famous of them from the past two or three hundred years, from our country and others in Europe, and as I was always a great admirer of old noble families I asked the governor to call up one or two dozen kings, with their ancestors stretching back eight or nine generations. But I had a great and unexpected disappointment. Instead of a great line of crowned heads, in one family I saw two fiddlers, three courtiers, and an Italian priest. In another there was a barber, an abbot and two cardinals. I have too much respect for royalty to dwell further on such a delicate subject. But I wasn't so discreet about counts, marquis, dukes, earls and so on, and I must admit it gave me some pleasure to follow back the features for which a family was noted to their origins. I could clearly see where one family got its long chin from, why another had been full of scoundrels for two generations and fools for two more; why a third tended to madness and a fourth were all cheats; how it came about, the thing which made Polydore Virgil say of a certain noble house that they had not one strong man nor one chaste woman. I saw how cruelty, lies and cowardice became the characteristics by which certain families were distinguished, as much by those as their coat of arms. I also saw who brought the pox into a noble house, which has given all their descendants scrofulous tumors. And this was no surprise, when I saw how these noble bloodlines had been invaded by pages, lackeys, valets, coachmen, gamblers, fiddlers, actors, sailors and pickpockets.

Most of modern history disgusted me. When I looked carefully at all the most famous men from the courts of princes for the last century I found that the world had been tricked, by sellout writers, into thinking that cowards had committed great acts of war, that fools were wise, that flatterers were sincere, that traitors were patriots, atheists were religious, sodomites were pure, informers were honest. I found that many innocent good people had been condemned to death or exile through great ministers using the corruption of judges, and the hatred of parties; how many villains had been promoted to positions of the highest trust, power, honor or profit; and what a great part in the affairs of courts, councils and senates was played by brothel keepers, whores, pimps, parasites and clowns. What a low opinion I got of human intelligence and integrity, when I saw the real cause of the great achievements and revolutions of the world, and of the stupid chances which let them succeed.

This is where I found out the cheating and ignorance of those who claim to know the secrets of history; writers who claim that a king was poisoned, who will report the conversation between a prince and a first minister to which there were no witnesses, write as if they know the inner thoughts, and the contents of the desks, of ambassadors and secretaries of state, and always be wrong. I found out here the true causes of many events that have shocked the world; how a whore can rule over the back stairs, the back stairs can rule over a council, and a council over a senate. A general confessed to me that he had won a victory completely through cowardice and mismanagement, and an admiral admitted that through stupidity he had beaten the enemy when in fact he had meant to hand them the entire fleet. Three kings told me that throughout their reigns they never gave a job to someone who deserved it, unless it was by mistake or they were tricked into it by some minister, and if they had their time again they would do the same, and they made a strong case that kings needed corruption, as positive, confident independent men always held up public business.

I had the curiosity to look closely at the ways in which huge numbers had managed to get hold of exalted titles, and grand estates. I only looked into very modern times, without going into the present, for I don't want to upset anybody, not even foreigners (for the reader will of course understand that I don't refer to my own country in any way here); I called up a large number of people, and found such shocking situation that it gave me pause for thought. Perjury, oppression, blackmail, fraud, pimping and other horrid things were some of the least bad things they did, and I gave as much forgiveness as I could for them. But when I found that some confessed they owed their title and wealth to sodomy or incest; to prostituting their own wives and daughters; to betraying their country or their ruler; to poisoning; and more to the perverting of justice, in order to destroy the innocent, I hope I may be forgiven if these discoveries made me lose some of that great respect which I am naturally accustomed to giving to people of high rank, who ought to be treated with the greatest respect due to their magnificent position by we inferiors.

I often read of great things done for princes and states, and asked to see the people who did them. When I asked I was told that their names usually couldn't be found, except for a few of them, whom history has recorded as the most terrible scoundrels and traitors. As for the rest, I had never heard of them. They all appeared depressed and were dressed in rags, and most of them told me that they had died in poverty and disgrace, and the rest had been executed.

Amongst all the others there was one whose case seemed to be unique. He had a youth of eighteen standing by his side. He told me that he had been the captain of a ship for many years, and in the battle of Actium he'd been lucky enough to break through the enemy lines and sink three of their main ships and capture a fourth, and that was the only reason Antony fled and the war was won; the youth standing with him was his only son, who was killed in the battle. He added that as he knew he had done well, he went to Rome at the end of the war and asked Augustus to give him command of a larger ship, whose commander had been killed. But, ignoring his ambitions, the command was given to a boy who had never been to sea, the son of Libertina, a servant to one of the emperor's mistresses. When he went back to his own ship he was accused of dereliction of duty, and the ship was given to one of the favorite servants of Publicola, the vice admiral. So he retired to a poor farm a long way from Rome, and died there. I was so interested in this story that I called up Agrippa, who had been an admiral in the battle, to conform the truth of it. He appeared and said it was all true, except the captain had been far too modest about his achievements.

I was surprised to discover that corruption had spread so rapidly in that empire, through the influence of luxury which had only just been discovered; it made me less surprised to see the same in other countries, where all kinds of vice have existed much longer, and where all the praise for victory, as well as all the loot, has gone to the commander in chief, perhaps the man who deserved it least.

As every person summoned looked exactly the same as they had done in life, I reflected sadly on how mankind has degenerated in the last hundred years. The pox, in all its forms, has changed the looks of the English completely: bodies are smaller; nerves are weaker; sinews and muscles are looser; complexions are sickly and the skin is loose and rotting.

I went back so far as to ask to see some old fashioned English farmer called up, of the type once so famous for their simple manners, diet and clothes, for their fair dealing, for their genuine love of freedom, for their bravery and their patriotism. And I couldn't help be sad, after I had compared the living and the dead, when I saw how all these pure native values were sold for cash by their grandchildren, who, selling their votes and fixing elections, have taken on every vice and corruption that can be found in court.

Chapter IX

[The author returns to Maldonada. He sails to the kingdom of Luggnagg. He is imprisoned. He is summoned to court. How he is welcomed. How merciful the king is to his subjects.]

The day for us to leave had arrived, so I said goodbye to his highness the governor of Glubbdubdrib and went back with my two friends to Maldonada, where, after a fortnight's wait, there was a ship ready to sail for Luggnagg. The two gentlemen and some other friends were kind enough to give me supplies and to see me on board. This voyage took a month. We experienced one violent storm and we had to steer to the west to pick up the trade wind, which blows for nearly two hundred miles. On the 21st of April 1708 we sailed into the river at Clumegnig, which is a seaport town on the southeast tip of Luggnagg. We anchored quite close to the town and signalled for a pilot. Two of them came aboard in less than half an hour, and we were guided by them between certain banks and rocks, which are very dangerous to cross, into a large harbor, where a whole fleet can safely anchor within a cable's length of the walls of the town.

Some of our sailors, whether through treachery or accidentally, had told the pilots that I was a stranger and a great traveller, so they alerted a customs officer, who questioned me very closely when I landed. He spoke to me in the language of Balnibari which, due to the amount of business they do with that country, is usually understood in that town, especially by sailors and the customs officers. I gave him a brief account of some details, keeping my story as believable and consistent as I could, but I thought I should hide my nationality, and say I was Dutch, because I wanted to go to Japan and I knew that the Dutch were the only Europeans allowed in that country. So I told the officer that I had been shipwrecked off the coast of Balinbarbi and thrown onto a rock, and I had been welcomed on to Laputa, or the flying island (which he had often heard of) and I was now trying to get to Japan, where I hoped to find a way of getting back to my own country. The officer said that I must be locked up until he could get orders from the court, which he would write off for at once, and he expected to get an answer within two weeks. I was taken to a comfortable room with a sentry on the door; however, I was allowed to walk in a large garden, and I was treated well enough at the king's expense. I was visited by several people, mainly because they were curious about the stories that I had been to faraway countries of which they had never heard.

I hired a young man, who had been on the same ship as me, as an interpreter; he was a native of Luggnagg, but he had lived for some years at Maldonada and was an expert in both languages. With his help I could hold a conversation with my visitors, but only in a stilted, question-and-answer way.

The message came from the court about the time we expected it. It was an order for myself and my servants to be taken to Traldragdubh, or Trildrogdrib (it is as far as I remember pronounced both ways) with an escort of ten horsemen. My only servant was that poor lad as interpreter, and I persuaded him to come with me; at my polite request we were each given a mule to ride. A messenger was sent half a day ahead of us, to notify the king that I was coming, and to ask if his majesty would please choose a day and time when I might be given the honor of being allowed to lick the dust in front of his footstool. This is the custom of the court, and I found that it wasn't just a figure of speech; when I was welcomed two days after my arrival I was told to crawl on my belly and lick the floor as I went. However, as I was a stranger the floor and been carefully cleaned beforehand so that the dust did not disturb me. But this was an unusual favor, not given to anyone but the most noble when they request an audience.

In fact sometimes the floor is covered in dust deliberately, when the person being welcomed happens to have powerful enemies in the court. I have seen a great lord with his mouth so full of dust that when he had crawled close to the throne he couldn't say a word. And there was nothing he could do, as spitting or wiping one's mouth in the presence of the king is punishable by death. There is another custom, of which I can't wholeheartedly approve: when the king decides to execute any of his noblemen with some kindness, he orders that the floor should be covered with a certain poisonous brown powder, which, when it is licked up, inevitably kills the victim within twenty-four hours. But to be fair to the king's great mercy, and the great care he takes of his subject's lives (which we should wish the monarchs of Europe would copy) it should be mentioned that there are strict orders for the poisoned parts of the floor to be well washed after every execution of this type, and if the servants forget to do this they are in danger of incurring his royal displeasure.

I myself have heard him give orders that one of his pages should be whipped, who should have given orders for the floor to be washed after an execution, but had maliciously failed to do this, and by his neglect a very promising young lord, who had come for an audience, was unfortunately poisoned although at that time the king had no plans to take his life. But this good prince was so merciful that he let the poor page off his whipping, on condition he wouldn't do it again without specific orders.

Anyway, to get back to my story: when I got to within four yards of the throne I got gently to my knees, and then beating my forehead seven times on the ground I said the following words, which had been taught to me the previous night, "Inckpling gloffthrobb squut serummblhiop mlashnalt zwin tnodbalkuffh slhiophad gurdlubh asht." This, by the law of the land, is the compliment everyone who goes in to see the king gives him. In English it means, "May your celestial majesty live a year longer than the sun!" The king gave some answer, which I did not understand, but I replied as I had been told to, "Fluft drin yalerick dwuldom prastrad mirpush," which means "My tongue is in the mouth of my friend," meaning that I would like to bring in my interpreter. So the young man I already mentioned was brought in, and with his help I answered his majesty's questions for over an hour. I spoke in Balnibarbian, and my interpreter translated into Luggnaggian.

The king was very pleased with my company, and ordered his Bliffmarklub, or high chamberlain, to give me and my interpreter rooms in the court, to provide us with food and give me a large purse of gold for everyday expenses.

I stayed in this country for three months, from respect for his majesty's wishes, and he made me some very favourable offers to stay. But I thought it was more proper and more sensible that I should live out my life with my wife and family.

Chapter X

[The Luggnaggians are commended. A detailed description of the Struldbrugs, with many conversations between the author and some high ranking people on the subject.]

The Luggnagians are a polite and generous people, and although they do have that tendency towards arrogance which is common in all eastern countries they are polite to strangers, especially those who are favored by the court. I knew many people at the top of society, and as I always had my interpreter with me we had some good conversations.

One day, when I was with a good crowd, one gentleman asked me if I had seen any of their Struldbrugs, or immortals. I said that I had not, and asked him what he meant by giving such a name to a mortal creature. He told me that sometimes, though very rarely, a family would have a child that was born with a red circular spot on its forehead, which was proof that it would never die. The spot, as he described it, was about the size of a silver threepence, but over time it got bigger, and changed color; at twelve it turned green, and stayed that way until twenty-five, when it turned deep blue; at forty-five it turned coal black, and was as large as an English shilling, and then stopped changing for good. He said that these births were so rare that he didn't think there were more than eleven hundred Struldbrugs in the kingdom, of either sex; he thought that there were about fifty in the capital and amongst the rest the last one was a young girl born about three years ago. These births didn't run in families but were pure chance, and the children of Struldbrugs were as mortal as everybody else.

I must admit that I was overjoyed to hear this story, and as the person telling me about it happened to understand Balnibarian, which I spoke very well, I couldn't keep myself from speaking out, perhaps a little extravagantly. I cried out rapturously, "What a happy country, where every child has at least a chance to be immortal! What a happy people, who have so many living examples of the ancient virtues, and masters who can teach them all the wisdom of days gone by! But the happiest people must be these Struldbrugs who, being born exempt from death, have their minds free and unburdened, not having to suffer the continual depression of thinking about it!" I spoke of my amazement that I had not observed any of these illustrious people at court, and the black spot on the forehead was such an obvious marker that I couldn't have missed it, and surely his majesty, a very sensible prince, wouldn't have missed the opportunity to have a good number of such wise and competent councillors. But perhaps the virtue of these venerable sages was too strict for the corrupt and loose morals of a court. We have often seen that young men are too opinionated and changeable to take any notice of the sensible guidance of their elders. However, since the king was kind enough to allow me to talk with him I decided that the next time I spoke to him I would tell him my opinions about this matter, with the help of my interpreter. Whether he would take my advice or not I was determined on one thing, and that was that I would accept the king's offer of a place in his country gratefully, and spend the rest of my life talking to these superior beings, the Struldbrugs, if they would let me.

The gentleman I was speaking to, because (as I have already mentioned) he spoke Balnibarian, said to me, with the sort of smile that usually comes from pitying the ignorant, that he was glad if there was anything which made me want to stop in their country, and would it be alright to tell the others what I had said. He did so, and they talked amongst themselves in their own language, which I didn't know a word of, and I couldn't see from their expressions what impression what I had said had made. After a little while the same person said to me that his friends and mine (which is how he thought it right to call them) were very pleased to hear the sensible remarks I had made about the great happiness and advantages of immortality, and they would like to know in detail how I would have lived my life, if I had been born a Struldbrug.

I answered that it was easy to say a lot about such a wide and delightful subject, especially for me, who often amused myself with fantasies about what I would do if I were a king, a general or a lord, and in this case I had often thought about what I would do with my life if I knew I was going to live forever.

I said that if I had been lucky enough to be born a Struldbrug, as soon as I knew how lucky I was, when I understood about life and death, I would firstly decide, in every possible way, to get rich. I could reasonably expect within two hundred years to be the richest man in the kingdom. In the second place, I would from childhood devote myself to the study of arts and sciences, so that eventually I would be more learned than all others. Lastly, I would carefully write down every important public event and action, impartially describe the characters of all the princes and great ministers of state and add my own opinions. I would note down all the changes in customs, language, fashion, diet and amusements. Doing all this I would become a living storehouse of knowledge and wisdom, and I would certainly be the wisest man in the nation.

I wouldn't marry after the sixtieth time, but live in a hospitable way, though frugally. I would spend my time teaching and directing the minds of promising young men, by convincing them, from my memories, experience and observation, backed up with many examples, of the importance of virtue in public and private life. But my chosen permanent companions would be from my own immortal brethren; I would choose a dozen of them, from the oldest down to my own generation. If any of them lacked money I would give them comfortable houses to live in on my estate, and always have them to dine with me. I would invite just a few of you mortals, the best ones; in time I would become used to losing you, and wouldn't be sad, and I would feel the same way about your successors, just as a man enjoys the flowers in his garden without mourning the loss of the ones that died the year before.

These Struldbrugs and I would share our ideas and our memories over time; we would observe the steps by which corruption creeps into the world, and oppose it at every turn, by always giving warnings and teaching mankind, and this, added to the great example we would set, would probably prevent the progressive degeneration of human nature which has so rightly always been complained of.

In addition I would have the pleasure of seeing the movement of states and empires, the changes on earth and in the skies; I would see ancient cities collapse in ruins and obscure villages become the thrones of kings. Famous rivers would become shallow streams, and the ocean would leave one coast dry and flood another. Many countries not yet known would be discovered, and the most civilised nations would become barbarians and vice versa. Then I would see the discovery of longitude, perpetual motion and the universal cure, and many other great inventions, all made absolutely perfect.

What great discoveries we would make in astronomy, by living to see the outcome of our predictions; we could observe the leaving and returning of comets and the changing motions of the sun, moon and stars.

I spoke of many other things, inspired by the natural desire for endless life and earthly happiness. When I finished, and the main points of my talk had been passed on as before to the rest of the company, there was a good deal of talk amongst them in the language of the country, as well as some laughter at my expense. At last the gentleman who had been my interpreter said that the rest had asked him to set me straight on in a few mistakes I had made, made through the usual stupidity of human nature, which was excusable. The Struldbrugs were unique to their country, for there were no such people either in Balnibarbi or Japan, where he had been honored to be his majesty's ambassador. He found that the natives of those kingdoms had found it hard to believe such a thing could be possible, and he could see from my astonishment when he mentioned it to me that I had never heard of such a thing, and could hardly believe it. In the two kingdoms he mentioned, where he had spoken with many of the inhabitants, he had observed that having a long life was the universal desire of mankind. A person who had one foot in the grave did their best to keep the other one out of it. Even the oldest wanted to live longer, and saw death as the worst thing possible and was always trying to escape it. It was only on this island of Luggnagg that people didn't hanker after a long life, because of the example they had seen of the Struldbrugs.

He said that the system of life I had invented was illogical and silly, because it assumed lifelong youth, health and strength, that no man would be so foolish as to hope he would get, no matter how much of a fantasist he was. So the question was not how a man would live with eternal prosperity and health but how he would live his immortal life through all the disadvantages that old age brings. For although few men would stick to their desire to be immortal under those harsh conditions, he had seen in the two kingdoms he mentioned, Balnibarbi and Japan, that every man tried to put off death, however late in life it came, and he had never heard of any man willingly take his life unless he suffered the most awful grief or pain.

After this introduction he gave me a detailed account of the Struldbrugs in their country. He said that they acted like ordinary people until they were about thirty, then they became sad and depressed, more and more so until they got to eighty. He learned this from what they said, because there weren't more than three or four of them born in any generation, so there were not enough of them to make proper studies. When they got to eighty, which is the longest anyone lives in this country, they not only had the stupidity and weakness of other old men but they had many more which came from the dreadful prospect of never dying. They were not only opinionated, peevish, miserly, depressive, vain and talkative but they could not make friends and had no natural affection, which died out with their grandchildren. Envy and unfulfilled desires are their main passions. The things which they seem most jealous of are the vices of the young and the deaths of the old. Looking at the first, they see that they are cut off from such pleasures, and whenever they see a funeral that complain and are sad that others have gone to a rest which they will never know. They can't remember anything except what they learned in youth and middle age, and even then not very well. For the truth or details of any fact it is best to rely on agreed tradition rather than their memories. The happiest ones amongst them seem to be the ones who become senile and completely lose their memories. Those get more pity and help as they lack many of the bad qualities the others have in abundance.

If a Struldbrug happens to marry one of his own kind, the marriage is automatically dissolved, with state approval, as soon as the younger one gets to eighty, because the law thinks it is reasonable that those who are condemned through no fault of their own to stay in the world forever shouldn't have their misery doubled by having to carry a wife as well.

As soon as they have reached eighty they are seen as non-existent in the law. Their heirs immediately inherit their estates, and only a tiny sum is kept for their support; the poor ones are looked after at the public expense. After that time they are thought to be incapable of any jobs which require trust or make a profit; they cannot buy or rent land, and they cannot be witnesses in any case, criminal or civil, not even in property disputes.

At ninety they lose their teeth and hair, and at that age they can't taste anything but eat and drink anything they can get, without enjoyment or hunger. The diseases they have carry on forever, without getting better or worse. When they talk they forget what things are called, and people's names, even those of their closest friends and relations. For the same reason they lose their pleasure in reading, because they can't remember a sentence from beginning to end, and because of this they lose the only pleasure they could have.

As the language of the country is always changing the Struldbrugs of one age do not understand the talk of those from another, and after two hundred years they can't converse (apart from a few common words) with their neighbors the mortals, and so they become like foreigners in their own country.

This was what I was told about the Struldbrugs, as far as I can remember. I saw afterwards five or six from different generations, the youngest of whom was not more than two hundred years old, brought to me at various times by some of my friends. But although they were told I was a great traveller, who had seen the whole world, they had no curiosity about me; they just asked to be given a "slumskudask", or something to remember me by, which is a subtle way of begging. They do this to avoid breaking the law which forbids them begging as they are paid for by the public, although only with a very small allowance.

They are despised and hated by all sorts of people. When one of them is born it is seen as a sign of bad luck, and great care is taken to note their birthdays, so that one can know their age by looking in the register, although it has not been kept for more than a thousand years, or at least the older records have been destroyed through time or public disturbances. The usual way of discovering their age is to ask them what kings or famous people they can remember, and then matching it with history, for it's always the case that the last prince they can remember didn't begin his reign after they were eighty years old.

They were the most distressing sight I ever saw, and the women were more horrible than the men. Besides the usual deformities of old age they had additional ones in proportion to their years, which cannot be described, and amongst half a dozen I could always tell who was the oldest, even if there was only a century or two between them.

The reader will find it easy to believe that what I had seen or heard certainly put me off the idea of immortality. I became very ashamed of the fantasies I had created, and I thought that no tyrant could invent a way of dying which I wouldn't embrace to avoid living in that way. The king heard of everything my friends and I had discussed and made fun of me very charmingly; he said he wished I could send a couple of Struldbrugs to my own country, to stop people being afraid of dying, but it seems that this is forbidden by the fundamental laws of the country, otherwise I would have been happy to shoulder the trouble and expense of sending them.

I could only agree that the laws of the kingdom relating to the Struldbrugs were based on sound thinking, and any other country would have to pass the same laws in the same circumstances. Otherwise, as greed always comes with old age, these immortals would soon own the whole nation, and take over the government, and as they didn't have the ability to manage it the country would be ruined.

Chapter XI

[The author leaves Luggnagg, and sails to Japan. From there he sails in a Dutch ship to Amsterdam, and on to England.]

I thought this account of the Struldbrugs might amuse the reader, as it seems to me rather unusual; at least I don't remember reading anything like it in any travel book I've ever come across. If it has been done before then I must be excused, as it is very necessary for travellers describing the same country to write about the same things, and they don't deserve to be accused of stealing or copying from those who went there before them. There is always business between this kingdom and the great empire of Japan, and it is very likely that the Japanese authors may also have given some description of the Struldbrugs, but my stay in Japan was so brief, and I was so ignorant of their language, that I could not ask. But I hope the Dutch, reading this, will be able to enquire and so make up for my lack of knowledge.

His majesty had often asked me to take a job in his court, but finding me completely determined to go back to my native country he kindly gave me permission to leave, and honored me with a letter of recommendation, signed personally, to the Emperor of Japan. He also gave me four hundred and forty-four gold pieces (this country loves round numbers) and a red diamond, which I sold in England for eleven hundred pounds.

On the 6th of May 1709 I took solemn leave of his majesty and all my friends. The prince was kind enough to order a guard to take me to Glanguenstald, which is a royal port on the southwest of the island. In six days I found a ship able to take me to Japan, and I spent fifteen days on the journey.

We landed at a small port town called Xamoschi, situated in the south-east of Japan. The town lies to the far west, where there is a narrow strait going north into a long stretch of sea, and the capital Yedo is there in the north-west. When I landed I showed the custom house officers my letter from the king of Luggnagg to his imperial majesty. They recognised the seal at once; it was as big as the palm of my hand. The impression it made was a picture of a king lifting a lame beggar off the ground. The magistrates of the town, hearing of the letter, treated me as though I was a government minster. They gave me carriages and servants, and sent news of me to Yedo. I was given an audience there, and handed over my letter, which was opened with great ceremony, and it was read to the Emperor by an interpreter who then informed me, on the orders of his majesty, that I should say what I wanted and whatever it was he would grant it out of respect for his royal brother of Luggnagg. This interpreter was employed to do business with the Dutch. He soon guessed from my appearance that I was a European, and so he translated his majesty's commands in Low Dutch, which he spoke perfectly well. I told him, as I had planned beforehand, that I was a Dutch merchant, shipwrecked in a very remote country, and I had travelled from there by sea and land to Luggnagg and then took a boat for Japan. I knew my countrymen often traded with Japan, so I was hoping that one of them could carry me back to Europe; so I must humbly asked that his majesty be kind enough to give me safe passage to Nangasac.

I added another plea to this, that for the sake of my patron the king of Luggnagg his majesty would allow me to avoid the ceremony usually demanded of my countrymen, being forced to trample on a crucifix, as I had landed in his country through misfortune, rather than intending to trade. When this plea was translated to the Emperor he seemed a little taken aback, and he said that I was the first of my countrymen to make a fuss about this point, and he wondered if I was really Dutch; he was beginning to suspect that I was a Christian. However, for the reasons I put forward, but mainly to please the king of Luggnagg with a great favor, he would allow my odd request. But he ordered that the business must be done subtly, and his officers should be told to let me miss the ceremony as if they had simply forgotten. For he assured me that if my Dutch countrymen found out about it they would certainly cut my throat on the journey. I thanked him, through the interpreter, for such a great favor, and as some troops were at that time marching to Nangasac the commanding officer had orders to get me there safely, with special orders about the crucifix business.

On the 9th of June 1709 I arrived at Nangasac, after a very long and troublesome journey. I soon met some Dutch sailors off the Ambonya, of Amsterdam, a stout ship of 450 tons. I had lived in Holland for a long time, studying at Leiden, and I spoke Dutch well. The sailors knew where I had come from most recently; they were curious about my voyages and my general life. I made up a story as short and believable as I could, keeping most things hidden. I was able to invent names for my parents, whom I pretended were nobodies living in the province of Gelderland. I would have given the captain (whose name was Theodorus Vangrult) anything he asked for passage to Holland, but when he heard I was a surgeon he was happy to offer me half price, on condition that I worked in that capacity. Before we sailed I was often asked by the crew if I had performed the ceremony I mentioned above. I evaded the question with general answers, saying I had done everything the Emperor and the court had asked. However, a malicious scoundrel of a boatman went to an officer and pointed at me, saying I had not yet trampled on the crucifix. But the officer, who had instructions to let me off, gave the rascal twenty strokes on the shoulders with a bamboo cane, and after that nobody asked any questions.

Nothing noteworthy happened on that voyage. We sailed with a fair wind to the Cape of Good Hope, where we stopped just to take on fresh water. On the 10th of April 170 we arrived safely at Amsterdam, having only lost three men from sickness on the voyage, and a fourth who fell from the foremast into the sea, not far from the coast of Guinea. From Amsterdam I soon set sail for England, in a small ship of the city.

On the 16th of April we reached the coast of Kent. I landed the next morning, and saw my native country again after an absence of five years and six months in total. I went straight to Redriff, arriving there at two in the afternoon on the same day, and I found my wife and family were in good health.

Part IV: A Voyage to the Country of the Houyhnhnms

Chapter I

[The author sets out as captain of his own ship. His men plot against him and lock him in his cabin for a long time, then put him ashore in a strange land. The Yahoos, a strange sort of animal, are described. The author meets two Houyhnhnms.]

I stayed at home with my wife and children for about five months, in a very happy state, if I had had the sense to know when I was well off. I left my poor wife heavily pregnant, and accepted a profitable offer to be captain of the Adventurer, a well built merchant ship of 350 tons, for I knew how to navigate and I was fed up with being a ship's surgeon, though I could still use those skills when necessary. I took a skilful young ship's surgeon, called Robert Purefoy, onto my ship. We set sail from Portsmouth on the 7th of September 1710; on the 14th we met Captain Pocock of Bristol at Tenerife; he was going to the bay of Campechy to collect firewood. On the 16th we lost contact with him in a storm; I have heard since I came back that his ship sank, and only one cabin boy escaped. He was an honest man and a good sailor, but a little too sure of himself, which was his downfall as it has been for several others; if he had followed my advice he, like me, might now be safe at home with his family.

Several men on my ship died of fever, so the merchants who employed me ordered me to recruit replacements from Barbados and the Leeward Islands. I soon had reasons to regret this, as I found out afterwards that most of them were pirates. I had a crew of fifty, and my orders were to trade with Indians in the Pacific and see what I could discover. These scoundrels I had picked up poisoned my other men against me and they hatched a plot to seize the ship and lock me up. They did this one morning, rushing into my cabin, tying me hand and foot and threatening to throw me overboard if I resisted. I told them that I was their prisoner and would do as they asked. They made me swear to this, and then they untied me, just leaving a chain tied to one leg and the other end to my bed. They put a sentry at my door with a loaded gun, with orders to shoot me dead if I tried to escape. They sent me my own food and drink and took charge of the ship for themselves. Their plan was to become pirates and rob Spanish ships, which they could not do until they had more men. But they decided first that they would sell the ship's cargo, then go to Madagascar for recruits, as several of them had died since they locked me up. They sailed for many weeks, and traded with the Indians, but I don't know what course they sailed as I was confined to my cabin and expecting to be murdered, as they kept threatening to do.

On the 9th of May 1711 a sailor called James Welch came down to my cabin and said he had orders from the captain to set me ashore. I argued with him, but in vain; he wouldn't even tell me who the new captain was. They forced me into the longboat, letting me wear my best suit of clothes, which were as good as new, and take a small bundle of shirts and underclothes, but they wouldn't allow me any weapons except my sword. They were polite enough not to search my pockets, into which I put what money I had, and some other little essentials. They rowed about three miles then put me on a sandbank. I asked them to tell me what country it was, but they swore that they did not know. They said that the captain (as they called him) had decided that after they sold the cargo they would get rid of me at the first land they saw. They pushed off at once, advising me to hurry to avoid being caught by the tide, and said farewell.

In this lonely state I went ahead and soon reached firm ground, where I sat down on a bank to rest and think about what I should do. When I was a little rested I went inland, planning to surrender to the first savages I met and buy my life from them with some bracelets, glass rings and other toys that sailors usually carry with them on these voyages; I had a few with me. The land was divided into sections with long rows of trees, not planted but growing naturally. There was plenty of grass and several fields of oats. I walked very cautiously, worried about being ambushed or suddenly shot with an arrow from behind or from either side. I found a well trodden road, where I saw many human footprints as well as cattle tracks, but mainly the hoofprints of horses. At last I saw several animals in a field, and one or two of the same kind sitting in trees. They seemed an unusual and deformed shape, which worried me a little, so I hid behind some bushes to get a better look at them. Some of them came near my hiding place, so I had an opportunity of getting a good look at them. Their heads and chests were covered in thick hair, some curly and some straight; they had beards like goats, and long lines of hair down their backs, shins and feet, but the rest of their bodies were bare so I could see their skins, which were a beige color. They didn't have tails, or any hair on their buttocks, except around the anus, which I assume nature put there for protection when they sat on the ground, which they often did, as well as lying down and standing on their back legs.

They climbed high trees as well as squirrels, because they had long strong claws front and back, which were hooked with sharp points. They would often spring, bound and leap with impressive agility. The females were not as large as the males; they had long straight hair on their heads, but none on their faces, and just a short downy coat on the rest of their bodies, except around the anus and genitals. Their breasts hung between their front feet, and almost touched the ground as they walked. The hair of both sexes was various colors, brown, red, black and yellow.

All in all I had never, on all my travels, seen quite such a revolting animal, or one to which I had taken such a dislike. I thought I had seen enough of them, so I got up, full of hatred and disgust, and got back on the road, hoping it would lead me to some Indian's cabin. I hadn't got far when I met one of these creatures right in my way, which came right up to me. The ugly monster, seeing me, pulled many faces and stared as if I was something he had never seen before. When he got closer he lifted up his front paw, whether out of curiosity or mischief I didn't know. I drew my sword and gave him a good blow with the flat of it, for I didn't dare use the edge in case some of the natives might attack me if they knew I had harmed any of their animals. When the beast felt the blow he retreated and roared so loud that a herd of at least forty of them came running at me from the next field, howling and making hideous faces. But I ran to the trunk of a tree and put my back to it, keeping them off by waving my sword. Several of this foul mob got hold of the branches round the back of the tree and climbed up into it, and from there they began to crap on my head. However, I avoided it pretty well by sticking close to the trunk, although I was almost choked with the filth, which fell around on all sides.

In the middle of this danger they all suddenly ran away as fast as they could, so I risked leaving my tree and following the road, wondering what had frightened them. Looking to my left I saw a horse walking quietly in a field; my tormentors had seen him before me, and this is what had made them run. The horse shied a little when he saw me, but soon pulled himself together and looked straight at me with obvious amazement. I would have carried on, but he stood right in my path, though he looked very peaceful and didn't threaten any sort of harm. We stood looking at each other for some time; eventually I had the nerve to reach out a hand and try to stroke its neck, using the gestures and noises that jockeys do, when they're handling an unfamiliar horse. But the animal seemed to dislike my politeness and shook his head, frowned, and lifted up his right front leg to push my hand away. Then he neighed three or four times, but in such different ways that I almost began to think he was talking to himself in some language of his own.

While he and I were doing his another horse arrived; going to the first in a very formal way they gently touched right front hoofs, and they neighed several times in turn, making different noises so it almost sounded like speech. They went some paces away, as if they were consulting together, walking side by side, to and fro, like people discussing some important business, but they often looked over at me as if making sure I wouldn't escape. I was amazed to see such actions and behavior from dumb animals, and thought that if the natives of this country had intelligence in proportion to their horses they must be the cleverest people on earth. This thought was so comforting that I decided to press on until I could find some house or village, or meet any of the natives, leaving the two horses to talk together as they liked. But the first horse, who was a dapple gray, seeing me sneak off, neighed after me in such an expressive way that I thought I understood what he meant, and I turned back and came close, expecting further orders. I hid my fear as well as I could, for I began to worry as to how this business might finish, and the reader will find it easy to appreciate I didn't like the position I was in.

The two horses came up close to me, looking very carefully at my face and hands. The grey horse rubbed my hat all over with his right front hoof, and disarranged it so much that I had to take it off and put it back on. This appeared to surprise him and his companion (who was a brown bay) very much. The latter felt the lapels of my coat, and finding it hanging loose about me they both stared with fresh amazement. He stroked my right hand, seeming to like the softness and color, but he squeezed it so hard between his hoof and leg that I was forced to yell out; after that they touched me as gently as they could. They were very confused by my shoes and stockings, which they often touched, neighing to each other and making various gestures, like a philosopher trying to solve a new and difficult problem.

All in all, the behavior of these animals was so orderly and rational, so sharp and sensible, that I decided that they must be magicians, who had transformed themselves for some purpose and, seeing a stranger on the road, had decided to amuse themselves with him. Or perhaps they really were amazed by the sight of a man so very different in dress, looks and complexion from those who probably lived in this remote land. Thinking this, I tried speaking to them: "Gentlemen, if you are magicians, as I have every reason to believe, you will understand my language. I would like to let you know that I am a poor Englishman in need of help, washed up on your coast through bad luck. I ask one of you to let me ride on your back, as if you were a real horse, to some house or village where I can get help. In return for this I will make you a present of this knife and bracelet." I took the things out of my pocket. The two creatures stood silent as I spoke, seeming to listen to me very intently, and when I was finished they neighed at each other as if they were having a serious conversation. I could see that their language was very expressive, and that the words could, with a little effort, be written down more easily than Chinese.

I frequently heard the word "Yahoo", which they each said several times. Although it was impossible for me to guess what it meant, while the two horses were busy in conversation I tried practising this word with my tongue, and as soon as they were quiet I boldly said, "Yahoo," in a loud voice, at the same time imitating as closely as I could the neigh of a horse. They were both obviously surprised by this, and the gray repeated the same word twice, as if he was trying to teach me the right accent. I copied him as well as I could and I could feel myself noticeably improving each time, though I was far from perfection. Then the bay tried me with another word, much harder to pronounce; if I try to put it into English writing it could be spelt Houyhnhnm. I didn't pronounce this as well as the first word, but after two or three tries I improved, and they both appeared amazed that I could manage it.

After some more discussion, which I thought might be about me, my two friends parted, with the same touching of hoofs, and the gray indicated that I should walk ahead of him. I thought it would be sensible to do so, until I could find a better guide. When I tried to slow down he would cry "Hhuun hhuun!" I guessed what he meant, and I told him, as well as I could, that I was tired and could not walk faster, and then he would stand still for a while and let me rest.

Chapter II

[The author is taken to a Houyhnhnm's house. The house is described. The author's welcome. What the Houyhnhnms eat. The author's discomfort at the lack of meat. He gets some at last. How the author ate in this country.]

Having walked about three miles, we came to a long building, made of timbers stuck in the ground with wood woven across; the roof was low and straw-covered. I now began to feel a little easier, and took out some toys which travellers usually carry as presents for the savage Indians of America and other parts, in the hope that the inhabitants of the house would give me a kind welcome. The horse indicated that I should go in first; it was a large room with a smooth clay floor, with a hay rack and a manger running the whole length of one side. There were three males and two females, not eating, but some of them were sitting on their back legs, which I was amazed by, but I was even more amazed to see the rest doing domestic things, as they seemed to be normal beasts. However, this backed up my first idea, that a people who could train brute animals like this must be the cleverest in the world.

The gray came in straight after me, and so prevented the others doing me any harm. He neighed to them several times as if he was in charge, and got answers.

Beyond this room there were three others, stretching the length of the house, and you could walk through the house in a straight line, following the doors one after the other. We went through the second room and towards the third. The gray walked in first, signalling me to follow; I waited in the second room and got my presents ready for the master and mistress of the house. They were two knives, three bracelets of false pearls, a small mirror and a bead necklace. The horse neighed three or four times and I waited to hear some answers in a human voice, but all I heard was a reply in the same language, though a little higher than his. I began to think that this house must belong to a very important person, as there was so much ceremony before I could enter. But the fact that a gentleman seemed to only have horses for servants baffled me. I worried that my brain had been disturbed by my suffering and misfortunes. I stood up and looked around the room where I had been left. It was furnished like the first, only rather more elegantly. I kept rubbing my eyes, but the same things were there. I pinched my arms and sides to wake myself up, hoping I might be dreaming. I then decided that everything I saw must have been produced by wizardry and magic. But I had no time to think about this, as the gray horse came to the door and signalled to me to follow him into the third room, where I saw a very pretty mare, together with a colt and a foal, sitting on their haunches on straw mats, quite skilfully made and perfectly neat and clean.

Soon after I came in the mare got up from her mat and came up close; after she had carefully examined my hands and face she gave me a very contemptuous look, and turning to the horse I heard that they both often said "Yahoo." I didn't, then, know what the word meant, though I was the first one I had learned to say. But I soon learned, to my eternal embarrassment, because the horse, signalling with his head, and repeating "hhuun, huhnn," as he had on the road, which I understood meant, "come with me", led me out into a kind of courtyard, where there was another building some distance from the house. We went in, and I saw several of those revolting creatures I had met when I landed, eating roots and some meat, which I later discovered to be ass or dog, and sometimes cow, which had died from an accident or disease. They were all tied by the neck to a beam with strong ropes; they held their food between the claws of their front feet and tore at it with their teeth.

The master horse ordered a sorrel nag, one of his servants, to untie the largest of these animals and take him into the yard. The beast and I were brought close together, and our faces were carefully compared by master and servant, who both then repeated the word "Yahoo" several times. I cannot describe my horror and amazement when I saw that this disgusting animal looked completely human. It's true that its face was flat and wide, its nose spread out, with large lips and a wide mouth, but these differences are normal in savage countries, where the lines of the face are distorted by the natives letting their children lie face down on the ground, or by carrying them on their backs with their faces pressed into their mothers' shoulders. The front feet of the Yahoo were only different from my hands in the length of the nails, the roughness and brownness of the palms, and the hairiness of the backs. Our feet were also the same, with the same differences; I knew this very well but the horses didn't because of my shoes and stockings. We were similar in every other part of our bodies as well, apart from hair and color, as I have already described.

The thing that seemed most to confuse the two horses was to see that the rest of my body was so different to that of a Yahoo, because of my clothes, which they had no idea about. The sorrel nag offered me a root which he held (in their way, which I shall describe later) between his hoof and leg; I took it in my hand, smelt it and returned it to him as politely as I could. He brought a piece of ass' flesh from the Yahoo's kennel, but it smelt so vile that I turned away in disgust. He threw it to the Yahoo who greedily gobbled it up. He then showed me a wisp of hay and a handful of oats, but I shook my head to show that these were not what I ate. And now I realised that I was going to starve if I didn't get to some of my own kind. As for those filthy Yahoos, although there were few at that time who loved mankind as much as I did I never saw a thinking being that was so disgusting in every way, and the better I got to know them the more revolting they became, the whole time I was in that country. The master horse saw this from my behavior and so sent the Yahoo back to its kennel. He then surprised me very much by lifting his front foot to his mouth, although he did it easily and the movement seemed perfectly natural; he also made other signs, asking what I wanted to eat. I couldn't answer him in any way that he would understand, and if he had understood I still couldn't see how I could have got any food. While we were doing this I saw a cow going past and I asked if I could go and milk her. This had an effect, because he took me back into the house, and ordered a mareservant to open a room where there was a good stock of milk in earthenware and wooden containers, all very neat and clean. She gave me a large bowlful, which I drank with great gusto, and found that I felt much better.

About noon I saw a vehicle like a sledge coming towards the house, drawn by four Yahoos. There was an old horse in it, who seemed to be a gentleman. He got out back feet first, having hurt his left forefoot in an accident. He had come to dine with our horse, who welcomed him very warmly. They dined in the best room, and had oats boiled in milk as their second course, which the old horse ate warm, though the rest had them cold. Their mangers were laid out in a circle in the middle of the room, divided into several sections, and they sat round them on their haunches on straw bales. There was a large rack in the middle, with sides facing every section of the manger, so that each horse and mare ate their own portion of hay, and their own mash of oats and milk, very nicely and with good manners. The behavior of the young colt and foal seemed very respectful, and the master and mistress seemed very cheerful and welcoming to their guest. The gray ordered me to stand next to him, and him and his friend spoke about me a lot, as I could see from the way the stranger kept looking at me and the fact that they both often said "Yahoo."

I happened to have put on my gloves, which confused the master gray, as he showed signs of astonishment, wondering what I had done with my front feet. He touched them three or four times with his hoof, as if to say I should return them to their former shape; I soon did, pulling off my gloves and putting them in my pocket. This caused more talk, and I saw that the company was pleased with my behavior, which I soon found had done me some good. I was ordered to speak the few words I understood, and whilst they ate the master taught me the names for oats, milk, fire, water and some others, which I could easily copy, as from my childhood I have always found it easy to learn languages.

When dinner was over the master horse took me to one side, and through signs and words he showed me that he was worried by the fact that I hadn't had anything to eat. In their language oats are called "hlunnh." I said this word two or three times, for although I had refused them to start with I began to think that I could make a sort of bread out of them which might be enough, with milk, to keep me alive until I could escape to another country and be with creatures of my own species. The horse immediately ordered a white mareservant of the household to bring me a good quantity of oats on a sort of wooden tray. I heated these at fire, as well as I could, and rubbed them until the husks came off, and I did my best to separate them from the grains. I ground and beat them between two stones, then took water and made them into a paste or dough, which I toasted on the fire and ate warm with milk. It was a very dull diet to begin with, though it's normal enough in parts of Europe, but I got used to it in time, and as I had often been reduced to short rations in my life it was not the first time I had seen how easily our needs can be satisfied. And I must say that I never had an hour of illness while I was on the island. It's true that I sometimes managed to catch a rabbit or bird with traps made from Yahoo hair, and I often gathered edible herbs, which I boiled and ate as salad with my bread. Every now and again, as a treat, I made a little butter and drank the whey. At first I missed salt very much, but I soon got used to not having it, and it's my belief that salt is just a luxury, and was only introduced amongst us to make us want drink. It is only really needed for preserving meat on long voyages, or in places far away from great markets. We can see that no animal apart from man likes salt, and when I left this country it was a long time before I could stand the taste of it on anything I ate.

That's enough about my diet; other travellers fill their books with details of what they eat, as if the reader gives a damn if we eat well or badly. However, I had to mention it, in case anyone should question how I managed to stay alive for three years in such a country, with such natives.

When it got towards evening the master horse ordered me a place to stay in; it was only six yards from the house and separate from the Yahoo's stable. I got some straw and, using my own clothes as a blanket, slept very well. But I was soon given a better place to stay, as the reader will learn, when I come to speak about my way of life in more detail.

Chapter III

[The author tries to learn the language. His master, the Houyhnhnm, helps him. The language is described. Several Houyhnhnms come to see the author through curiosity. He gives his master a brief account of his journey.]

The main thing I wanted to do was to learn the language, which my master (as I shall call him from now on) and his children, and every servant in the house, were keen to teach me, for they thought it was incredible that a dumb animal should show such signs of intelligence. I pointed to everything and asked what it was called, which I wrote down in my journal when I was alone, and corrected my poor pronunciation by asking the members of the family to say the words over and over. A sorrel nag, one of the under-servants, was very keen to help me with this.

When they spoke, they talked through the nose and throat, and of the European languages I know it is closest to High-Dutch, or German, though far more graceful and expressive. The emperor Charles V said almost the same thing, when he said that if he spoke to his horse he would speak in High-Dutch.

My master was so impatient to hear about me that he spent much of his free time teaching me. He was convinced (he told me afterwards) that I must be a Yahoo, but my ability to learn, politeness and cleanliness amazed him, as these were qualities no Yahoo had. He was most confused by my clothes, debating to himself whether they were a part of my body, because I never undressed until the family were asleep and dressing before they rose in the morning. My master was keen to learn where I had come from, and how I had come by my learning, which he could see in everything I did, and he was looking forward to hearing my story from my own lips, which he hoped he would soon thanks to the great strides I had made in learning and pronouncing their words and sentences. To help my memory I wrote down everything I learned in the English alphabet, with translations. After a while I did this in my master's presence, and it was very difficult to explain to him what I was doing, as the inhabitants don't have any concept of books or literature.

In about ten weeks' time I could understand most of his questions; in three months I could answer him quite well. He was extremely curious as to where I came from, and how I was taught to imitate a rational creature, because the Yahoos (whom he could see I exactly resembled in my face, head and hands, which were all he could see) were cunning troublemakers and the most unteachable of all the brutes. I told him that I had come from over the sea, from a faraway place, with many others of my own sort, in a great hollow container, and that my companions had forced me to land on this coast and then left me to fend for myself. With some difficulty, and using much sign language, I managed to make him understand me. He replied that I must be mistaken or saying the thing which was not (for they have no word for lying); he knew that there could not be a land beyond the sea, or that a group of animals could move a wooden vessel wherever they wanted to on the water. He was sure that no Houyhnhnm could make such a thing, and if they could they would not trust Yahoos to handle it.

The word Houyhnhnm in their language means horse and is derived from a phrase meaning "Perfection of nature." I told my master that I couldn't explain at the moment, but I would get better as fast as I could and then I would be able to tell him wonderful things. He was kind enough to tell his own mare, colt, foal and the family servants to take every chance to teach me, and he did so himself, for two or three hours every day. Several horses and mares of the upper classes in the neighborhood often came to our house, as the report spread that there was an amazing Yahoo that could speak like a Houyhnhnm and seemed, in his words and actions, to have some form of intelligence. They loved talking to me; they asked me many questions, which I answered as well as I could. Through all this help I made such great progress that after five months I understood whatever was said and could express myself reasonably well.

The Houyhnhnms, who came to see my master as an excuse for seeing me, could hardly believe that I was a true Yahoo, as my body had a different covering from the others of my kind. They were amazed to see that I didn't have the usual hair and skin, except on my head, face, and hands; but I had shown the secret of that to my master, due to an accident which had happened about a fortnight before.

I have already told the reader that every night, when the family had gone to bed, I would strip off and cover myself with my clothes. It happened, early one morning, that my master sent the sorrel nag, who was his valet, to get me. When he came I was fast asleep, my clothes had fallen off to one side and my shirt was above my waist. I was woken by the noise he made and he delivered his message in a rather disturbed way, after which he went to his master and in a great fright he gave him a very confused story of what he had seen. I soon found this out, for as soon as I was dressed I went to see his honor, and he asked me what this thing that his servant had reported meant; his valet had told him that I was part white, part yellow (or at least not so white) and part brown.

Up until then I had kept my clothes a secret, to make myself as different as possible from the cursed race of Yahoos, but now I saw it was pointless to try and do so any longer. Besides, I knew that my clothes and shoes would soon wear out, as they were already in a bad way, and I must get some more from the hides of the Yahoos or other animals, and then the whole secret would be revealed. So I told my master that in the country I came from my kind always covered their bodies with the hairs of certain animals, prepared through skill, for decency as well as to avoid the variations in temperature, hot and cold. I would show him everything, if he wished, though I asked that he allowed me to keep the parts hidden which nature wished us to. He said that my speech was very strange, especially the last part, which he couldn't understand at all – why should nature have taught us to hide what it had given us? But, he said, I could do as I wished. So I unbuttoned my coat and took it off, and the same with my waistcoat. I took off my shoes, stockings and breeches. I let my shirt down to my waist, and pulled up the bottom part, so it fastened around my middle like a belt to hide my nakedness.

My master watched the whole performance with much curiosity and interest. He picked up my clothes with his leg, one piece after another, and examined them closely. Then he stroked my body very gently and looked round me several times. After that he said I must be a perfect Yahoo, but that I was very different from the rest of my species in the softness, whiteness and smoothness of my skin, my lack of hair on several parts of my body, the shape and shortness of my claws on hands and feet and my habit of always walking on my hind legs. He wanted to see no more, and gave me permission to get dressed, as I was shivering with cold.

I said that I was not happy with him always calling me a Yahoo, a revolting animal for which I had so much hatred and contempt; I begged that he would stop calling me that, and ask his family, and the friends he allowed to see me, to do the same. I also asked that the secret of my having a false covering on my body could be kept between us, at least as long as my current clothes held out, and as for what his valet, the sorrel nag, had seen, he might order him to keep it secret.

My master very kindly agreed to all this, and so the secret was kept until my clothes began to wear out, and I was forced to make up for that with several tricks I'll mention later. He asked that in the meantime I should carry on doing my best to learn their language, because it was my capacity for speech and thought that really amazed him, not my body, covered or not, and he was waiting impatiently to hear the wonderful things I had promised to tell him about.

After that he made twice the effort he had before to teach me; he introduced me to everyone and told them to treat me politely, telling them privately that this would make me happy and so more entertaining.

Every day, when I attended him, as well as the efforts he made in teaching me he would ask me several questions about myself, which I answered as well as I could, and through these he had already got some rough ideas, though very limited ones. It would be boring to tell all the steps I took to get to a more normal conversation, but the first account I gave of myself which had any order and length was like this:

That I came from a very far off country, as I had already tried to tell him, with about fifty of my own species; we had travelled on the seas in a great hollow vessel made of wood which was larger than my master's house. I described the ship to him as well as I could, and used my handkerchief to show how it was blown forward by the wind. Due to an argument I had been put ashore on this coastline, and I had walked inland, not knowing where I was going, until he had rescued me from the attacks of those disgusting Yahoos. He asked me who had made the ship, and why did the Houyhnhnms of that country leave it to brutes to operate it. I told him that I could not go on with my tale unless he would give me his word of honor that he would not be offended, and then I would tell him the amazing things I had promised. He agreed, and I continued by promising him that the ship was made by creatures like myself, and that in all the countries I had visited, as well as my own, we were the only ruling intelligent creatures. I told him that when I had arrived in his land I was as amazed to see Houyhnhnms acting like intelligent beings as he or his friends were to find intelligence in a creature which he called a Yahoo. I admitted that I looked exactly like them, but I could not understand their brutal and degenerate nature. I also said that if I ever had the good luck to return to my homeland, as I hoped to, everybody would believe that I was saying the thing that was not, and that I had invented the story from my imagination. With all due respect to him and his family, and as he had promised not to be offended, our countrymen would not believe it possible for Houyhnhnms to be the ruling creatures of a nation, and the Yahoos the animals.

Chapter IV

[The Houyhnhnm's ideas of truth and lies. The author's speech is disliked by his master. The author gives a more detailed account of himself and the mishaps on his voyage.]

My master looked extremely uneasy when he heard me saying this. Because doubt or disbelief are so uncommon in that country the inhabitants don't know how to behave when they find themselves in that position. And I remember when, in the frequent talks I had with my master about the nature of men in other parts of the world, I had to mention lying and deceit, and he found it very difficult to understand what I meant, although otherwise he was very intelligent. He thought that the point of speech was to allow us to understand one another and to pass on facts; if anything was said which was not true, that purpose is defeated, because I can't be said to understand him, and far from receiving facts he would be leaving me in a state worse than ignorance, if I believe a thing is black when it is white and short when it is long. That is all he had to say about the skill of lying, which is so perfectly understood and widely practised by mankind.

To come back to the point; when I said that Yahoos were the only governing creatures in our country, which my master found beyond belief, he asked if there were any Houyhnhnms in our country, and what they did. I told him that we had a great many, and that in summer they grazed in the fields, and in winter they were kept in houses with hay and oats, with Yahoo servants who rubbed them down, combed their manes, cleaned their hooves, brought them food and made their beds. "Now I understand," my master said, "I can clearly see now that from everything you've said, whatever intelligence the Yahoos think they have, the Houyhnhnms are your masters; I dearly wish our Yahoos would be so helpful." I begged that his honor would allow me to stop, because I was sure that the story he was asking for would be very upsetting for him. But he insisted and told me to let him know the best and the worst of it.

I told him that I would do as he asked. I admitted that the Houyhnhnms of our country, whom we called horses, were the most well made and beautiful animals we had, which excelled in strength and speed. When they belonged to high class people they were used for travel, racing or pulling carriages; they were very well looked after until they got diseases, or started to get weak; but then they were sold and used in all kinds of hard labor until they died, when their skins were stripped off and sold for what could be got, and their bodies were left to be eaten by dogs and birds of prey. But ordinary horses weren't so lucky, as they were kept by farmers and carriers and other low people, who made them work harder and gave them worse food. I described as well as I could the way we ride, the shape and purpose of a bridle, saddle, spur and whip, as well as harness and wheels. I added that we fastened plates of a hard substance called iron to the bottom of their feet, to stop their hooves getting cracked on the stony paths which we often travelled on.

My master, after expressing his outrage at this, wondered how we dared to climb on a Houyhnhnm's back, for he was sure that the weakest servant in his house would be able to throw off the strongest Yahoo, or by falling down and rolling on his back he could squash the brute to death. I said that our horses were trained from the age of three or four for the tasks we meant for them; if any of them turned out to be intolerably vicious they were used for carriages. I told him they were severely beaten when they were young for any mischievous tricks and that the males who were destined for normal riding or pulling were usually castrated at about two years old, to calm their spirits and make them more tame and docile. I said that although it was true that they could respond to rewards and punishments I would ask his honor to consider that they didn't have a drop of intelligence, any more than the Yahoos of his country did.

I had to try many different ways of speaking to give my master the right impression of what I was talking about; their language does not have an enormous vocabulary, because their needs and emotions are less varied than ours. But I cannot describe his great resentment at our savage treatment of Houyhnhnms, particularly after I had explained the ways we castrated horses to stop them breeding and make them more docile. He said if it was possible that there was a country where only the Yahoos were intelligent then they would certainly be the rulers, as in time intelligence will always win over brute force. But looking at the size of us, especially me, he couldn't think of any creature of that bulk that was so poorly designed to use that intelligence in everyday life. He asked if my countrymen looked like me, or the Yahoos of his own country. I told him that I was as well built as most people my age, but that young people and women were softer and had skins as white as milk. He said that I did seem different from other Yahoos, as I was much cleaner and not so deformed. But in terms of which was really best, he thought that I was actually worse, because my nails were useless on my front and back feet; as for my forefeet he couldn't really even call them that, because he had never seen me walk on them, and they were too soft to cope with the ground. Also I usually had them uncovered, and the covering I did put on them was not the same shape nor as strong as the one on my back feet; and I could not walk safely, as if one of my back feet slipped I must inevitably fall over.

He then began to find fault with the rest of my body, the flatness of my face, my prominent nose, my front facing eyes, so that I could not look to the side without turning my head. He also pointed out that I couldn't feed myself without putting one of my forefeet to my mouth, and so my feet were oddly shaped to help me do that. He said he couldn't see what use the divisions in my back feet were, and they were too soft to cope with hard and sharp stones unless they were covered with the skin of another animal. My body needed a barrier against heat and cold, which I had to put on and take off every day, which was tedious and took effort. Lastly, he knew that every animal in his country naturally hated the Yahoos, with the weaker avoiding them and the stronger driving them away. So, supposing we had intelligence, he could not see how we could get past that natural hatred which every creature had for us, and so he couldn't see how we could tame them and make them useful. However, he said, he would not talk about this matter any further, as he was more interested in getting my story, about my homeland and the things that had happened in my life before I came to his country. I promised him that I was extremely keen to tell him everything he wanted to know, though I was very doubtful that I would be able to explain various subjects to him which he could not have any understanding of, as I had seen nothing in his country I could compare them to. However, I would do my best and try to explain myself with similes, humbly asking that he would help me out when I didn't know the vocabulary, which he kindly promised to do.

I told him that I was the child of honest parents in an island called England, which was as far away from his country as the distance his strongest servants could travel in a year. That I was taught to be a surgeon, whose job is to cure wounds and pains in the body, got through bad luck or violence. That my country was ruled by a female human, whom we called queen. That I left the country to try to get money that I could use to support myself and my family when I got back; that on my last voyage I was captain of the ship and had about fifty Yahoos at my command, many of whom died at sea, and I was forced to replace them with others from different countries. I told him our ship was nearly sunk twice, once in a great storm and once by running into a rock. My master interrupted me here, asking how I managed to persuade strangers from other countries to come with me, considering the losses I had suffered and the dangers I had faced. I told him that they were desperate fellows, forced to run from their homelands because of poverty or their crimes. Some were brought down by lawsuits; others had spent all they had drinking, whoring and gambling; others fled because they had committed treason; many had committed murder, theft, poisoning, robbery, perjury, forgery, coining, rape or sodomy, cowardice or desertion. Most of them were on the run from prison, and none of them dared go back to their homelands lest they should be hanged or starve in a jail, and so they had to get their livings elsewhere.

While I told him this my master interrupted me several times. I had had great trouble explaining the nature of the different crimes for which our crew had been forced to run from their country. It took several days of conversation before he understood me. He couldn't understand at all what the purpose or need for those vices was. To explain this, I tried to give him some idea of the desire for power and wealth, and the terrible effects of lust, drunkenness, hatred and envy. I had to explain this by giving examples and making guesses. When he understood he would raise his eyes in amazement and indignation, like one who has just had their mind battered with something he had never heard of or seen before. Power, government, war, law, punishment and a thousand other things had no terms in that language to express them, which made it almost impossible to give my master any idea what I was talking about. But as he was very intelligent and had thought about and discussed matters deeply he finally got a working knowledge of what human nature, in our part of the world, is capable of, and he asked me to give him a detailed account of the land we call Europe, and particularly of my own country.

Chapter V

[At his master's command the author tells him how things are in England. What causes war between kings in Europe. The author begins to explain the English constitution.]

I would like the reader to note that the following account of the many conversations I had with my master contains a summary of the most important points we discussed several times over more than two years, as his honor often asked for more details as my knowledge of the language of the Houyhnhnms improved. I showed him, as well as I was able, what all of Europe was like. I told him about business and factories, arts and sciences, and the answers I gave to his questions as they came up on many subjects meant that we never ran out of conversation. But I'll just put down here the essence of what we spoke of about my own country, putting it into the best order I can, regardless of time or place, while still keeping strictly truthful. The only thing that worries me is my inability to do justice to my master's arguments and expressions, which must be spoilt by my lack of ability as well as the translation into ugly English.

Following his honor's commands then, I told him about the revolution led by the Prince of Orange and the long war with France which he had begun and which was continued by his successor, the current queen, which involved the greatest nations in Christendom and was still going on. I calculated, when he asked me, that about a million Yahoos might have been killed in the whole war, with about a hundred cities captured, and five hundred ships sunk or burnt. He asked me what were the normal reasons that countries went to war. I told him that there were countless reasons, but I would just tell him the main ones. Sometimes it's the ambition of princes, who always want more land and people to govern; sometimes the corruption of ministers, who get their master involved in a war in order to quash, or distract the people from their, protests at their evil government. Differences of opinion have cost many lives, for instance whether flesh is bread or bread is flesh; whether the juice of a certain berry is blood or wine; whether whistling is good or bad; whether one should kiss a statue or throw it in the fire; whether a coat should be black, white, red or gray, long or short, dirty or clean, and there are many others.

And there are no wars so passionate and deadly, or which go on so long, as ones caused by differences of opinion, especially if they concern unimportant matters.

Sometimes two princes will fight to decide which of them shall take the lands of a third, which neither of them pretend they have any rights to. Sometimes one prince will fight another because he's worried the other might attack him first. Sometimes a war begins as the enemy is too strong, other times because he is too weak. Sometimes out neighbors want the things we have, or have the things we want, and we both fight until they have our things or they give us theirs. It's seen as a very good reason for war to invade a country after its people have been weakened by famine, destroyed by plague or have had a civil war. It is allowed to enter into war against our closest friend, if one of his towns looks easy to take, or if there's a piece of his land that would make our kingdom round and whole. If a prince sends forces into the nation where the people are poor and ignorant he may lawfully put half of them to death, and enslave the rest, in order to civilize them and take them away from their barbarous way of life. It is a very kingly, honorable and frequent thing, when one prince wants the help of another to help protect him against invasion, for the assistant, when the invader is beaten, to grab the lands for himself, and kill, imprison or exile the prince he came to save. Alliances through family, or marriage, often cause wars, and the closer they are related the more likely they are to quarrel. Poor nations are hungry and rich nations are proud, and pride and hunger will always clash. For these reasons the job of a soldier is thought to be the most noble of all, because a soldier is a Yahoo hired to kill, in cold blood, as many of his own species who have never done him any harm as he can.

There is also a type of poor prince in Europe, unable to make war themselves, who hire out their troops to richer nations, for so much per day per man, and they keep three quarters of the fee themselves and it's their biggest source of income. There are many like that in northern Europe.

"What you have told me," my master said, "about war, shows that you do indeed have that intelligence you claim. It's lucky that the nastiness of it is greater than the actual danger, as nature has left you totally incapable of doing much damage. With your mouths lying flat against your faces you can't bite each other with any success, unless you allowed it. As for the claws on your front and back feet they are so short and soft that one of our Yahoos could thrash a dozen of yours. And so, when you talk of those who have died in battle, I can't help thinking you have said the thing that is not."

I couldn't help shaking my head and smiling a little at his ignorance. As I was no stranger to the art of war, I told him about cannons, culverins, muskets, carbines, pistols, bullets, powder, swords, bayonets, battles, sieges, retreats, attacks, undermines, countermines, bombardments, sea fights, ships sunk with a thousand men, twenty thousand killed on each side, dying groans, limbs flying in the air, smoke, noise, confusion, people trampled to death under horses' feet, flight, pursuit, victory; fields covered in carcases, left for food for dogs and wolves and birds of prey; plundering, stripping, raping, burning, and destroying. And to demonstrate the bravery of my own dear countrymen I told him that I had seen them, in a siege, blow up a hundred enemies at once, and the same number on a ship, and I'd seen the dead bodies come falling in pieces from the clouds, much to the amusement of onlookers. I was going to give more details when my master commanded me to be silent. He said that anyone who understood what Yahoos were like could easily believe that such a vile animal was capable of all the things I had described, if they had the strength and cunning to match their hatred. But my talk had increased his disgust at the whole species, and he found it had upset him in a way that he had never known before.

He said that he thought his ears, when they got used to such horrible words, might in time hear them with less revulsion. Although he hated the Yahoos of his country he didn't blame them for their revolting qualities, any more than he did a Gnnayh (a bird of prey) for its cruelty, or a sharp stone for cutting his hoof. But when a creature that was supposed to be intelligent did such terrible things he was worried that the perverted intelligence might actually be worse than brutality. So he was sure that we didn't have intelligence, just some quality which increased our natural vices, like a rippling stream reflects a body, making it look poorly shaped and bigger than it is.

He also said that he had heard too much about war, in this and some of our previous conversations. There was something else which rather confused him at the moment. I had told him that some of our crew had left their country as their lives had been ruined by the law. I had already explained to him what the law was, but he couldn't understand how the law, which was designed to look after every man, could also ruin a man. So he wanted to know more about what I meant by law, and the people who operated it, as it worked in my country. He thought that nature and common sense were good enough guides for an intelligent animal, which is what we thought we were, to show what ought to be done and what ought to be avoided.

I told his honor that law was an area I hadn't been involved in much, apart from hiring lawyers, pointlessly, to correct some wrongs that had been done to me. However, I would tell him all I could.

I told him that there was a group of men amongst us who learned from youth to prove, with a great number of words, that white is black or black is white, depending on who is paying them. All the rest of the people are enslaved to this group. For example, if my neighbor wants my cow, he gets a lawyer to prove that he should have it. So then I must hire another one to say I should keep it, as it's against the rules of law that any man should speak for himself. Now in this case I, the proper owner, have two great disadvantages. The first is that my lawyer, having been brought up almost from the cradle to defend lies, is completely lost when he has to speak for justice, which is unnatural to him and he always does it clumsily, if not unwillingly. The second disadvantage is that my lawyer must be very careful or he will be reprimanded by the judges and hated by his comrades, as being someone who wants to diminish the law. And so I only have two ways of keeping my cow. The first is to bribe my adversary's lawyer with a double fee to betray his client by implying that he has justice on his side. The second way is for my lawyer to make my cause look as unjust as possible, by saying that the cow belongs to my opponent, and if he does this skilfully it will certainly win over the judge. I told his honor that he must realise that these judges are people appointed to decide all property disputes as well as criminal trials, and they are chosen from the most cunning lawyers, once they have got old or lazy. They have been biased against truth and justice all their lives, and so they will always favor fraud, perjury and oppression; I have known some of them refuse a large bribe from the side which had justice with it, rather than harm their profession by doing anything which would go against the nature of their office.

It is a tradition amongst these lawyers that whatever has been done before may legally be done again, and so they take special care to record all the decisions that have been made against common justice or common sense in the past. They call these precedents, and they produce them to justify the most unfair opinions, and the judges always go along with them.

When they speak in court they are careful not to mention the facts of the case; they are loud, passionate and boring about everything which has nothing to do with it. For instance, in the case I mentioned, they never want to know what rights my adversary has to my cow; they ask if the cow is red or black, with short or long horns, whether the field I keep her in is round or square, whether she was milked at home or elsewhere, what diseases she has had and so on. After that they look at precedents, adjourn the case from time to time, and in ten, twenty or thirty years they come to a decision.

It should also be noted that this group has a particular slang and language of its own, that no other person can understand, and all their laws are written in it, and they make sure there are plenty of them. Using them they have managed to mix up the essence of truth and lies, right and wrong, so it will take thirty years to decide whether a field that has been in my family for six generations should belong to me or some stranger who lives three hundred miles away.

When people are accused of crimes against the state the method is much quicker and more admirable: the judge first finds out what the people in power want, and then he hangs or pardons the criminal, still sticking to all the proper forms of law.

My master interrupted here and said that it was a shame that creatures of such intelligence, as these lawyers must be, from my description of them, didn't teach others wisdom or knowledge. I told him that in everything except their own profession they were usually the most ignorant and stupid people born, the dullest in ordinary conversation, sworn enemies of knowledge and learning and just as keen to pervert the intelligence of mankind in everything spoken of as they are in their own profession.

Chapter VI

[A continuation of the report on the state of England under Queen Anne. What a first minister of state in European courts is like.]

My master was still completely unable to understand why this race of lawyers would want to confuse, upset and tire themselves, and join in a conspiracy of injustice, just for the sake of harming their fellow animals. He couldn't understand either what I meant when I said that they did it for hire. So I had great trouble explaining to him what money was, what it was made of and what the various metals were worth. I told him that when a Yahoo had got a great stock of this stuff then he could buy whatever he wanted; the best clothes, the greatest houses, enormous areas of land, the most expensive food and drink, and he could have his pick of the loveliest women. Since it was only money that could do all this, our Yahoos thought they would never have enough of it to spend or save, as they wanted, depending on whether they were naturally spendthrift or miserly. I told him the rich man got the fruit of the poor man's work, and there were a thousand poor men for every rich man; most of our people were forced to live miserable lives, working every day for small wages, so that a few could have good lives.

I told him much about this, and many other similar things, but his honor was still questioning. He thought that every animal had a right to their share of what the earth produced, especially those who ruled. So he wanted to know what these costly meats were, and why any of us wanted them. So I told him as many things as I could think of, and the various ways of preparing them which could not be performed without sending ships to all parts of the world, as much as to get liquors to drink with them as the ingredients for sauces as well as many other fine things. I assured him that someone would have to go three times round the planet to get enough for one of our higher class female Yahoos to have enough for her breakfast and a cup to put it in. My master remarked that it must be a miserable country that couldn't feed its own people. But what he was really amazed by was how such great areas of land could be without fresh water, so that people would have to send for it from overseas in order to have enough to drink. I replied that England (the dear country of my birth) was reckoned to produce three times as much food as its inhabitants could eat, as well as liquors made from grain, or pressed out of the fruit of various trees, which made excellent drink, and we had the same amount of things in every other necessity of life. But to satisfy the greed and indulgence of our males, and the vanity of our females, we sent away the largest part of our necessities to other countries, in exchange for things which created disease, stupidity and vice for ourselves.

And so in consequence great numbers of our people had to make their livelihood by begging, robbing, stealing, cheating, pimping, flattering, bribing, giving false evidence, forging, gambling, lying, flattering, hectoring, voting, scribbling, star-gazing, poisoning, whoring, hypocrisy, libelling, freethinking, and similar professions (I had great difficulty in getting him to understand these terms).

I told him that wine wasn't imported from other countries as we were lacking in water or other drinks, but because it was the sort of liquid which made us happy by making us stupid, pushing away sad thoughts, creating extravagant fantasies, raising our hopes and banishing our fears, blocking all common sense for a time and depriving us of the use of our limbs until we fell asleep. Though it had to be admitted that we always woke up sick and depressed, and that using this liquor gave us diseases which made our lives miserable and short.

But apart from all this most of our people supported themselves by selling the necessities and luxuries of life to the rich and to each other. For example, when I am at home in my normal clothes, I am carrying on my back the labor of a hundred tradesmen; the building and the furniture of my house took as many more, and five times more were needed to dress my wife.

I was going on to tell him about another type of people who made their living looking after the sick, as I had at some points told my master that many of my crew had died from disease. But here I had great difficulty explaining what I meant. He could easily understand that a few days before his death a Houyhnhnm would feel weak and heavy, or he might hurt a leg in some accident. But he thought it was impossible that nature, which creates everything so perfect, would allow our bodies to suffer pain from inside, and he wanted to know the reason for this inexplicable evil.

I told him that we ate a thousand things which fought against each other; that we ate when we were not hungry and drank when we were not thirsty; that we sat up all night drinking strong liquor and not eating, which made us lazy, made our bodies swollen and hurried or blocked our digestion. I told him that prostitute female Yahoos had a certain illness which made the bones of those who had sex with them rot, and that this, and many other diseases, could be passed on from father to son, so that many were born already with difficult illnesses. It would take forever to give him a list of all the diseases human bodies could get, but it couldn't be fewer than five or six hundred, which could affect every limb and joint; in fact, every part of the body, inside and out, had its own diseases. To fight this there were people among us who had the job of curing the sick, or pretending to. And as I had some skill in this profession myself I would, as a show of gratitude to his honor, let him know all their secrets and techniques.

The main thing they say is that all disease comes from fullness, so they think that the body must be flushed out, either through the natural passage or through the mouth. The next thing they do is to make, from herbs, minerals, gums, oils, shells, salts, juices, seaweed, excrements, barks of trees, serpents, toads, frogs, spiders, dead men's flesh and bones, birds, beasts, and fishes a potion that is as horrid, nauseating and disgusting in smell and taste that they possibly can. The stomach immediately rejects this, and they call this a vomit. Otherwise, from the same ingredients, with other poisonous additions, they tell us to take, orally or anally (as the doctor happens to feel at that moment) a medicine which is equally irritable and revolting to the bowels; it relaxes the belly and forces everything out of it, and they call this a purge or clyster. For these doctors claim that nature meant our mouths to only have things put in them and our anuses only to get rid of things; these artists have cleverly decided that these diseases have pushed nature out of her normal place, so to get her back the body must be treated in the opposite way to normal, by swapping around the purposes of the orifices, forcing solids and liquids into the anus and making stuff come out of the mouth.

But as well as real diseases we suffer from many that are just imaginary, which the doctors have invented imaginary cures for. These have their own names and their own drugs to cure them, and our female Yahoos suffer from them all the time.

One of the great skills of this crew is in predicting the future, and they are almost always right. When real diseases get at all serious they nearly always predict death, which is in their power when a cure is not. If, after they have made their prediction, things look like getting better, they can avoid looking like false prophets and show their wisdom by just giving another drop of medicine.

This makes them very useful to husbands or wives who are fed up with their spouses, to eldest sons waiting to inherit, to great ministers of state and often to princes.

I had before, from time to time, told my master about the nature of government in general, and especially about our own wonderful constitution, which was deservedly admired and envied throughout the world. But as I had happened at this point to mention a minister of state he asked me, a little while later, to tell him what sort of Yahoo I meant by that name.

I told him that a first or chief minister of state, the person I was going to describe, was a creature who felt no grief, joy, love, hatred, pity or anger, or at least he never used those feelings and was only interested in wealth, power and titles. He could use words for anything, except to show what he was thinking. Whenever he tells the truth he wants you to think he's lying, and when he lies he wants you to think it's the truth. He promotes the ones he speaks worst of behind their backs, and when he begins to praise you to others or to your face then you're really in trouble. The worst thing you can get from him is a promise, particularly if it's backed up with an oath; that's when every sensible person leaves and gives up all hope. There are three ways in which a man can become a chief minister. The first is to know sensibly how to pimp out his wife, sister or daughter. The second is to betray or undermine his predecessor. The third is to show a great opposition, in public meetings, to the corruption of the court. A wise prince would prefer to choose someone who uses that last method, because those who seem that passionate always end up the most fawning and most in agreement with the wishes and emotions of their master. These minsters have all the state jobs at their command, so they use them to stay in power by bribing the majority of a senate or great council, and in the end, by using a trick called an Act of Indemnity (which I described to him at great length), they exempt themselves from any punishment and retire from public life carrying the nation's wealth with them.

The palace of a chief minister is a school to teach others following his trade; the pages, lackeys and porters copy their master and so become ministers of state in their own areas, and they learn to be perfect in the three main skills of insolence, lying and bribery. And so they are supported by people of the highest rank, and sometimes, through their cunning and cheek, they will rise up through the ranks and become a first minister themselves.

He is usually ruled by some faded old tart, or a favorite footman, who are the tunnels through which all his favors are passed, and who are, when all's said and done, the real governors of the kingdom.

One day, when we were talking, my master, having heard me mention my country's noblemen, paid me a compliment which I couldn't accept, that he was sure I must have been born into some noble family, because I was far better in shape, color and cleanliness than all the Yahoos in his country (although I was not as great in strength and agility, which he put down to my different lifestyle to those other brutes) and I also not only could talk but had some basic intelligence, to the extent that all of his friends thought I was a marvel.

He pointed out to me that amongst the Houyhnhnms the white, the sorrel and the iron gray were not as nicely shaped as the bay, the dapple-gray and the black, and they were not born as intelligent or with the ability to become so, so they always were the servants, and never wanted to mate out of their own race, which in that country would be thought of as monstrous and unnatural.

I gave his honor my lowest bow for the kind opinion he had of me, but at the same time I promised him that I was of quite common birth, with ordinary parents who just managed to give me a reasonable education, and that nobility, amongst us, was quite different his ideas of it. Our young noblemen grow up amongst idleness and luxury, and as soon as they are old enough they ruin their health and contract horrible diseases from lewd women. When they have spent nearly all their fortune they marry some woman of low birth, unpleasant personality and weak body whom they hate and despise, just for the sake of her money. The offspring of these marriages are usually degenerate, rickety or deformed children, and so the family won't usually last more than three generations, unless the wife finds a healthy father, amongst her neighbors and servants, to carry on and strengthen the line. The true marks of noble blood are a diseased body, yellow skin and a weak face, and if a nobleman has a healthy robust appearance then the world assumes that his real father was a groom or a coachman. The poorness of his body is matched by the poorness of his mind, made up of depression, stupidity, ignorance, changeability, lust and pride.

Without the agreement of these great men no law can be passed, abolished or changed, and they make rulings concerning everything we own, without appeal.

Chapter VII

[How much the author loves his native country. What his master said about the constitution and government of England, as the author has described it, with parallels and comparisons.]

The reader might wonder how I could bring myself to give such an honest appraisal of my own species to a race who already thought the worst of humankind, because of the similarity between me and the Yahoos. But I must admit that the great goodness of these wonderful quadrupeds, contrasted with human corruption, had opened my eyes and changed my thinking so much that I began to see the actions and passions of men very differently, and I didn't think the honor of my race was worth protecting. Anyway, it would have been impossible to do, in front of someone with the sharp judgment of my master, who daily indicated a thousand faults in me which I had never noticed before, and which, with us, wouldn't have even been called faults. I also developed, following his example, complete hatred of all lies and deceit, and truth seemed so good to me that it won over everything.

Let me be honest enough with the reader to admit that there was another, even stronger, reason I was so open in my descriptions. I had not been in the country for a year before I developed such love and admiration for the inhabitants that I had firmly decided that I would never go back to humanity, but would spend the rest of my life with the excellent Houyhnhnms, contemplating and practising every virtue, and here there was no example of vice, or encouragement of it, to follow. But luck, my old enemy, ruled that I would not have this great privilege. However, it is now some consolation to think that in describing my countrymen I made as many allowances for their faults as I dared before such a sharp questioner, and gave everything as favourable a spin as I could. For in fact is there anyone alive who won't be influenced by bias and partiality towards the land of his birth?

I have described several of the conversations I had with my master during the majority of the time I had the honor of being in his service, but I have, to remain concise, left out much more than I have written here.

When I had answered his questions, and his curiosity seemed to be fully satisfied, he called for me early one morning and told me to sit down some distance away (an honor he had never done me before). He said that he had been thinking very seriously about my whole story, as far as it concerned myself and my country. He thought we were some kind of animals, to whom some small measure of intelligence had been given, by what accident he couldn't imagine. We had made no other use of this intelligence than to increase our inbred vices and to invent new ones, which nature had not given us. We had thrown away the few advantages she had given us, and been very good at inventing things we thought we needed and then spending our whole lives trying to get them. As for myself, it was obvious that I did not have the strength or agility of an ordinary Yahoo; that I walked shakily on my back legs; that I had got an invention to make my claws no use as a tool or a defence, and to take the hair off my chin which was there to be a shelter against wind and weather, and lastly I couldn't run fast or climb trees like my brothers (that's what he called them) the Yahoos of his country.

Our institutions of government and law plainly showed our lack of intelligence, and so of goodness; intelligence alone is enough to rule an intelligent creature, and so we had, by my own account, no right to think that we were intelligent, even though he could tell that I had tried to defend my race by hiding many things and saying the thing that was not.

He was more convinced about this as he could see that I was in my body exactly the same as the other Yahoos except for the things in which I was worse, strength, speed, agility and length of claws, and some other things nature had nothing to do with, and from the account I had given him of our lives, manners, actions he thought that our minds were very much of the same type too. He said that the Yahoos were known to hate each other more than they hated other animals; it was usually thought that this was because they looked so revolting, which they could see in all the others but not in themselves. He had therefore begun to think that we were sensible in covering up our bodies, and in doing so we could hide many of our deformities from each other, which otherwise would be unbearable. But now he found that he had been wrong, and the divisions amongst the brutes of his own country came from the same causes as ours, as I had described them. He said that if you throw amongst five Yahoos enough food for fifty they will, instead of eating peacefully, all start to fight, with each one wanting everything for itself. For this reason if they were eating outside a servant was usually employed to stand guard, and the ones kept at home were tied up some distance from each other. If a cow died from age or from an accident and a Hounyhnhnm could not get to it soon enough, for his own Yahoos, the ones in the neighborhood would come and seize it, and a battle would follow as he had described, with terrible claw wounds given and taken, though they didn't often kill each other as they didn't have such clever weapons as we had invented. At other times the same type of battles had been fought between the Yahoos of different neighborhoods, without any apparent cause; those in one district watched out for a chance to catch the next unprepared. But if they find their plans don't work out then they go home and, lacking enemies, start a civil war amongst themselves.

He said that in some parts of the country there were certain shiny stones of various colors of which the Yahoos are passionately fond, and when one of these stones is partly buried in the earth, as it sometimes is, they will dig with their claws for days to get them out. Then they carry them away and hide them in heaps in their kennels, being very wary in case their comrades should find their treasure. My master said that he had never been able to find out the reason for this unnatural desire, or see how those stones could be of any use to a Yahoo, but now he thought it might come from the same principle of avarice which I had described in mankind. Once, as an experiment, he had taken a heap of these stones away from the place where one of the Yahoos had hidden it; the revolting animal, missing its treasure, began wailing so that the whole herd came to the place, and he howled miserably and began biting and scratching the rest, began to pine away and would not eat, sleep nor work, until he told a servant to secretly put the stones back in the same hole and hide them like before. Once his Yahoo found them he recovered his spirits and good humor (though he took good care to put them in another hiding place) and has been a very useful brute ever since.

My master also told me something I had seen for myself, that the fields where there are many shining stones are the ones where the fiercest and most frequent battles are fought, caused by the constant invasions of the neighboring Yahoos.

He said it was quite usual, when two Yahoos found such a stone in a field, and were fighting over its ownership, for a third to take advantage and carry it away from them both. My master thought that this in some way resembled our lawcourts, and I thought it would be better for our reputation not to put him right, since the result he mentioned was much fairer than many in our courts; the plaintiff and defendant he mentioned lost nothing apart from the stone that they had fought for, whereas in our fair courts the case would never have ended while either of them had anything left.

My master carried on by saying that there was nothing which made the Yahoos quite as revolting as their indiscriminate manner of eating anything which came their way, whether it was herbs, berries, roots, the rotten flesh of animals, or all of these mixed together. It was an odd thing about them that they preferred what they could get through robbery and cunning, farther away, to the far better food they were given at home. If they had enough supplies they would eat until they were ready to burst, after which nature had shown them a certain root which would work as a laxative. There was also another kind of root, very juicy but rather rare and hard to find, which the Yahoos looked for very keenly, and they would suck it with great delight. It caused the same effects in them as wine has on us. Sometimes it made them hug, sometimes fight; they would howl, grin, chatter, reel and tumble and then fall asleep in the mud. I had in fact noticed that the Yahoos were the only animals in the country who had any diseases, although they were fewer than the diseases our horses get and were not caused by any ill treatment but by the unpleasant brutes' greed. Neither language has anything more than a general name for these illnesses, which is borrowed from the name of the beast, and called "Hnea-Yahoo", or Yahoo's Evil. The cure is a mixture of their own dung and urine, forced down the Yahoo's throat. I have seen this work successfully, and I recommend it to my countrymen, for the public good, as a fine cure for diseases produced by over-consumption.

As for learning, government, arts, factories and so on, my master confessed that he could not find any resemblance between the Yahoos of his country and ours, for he only meant to comment on the things that were the same in us. He had in fact heard some curious Houyhnhnms observe that in most herds there was a sort of ruling Yahoo (as in our country there is usually a leading or chief stag in a park) who was always more bodily deformed, and wicked in character, than the rest, and this leader usually had a favorite as similar to himself as he could get, whose job was to lick his master's feet and backside and drive the female Yahoos to his kennel – now and then he would be rewarded for this with a piece of ass' flesh. This favorite is hated by the rest of the herd, and so to protect himself he always stays very close to the leader. He usually keeps his position until a worse one can be found. As soon as he is sacked his successor, leading all the Yahoos in the area, young and old, male and female, comes to him and they all crap on him from head to foot. But my master said I was the best one to decide how closely this compared to our courts, favorites and ministers of state.

I dared not reply to this wicked implication, which placed human intelligence below that of a common hound, who has the judgement to be able to recognise and follow the cry of the best dog in the pack, and never makes a mistake.

My master told me that there were some qualities which were unique to Yahoos, which he had not observed, or only a very little, in my accounts of mankind. He said that these animals, like other brutes, shared their females; but they differed in this, in that the female would have sex with the males while she was pregnant, and that the males would fight with the females as fiercely as with each other. Both these things showed a level of appalling brutality which no other thinking creature could match.

273

Another thing which amazed him about the Yahoos was that they seemed to love muck and dirt, whereas all other animals seemed to have a natural love of cleanliness. As for the first two allegations I was glad not to reply to them, as there was nothing I could say on that subject in defence of my own kind, although I could have defended myself as an individual. But I could have easily proved that humans were not unique under the last charge, if there had been any pigs in that country (unfortunately for me there were not); although they might be nicer than a Yahoo they cannot, I humbly submit, in all justice, be said to be cleaner, and his honor would have had to admit this if he had seen their filthy way of feeding and their custom of rolling, and sleeping, in the mud.

My master also mentioned another quality which his servants had found in several Yahoos which he couldn't understand in the least. He said that sometimes a Yahoo would retire into a corner, lie down, howl, groan and push away everyone who came close to him, even if he was young and fat, didn't need food or water and the servant couldn't see anything that could be bothering him. The only cure they found for it was to make him work hard, and after that he would inevitably return to his normal self. I didn't say anything about this due to bias towards my own kind, but I could see here the true origin of ennui, or melancholy, which only affects the lazy, luxurious and rich, and if they were given the same medicine I would back it to cure them.

Another thing his honor had noticed was that a female Yahoo would often stand behind a bank or bush to look at the young males passing by, and then appear then hide again, using many mad gestures and faces; it was observed that at this time she smelt atrocious. When any of the males advanced she would slowly retire, often looking back, and she would pretend to be afraid and run off to some secluded place where she knew the male would follow.

At other times if a female stranger arrived three or four of her own sex would gather round her and stare, chatter and grin and smell her all over, and then turn away with gestures which seemed to show contempt and aloofness.

Perhaps my master might have refined these speculations a little, which he had made from what he had seen himself or been told by others. However, I could not think with some amazement, and much sadness, that the essentials of lewdness, flirtation, criticism and gossip should be a part of womankind's natural makeup.

I expected that at any moment my master was going to say that Yahoos of both sexes had these flaws, which were so normal in us. But it seems nature hasn't been such a good teacher, and we have created these pleasures ourselves from our skill and intelligence.

Chapter VIII

[The author gives several details about Yahoos. The great goodness of Houyhnhnms. The education and exercise of their youth. Their general assembly.]

As I should have been able to understand human nature much better than my master, it was easy to see the similarities between his description of the Yahoos and my own countrymen, and I believed that I could make further discoveries of this sort if I was allowed to see for myself. So I often begged his honor to let me walk amongst the herds of Yahoos in his neighborhood, which he always very kindly agreed to, being utterly convinced that my hatred for these brutes would not allow me to be corrupted by them. He ordered one of his servants, a strong sorrel nag, very honest and good-natured, to be my guard; without his protection I would never have dared risk such a thing. I have already told the reader how much I was bothered by these horrible creatures when I arrived, and afterwards I very nearly fell into their clutches, two or three times, when I happened to wander any sort of distance without my sword. I have reason to believe that they thought I was one of them, and I helped this belief by rolling up my sleeves and allowing them to see my naked arms and chest, when my protector was with me. At these times they would come as close as they dared, and imitate my actions as monkeys will, but always with great signs of hatred. It was like when a tame jackdaw in cap and stockings is persecuted by the wild ones, if he happens to get amongst them.

They are amazingly agile from childhood. However, I did once manage to catch a young three year old male and tried, by showing it tenderness, to keep it quiet, but the little devil screamed, scratched and bit with such violence that I was forced to let it go. I was just in time, for a whole troop of adults came flocking at the noise, but they found that the cub was safe (for it had run away) and as my sorrel nag was with me they did not dare come too close. I noticed the young animal's flesh smelt quite revolting, the stink being like a combination of weasel and fox, though much worse. I forgot another thing (which the reader would probably forgive me for not mentioning at all), that while I held the disgusting vermin in my hands it squirted its filthy excretions, in the form of a yellow liquid, all over my clothes; luckily there was a stream close by, where I washed myself as clean as I could, although I did not dare see my master until the clothes had had a good airing.

From what I could discover, the Yahoos seem to be the most unteachable of all animals, they never learn more than how to pull or carry loads. But I think this defect comes mainly from their twisted, fidgety character, because they are cunning, malicious, treacherous and hold grudges. They are strong and fit, but cowardly, and because of that they are rude, unpleasant and cruel. It has been noted that the red haired ones of both sexes are more lustful and mischievous than the rest, whom they also exceed in strength and energy.

The Houyhnhnms keep the Yahoos they are using at present in huts close to the house, but the rest are sent away to specific fields, where they dig up roots, eat different types of herbs, and search for carrion, sometimes catching weasels and "luhimuhs" (a kind of wild rat) which they gobble up. Nature has taught them how to dig deep holes with their nails into the side of slopes, where they sleep alone; only the holes of the females are larger, big enough for two or three cubs.

They swim like frogs from childhood, and can stay under water for a long time, where they often catch fish, which the females take home to their young. And I hope the reader will now forgive me for telling him about an odd adventure.

I was out one day with my bodyguard the sorrel nag. And as it was a very hot day, I begged him to let me bathe in the nearby river. He agreed, and I immediately stripped completely and went quietly into the stream. It happened that a young female Yahoo, hiding behind a bank, saw the whole thing, and, as the nag and I presumed afterwards, became inflamed with desire and came running at top speed and leaped into the water within five yards of the place where I was bathing. I was never so scared in all my life. The nag was grazing some way away, not knowing there was anything wrong. She embraced me in a very "full-on" manner. I shouted as loudly as I could, and the nag came galloping up, at which she let go, very reluctantly, and jumped onto the opposite bank, where she stood watching and wailing all the time I dressed.

This was a matter of amusement for my master and his family, as well as a great embarrassment for myself. I could now no longer deny that I was a real Yahoo in every physical way, since the females took a natural fancy to me as one of their own species. And the hair of this brute wasn't red (which meant I could have used that as an excuse, saying she had unnatural appetites) but as dark as blackthorn, and her face wasn't quite as hideous as the rest of her species; I guess she could not have been much more than eleven years old.

Having lived in this country for three years I suppose the reader expects me, like other travellers, to give some account of the manners and customs of its natives, which was in fact what I spent most of my time learning.

As these noble Houyhnhnms have been made by nature to have a general inclination towards all things good, and have no idea of how evil could be part of a thinking creature, so their great rule is to cultivate reason and be ruled by it in all things. They do not see reason as something questionable, as we do, where men can argue the case on either side of the question, but as something that one sees straight away, as one always will if it is not mixed with, hidden behind, or discoloured by, passion or bias. I remember what trouble I had to explain to my master the meaning of the word opinion, or how a point could be argued. Reason has taught us to agree or deny only when we are certain, and if something is beyond our understanding we cannot do either. So controversies, wrangling, disputes and people arguing for false or dubious ideas are unknown amongst the Houyhnhnms. In the same way, when I explained to him our different scientific systems, he would laugh at the idea that a creature which pretended to be intelligent would be proud of itself for knowing other people's guesses – and in matters where even if their guesses were correct the information would be of no use. So he entirely agreed with the ideas of Socrates, as reported by Plato, and I say that as a compliment to that greatest philosopher. I have often though what damage this concept would do to the libraries of Europe, and how many paths to fame in the academic world would be blocked.

Friendship and kindness are the two most prized virtues amongst the Houyhnhnms, and not just to their friends and family but to the whole race. A stranger from the most far-flung region is treated the same as the nearest neighbor, and feels at home wherever he goes. They value decency and manners highest of all, but they know nothing about formal ceremonies. They have no forced affection for their colts and foals, but the care they take over their education is entirely logical. I have seen my master show the same affection for his neighbor's children as he had for his own. They say that nature teaches them to love the whole species, and only intelligence separates people, where one is more virtuous than another.

When the Houyhnhnm mothers have produced one child of each sex they no longer have sex with their mates, unless they lose one of their offspring through some accident, which very rarely happens. If it does happen they get back together, or if the same thing happens to someone whose wife cannot have more children some other couple will give them one of their colts and get back together until the mother is pregnant. This practice is necessary to stop the country becoming overpopulated. But the lower type of Houyhnhnms, raised as servants, are not so strictly limited in this matter: they are allowed to have three offspring of each sex, to serve as domestics for the noble families.

When they marry they are very careful to join colors which will not have any bad affect on the purity of the breed. Strength is the main thing looked for in a male, and beauty in the female. This is not due to love, but to stop the race from degenerating, because if a female happens to be very strong her mate is chosen for his looks.

Courtship, love, gifts, contracts and dowries have no place in their thoughts, and there are no terms to express them in their language. The young couple meet, and mate, as it is what their parents and friends have decided. They see it happen all the time and they regard it as one of the normal actions of an intelligent being. But adultery, or any other unchaste behavior, is unheard of. The married couple spend their lives together with the same friendship and respectful kindness which they have for all the others of their species they meet, without jealousy, bias, quarrelling or unhappiness.

In educating the youth of both sexes their method is admirable and should definitely be copied by us. They are not allowed to taste a single oat, except on certain days, until they are eighteen, and they are only very rarely allowed milk. In the summer they graze for two hours in the morning and two in the evening, the same as their parents. The servants only get half that time, and a large part of their grass is brought home and they eat it at the most convenient times, when they have the least work.

Temperance, hard work, exercise and cleanliness are all taught equally to the young of both sexes. My master thought it was monstrous of us to have a different sort of education for females (excepting some lessons about household management). As he rightly observed, this meant that half of our natives were no good for anything except breeding, and to have such useless animals looking after our children was, he thought, even worse.

But the Houyhnhnms train their young to build strength, speed and stamina by making them take part in races up and down steep hills and over hard stony ground, and when they are sweaty they are ordered to leap into a pond or river and completely submerge themselves. Four times a year the youth of a particular area will meet to demonstrate their skill in running and jumping and other feats of strength and agility, and the winner is rewarded with a song in praise of them. At these celebrations the servants drive a herd of Yahoos into the field carrying hay, oats and milk as a meal for the Houyhnhnms, and then the brutes are immediately driven back again so they don't offend the meeting. Every fourth year, at the spring equinox, there is a representative council of the whole nation, which meets on a plain about twenty miles from our house, and goes on for five or six days. They look into how things are progressing in various districts, whether they have plenty, or are short, of oats, cows or Yahoos; wherever anything is lacking (which is not very often) it is immediately supplied through unanimous agreement and contributions from everyone. This is also where the distribution of children is organised: for example, if a Houyhnhnm has two males he exchanges one of them with another who has two females, and when a child has been lost through some accident it is decided which family in the district will breed another to make up for the loss.

Chapter IX

[A grand debate at the general assembly of the Houyhnhnms, and the outcome. The Houyhnhnms learning, their buildings and the way they bury the dead. Flaws in their language.]

One of these grand assemblies was held in my time, about three months before I left, and my master went as the representative of our district. In this council they resumed their old debate, which was in fact the only debate they ever had in that country; when my master returned he gave me a very detailed account of it.

The question debated was whether the Yahoos should be exterminated from the face of the earth. One of the members for a yes vote offered several very powerful arguments, saying that the Yahoos were the filthiest, smelliest, most deformed animals that nature had ever produced, and also the most stubborn and untameable, mischievous and malicious. If they were not continually watched they would secretly suck the teats of the Houyhnhnms' cows, kill and eat their cats, trample their crops and commit a thousand other outrages. He remarked on the well accepted tradition that Yahoos had not always been part of the country, but that many ages ago two of the brutes had appeared on a mountain (whether produced by the heat of the sun on mud and slime, or from the ooze and scum of the sea, was not known); they had bred and their offspring quickly became so numerous that they overran and infested the whole country. The Houyhnhnms, to get rid of this evil, had held a great hunt, and eventually captured the whole herd. They killed the elders and every Houyhnhnm kept two young ones in a kennel and made them as tame as such a naturally savage animal can be, using them as pack animals and to pull carriages. He said that there seemed to be much truth in this tradition, and these creatures could not be "Yinhniamshy", or aborigines, because the Houyhnhnms and other animals hated them so much; although they deserved this, if they had been here from the start they couldn't have caused such great hatred, as they would already have been exterminated. Because they took a fancy to having Yahoos serving them the inhabitants had foolishly failed carefully to breed asses, which are a good looking animal, easy to keep, more tame and well behaved, with no offensive smell, strong enough for work even if they are not as agile as Yahoos, and if their braying wasn't pleasant to listen to it was at least much nicer than the revolting howling of the Yahoos.

Several others spoke in the same vein, then my master proposed a solution to the assembly which was in fact inspired by me. He said that he believed the tradition spoken of by the former speaker, and confirmed that the first two Yahoos had been driven here over the sea, and coming to land, abandoned by their companions, they had retreated to the mountains and had gradually degenerated, over time becoming much more savage than their own species in the country of origin of the original two. The reason for this claim was that he now owned an amazing Yahoo (meaning me) which most of them had heard of and many of them had seen. He told them how he had found me; that my body had an artificial covering of the skins and hair of other animals; that I had my own language, and had learned their language well; that I had told him the accidents that had brought me there; and that when he saw me without my covering I was exactly like a yahoo in every respect, except I was whiter, less hairy and had shorter claws.

He added that I had tried to persuade him that in my country and others the Yahoos were the ruling, intelligent animal and kept the Houyhnhnms as servants. He saw all the qualities of a Yahoo in me, except that I was a little civilised with a drop of intelligence; however, my intelligence was as far below that of a Houyhnhnm as the Yahoos of their country were inferior to me. He said that among other things I mentioned that we had a custom of castrating Houyhnhnms when they were young in order to tame them, and that the operation was easy and safe. It was no shame to learn wisdom from animals, as we learn about hard work from the ant and building from the swallow (this is how I translate "lyhannh", although it is actually a much larger bird). He proposed that this invention should be tried on the younger Yahoos, because besides making them tamer and more useful it would in one generation put an end to the whole species. In the meantime the Houyhnhnms should be encouraged to breed asses, which are not only more useful animals but are ready for work at five years old, which the others are not until they are twelve.

That was all my master saw fit to tell me at the time of what passed in the grand council. But it suited him to hide one detail which related to me particularly; I soon felt the unhappy effect of it, as the reader shall learn in the appropriate place, and I date all the following unhappiness of my life from that moment.

The Houyhnhnms do not write, and so all their knowledge is handed down. But as there are few big historical moments amongst a people who are so united, naturally good, ruled by the mind and completely isolated from other nations their history can easily be remembered without straining their memories. I have already noted that they do not suffer from any diseases, and so do not need doctors. However, they have excellent medicines made from herbs to cure accidental bruises or cuts on the legs or soft part of the hoof from sharp stones, as well as other knocks and grazes on other parts of the body.

They reckon the passing of a year by observing the sun and the moon, but they do not split the year into weeks. They know all about the movements of these two planets, and know what causes eclipses; this is all they know about astronomy.

In poetry it must be admitted that they beat all other mortal creatures; the perfection of their similes and the detail as well as accuracy of their descriptions are inimitable. Their verses are full of both these things, and usually have a theme of high friendship and kindness or are in praise of those who won in races and other sporting contests. Their buildings, although they are very crude and simple, are not uncomfortable and are well suited to protect them against all harm from heat and cold. They have a kind of tree which at forty years old becomes unstable and falls in the first storm. It grows very straight, and they sharpen the ends like stakes with a sharp stone (the Houyhnhnms do not know about iron) and stick them upright in the ground, about ten inches apart, and weave oat straw, or sometimes stripwood, between them. The roof is made in the same way and so are the doors.

The Houyhnhnms use the hollow between the leg and hoof of their forelegs as we use our hands, and they are far more skilled at this than I could have imagined at first. I have seen a white mare of our family thread a needle (which I lent her to see what she could do) with that joint. They milk their cows, harvest their oats and do all the work which needs hands in the same way. They have a kind of hard flint which they grind against other stones and form them into tools which they use instead of chisels, axes and hammers. With tools made from these flints they also cut their hay and harvest their oats, which grow naturally there in different fields. The Yahoos pull the sheaves home in carts and the servants tread them in special covered huts to separate the grain, which they keep in stores. They make rough clay and wooden vessels, baking the clay ones in the sun.

If they can avoid accidents they only die of old age, and they are buried in the most out of the way places possible. Their friends and relatives do not express either joy or grief at their departure, and the dying person does not show the least regret that he is going, any more than he would if he were coming home from a neighbourly visit. I remember my master once made an appointment for a friend and his family to come to his on some important business; on the selected day the wife and her two children came very late; she made two excuses; the first was for her husband, who, she said, happened that morning to "shnuwnh". The word is very clear in meaning in their language, but it is not easy to put into English; it literally means, "to retire to his first mother." Her second excuse was for herself, for not coming sooner, and it was that as her husband had died very late in the morning she had to spend a fair time discussing with the servants the best place for him to be buried. I noticed that she was just as cheerful as all the others in our house. She died about three months later.

They usually live to about seventy or seventy-five, very rarely to eighty. Some weeks before they die they feel gradually worn out, but they do not feel pain. During this time their friends pay them many visits, because they cannot travel as easily and comfortably as usual. However, about ten days before their death (which they usually calculate accurately) they return the visits that have been made by their nearest neighbors, being pulled on a comfortable sledge by Yahoos. They use this vehicle not only at this time but when they are old, when they go on long journeys or when they are lame from an accident. So when the Houyhnhms make these return visits they say solemn farewells to their friends as if they were going to some distant part of the country where they planned to spend the rest of their lives.

I don't know if it's worth noting that the Houyhnhnms have no word in their language to describe anything evil, except what they borrow from the deformities and poor qualities of the Yahoos. So they speak of the stupidity of a servant, a child's error, a stone that cuts their feet, continued bad or unseasonable weather and so on, by adding the word Yahoo to the thing they are speaking of. For example, "hhnm Yahoo"; "whnaholm Yahoo"; "ynlhmndwihlma Yahoo"; and a poorly built house is "ynholmhnmrohlnw Yahoo."

I would like nothing better than to talk more about the manners and virtues of this wonderful people, but I mean in a little while to publish a separate book devoted to the subject, and I refer the reader to that; in the meantime I'll tell my own sad tale.

Chapter X

[The author's home and happy life amongst the Houyhnhnms. How he becomes much more virtuous by speaking with them. Their conversations. The author is told by his master that he must leave the country. He faints with grief but agrees. He designs and builds a canoe with the help of a fellow servant, and takes his chances on the sea.]

I had my little home set up to my heart's content. My master had ordered that a room be made for me, in their fashion, about six yards from the house. I plastered the floor and sides with clay, which I covered with rush mats I made myself. I had beaten hemp, which grows wild there, and made it into a sort of sacking, and I filled it with the feathers of several birds I had caught with traps made from Yahoo's hair, which were excellent eating. I had made two chairs with my knife, with the sorrel nag helping me in the rough, harder part.

When my clothes had completely worn out I made myself others with rabbit skins and those of a certain lovely animal, about the same size, called "nnuhnoh", which has a skin covered in very fine fur. I also made very serviceable stockings out of these. I made the soles of my shoes from wood cut from a tree, fitted to a leather upper. When the leather wore out I replaced it with the skin of Yahoos dried in the sun. I often got honey out of hollow trees which I mixed with water or ate with my bread. No man is as well qualified as I to confirm the truth of the two sayings, "Nature is easily satisfied" and "Necessity is the mother of invention." I had perfect physical health and perfect peace of mind. I did not suffer the treachery or fickleness of friends, or the harm of a secret or open enemy. I did not have to bribe, flatter or pimp to get the favor of any great man or his underlings. I didn't need protection from fraud or oppression. There was no doctor to destroy my body, nor lawyer to destroy my fortune. There was no informer to watch my words and actions to make false accusations against me for money. There were no mockers, censors, backbiters, pickpockets, highwaymen, housebreakers, attorneys, bawds, buffoons, gamblers, politicians, wits, depressives, tedious talkers, controversialists, rapists, murderers, robbers, experts; no leaders, or followers, of party and faction; no encouragers to vice, by seduction or example; no dungeon, axes, scaffolds, whipping-posts, or pillories; no cheating shopkeepers or tradesmen; no pride, vanity, or affectation; no fops, bullies, drunkards, strolling whores, or venereal disease; no ranting, lewd, expensive wives; no stupid, proud pedants; no nagging, overbearing, quarrelsome, noisy, roaring, empty, conceited, swearing companions; no scoundrels raised from the dirt because of their vices, or nobility thrown into it on account of their virtues; no lords, fiddlers, judges, or dancing-masters.

I had the honor of being welcomed by several Houyhnhnms who came to visit or to dine with my master. His honor would kindly allow me to wait in the room and listen to their talk. Both he and his company would often lower themselves so far as to ask me questions and listen to my answers. I also sometimes had the honor of going with my master when he visited others. I never had the nerve to speak, except to answer a question, and I did that with secret regret, because it cut into the time I had to improve myself. But I was hugely delighted with the position of being a humble listener in such conversations, where nothing was spoken of except things that were useful, expressed in the fewest and best words. As I have already said, the best manners were shown without any sort of formality; no person spoke without pleasing both himself and his companions, there were no interruptions, no boredom, anger or disagreement. They have an idea that when people meet a short silence is a great help for improving conversations. I found that this was true, for in those little pauses they would form new ideas, which certainly freshened up the conversations.

Their usual topics of conversation are friendship and kindness, order and economy; sometimes they talked of what can be seen of nature's work, or ancient history; of the restrictions and limits of virtue; of the eternal rules of reason, or some decision which would be discussed at the next great assembly, and often of the various joys of poetry. Without being vain I can say that my presence often gave them plenty to talk about, because it gave my master the chance of telling his friends my story and the history of my country. They all liked to give their opinions on this, in a way which wasn't very flattering to mankind, so I won't repeat what they said. However, I must say that my master, to my great admiration, appeared to understand the nature of Yahoos better than I did. I listed all our vices and stupidities and mentioned many that I hadn't told him about; he had deduced them by imagining what a Yahoo of his country, with a tiny bit of intelligence, might get up to, and he concluded, all too accurately, what a vile and miserable creature such a one would be.

I freely admit that the small quantity of knowledge I have which is of any value was got through the lectures I had from my master, and from hearing him and his friends talking. I counted it a greater honor to listen to them than I would to be allowed to speak to the greatest and wisest gathering in Europe. I admired the strength, beauty and speed of the natives, and such a meeting of virtues in such kind people created the most profound respect in me. At first I did not feel the natural awe that they inspired in the Yahoos and all other animals. But it came to me by stages, much more quickly than I would have thought, and it was mingled with respectful love and gratitude that they condescended to treat me differently to the rest of my species.

When I thought of my family, friends and countrymen, or the human race in general I saw them for what they really were, Yahoos in shape and character, perhaps a little more civilised and being able to speak, but using their intelligence for no other purpose than increasing and strengthening those vices of which their brothers in this country had only the natural form. When I happened to see my own reflection in a lake or spring I turned my face away in disgust and hatred of myself, and I could bear the sight of a common Yahoo better than that of my own body. By talking with the Houyhnhnms and looking at them with pleasure I began to imitate their walk and gestures, which have now become a habit. My friends often say rudely that I "trot like a horse," but I take this as a great compliment. And I will not deny that when I speak I tend to imitate the voice and mannerisms of the Houyhnhnms, and it doesn't bother me in the slightest that I am mocked for it.

In the middle of all this happiness, when I thought I had settled down for life, my master sent for me one morning a little earlier than usual. I saw from his face that he was a little confused and was at a loss as to how to begin what he had to say. After a short silence he told me that he didn't know how I was going to react to what he had to tell me: in the last general assembly, when the business of the Yahoos was discussed, the other representatives had objected to his keeping a Yahoo (meaning me) in his family, treating me more like a Houyhnhnm than a brute animal. They knew that he often spoke with me, as if there was some pleasure to be gained, or something to be learned, from it. They thought this practice was an insult to nature and reason, and was without precedent amongst them. So the assembly told him that he should either put me to work like the rest of the Yahoos or order me to swim back to the place I had come from. The first of these ideas was completely rejected by the Houyhnhnms who had seen me at his house or in theirs; they said that because I had some glimmerings of intelligence added to the natural depravity of a Yahoo I might lead them off to the wooded and mountainous parts of the country and bring them in gangs at night to destroy the Houyhnhnms' cattle, as we were naturally greedy and lazy.

My master added that the Houyhnhnms in the neighborhood were continually urging him to carry out the wishes of the assembly, and he couldn't put it off much longer. He didn't think that it would be possible for me to swim to another country, and so he wanted me to build some kind of vehicle, like the ones I had described to him, to carry me on the sea. He would tell his servants to help me with this, and his neighbors would help as well. He finished by saying that he would have been happy to keep me in his service as long as I lived, as he knew I had cured myself of some of my bad habits and thoughts by trying, as far as my inferior nature permitted, to copy the Houyhnhnms.

I should point out to the reader that a decree from the general assembly of the country is called a "hnhloayn", which means a wish, as best as I can translate it, as they have no concept of forcing a rational being to obey, thinking he can only be advised or encouraged, as no person can disobey reason without giving up his claim to have it himself.

I was struck down with terrible grief and despair at what my master said, and as I couldn't cope with the agony of it I fell in a faint at his feet. When I came round he told me that he thought I had died, for these people do not suffer from such natural stupidity. I answered in a faint voice that death would have been far preferable, and although I could not criticize the assembly's wish or the urgency his friends were showing, in my weak and corrupt judgment I thought it would not be unreasonable to be less harsh. I could not swim over three miles, and the nearest land might be over a hundred times that away. I also said that this country completely lacked the many materials I would need to make a small vessel to carry me off; I would try it, out of obedience and gratitude to his honor, but I thought that it was impossible and so looked on myself as being dead already. This certainty of an unnatural death was the least of my worries, for supposing I did escape with my life through some strange adventure how could I resign myself to spending the rest of my days with Yahoos and falling back into my bad old ways, lacking examples to lead me and keep me virtuous? I fully accepted what sound reasoning all the decisions of the wise Houyhnhnms were based on, and that they wouldn't be changed by the arguments of a miserable Yahoo like me. So, after giving him my humble thanks for offering the help of his servants to build a vessel, and asking him for a reasonable amount of time for such a difficult task, I told him that I would try and save my wretched life. I also said that if I ever got back to England I hoped that I could be some use to my species by singing the praises of the wonderful Houyhnhnms and preaching their virtues for mankind to copy.

My master gave me a brief and very gracious reply and permitted me two months to finish my boat; he ordered the sorrel nag, my servant (this is what I will cheekily call him, now I am so far away) to follow my orders. I told my master that this sorrel nag's help would be enough, and I knew he was fond of me.

My first task was to go to the part of the coast where my rebellious crew had ordered that I be put on the shore. I got on some high ground and looked all round the sea; I thought I saw a small island to the northeast. I took out my pocket telescope and could then clearly see that it was, I estimated, about fifteen miles away. To the sorrel nag it seemed to just be a blue cloud; as he had no idea of the existence of any land besides his own he could not be expected to be as good at making out distant objects in the sea as we who have so much experience in that element.

After I had discovered that island I thought no further but decided that if I could I would make that the first stage of my exile, and leave the rest to fate.

I returned home, and on the advice of the sorrel nag we went into a small wood some way away where we cut down several strips of oak, about as thick as a walking stick, and some bigger pieces, me with my knife and he with a sharp flint fixed, very cunningly after their fashion, to a wooden handle. But I will not bore the reader with a description of all my labours. Suffice it to say that in six weeks, with the help of the sorrel nag, who did the parts which needed the most work, I had finished a sort of Indian canoe, though it was much larger; I covered it with the skins of Yahoos, tightly stitched with hemp threads I had made myself. My sail was also made of the skins of that animal, but I used the youngest I could get, as the skins of the older ones were too tough and thick. I made myself four paddles in the same way. I laid in a stock of boiled meat (rabbits and birds) and took two vessels with me, one full of milk and the other of water.

I tested my canoe in a large pond near my master's house, and fixed its faults; I filled in all the cracks with Yahoo grease until it was watertight and able to carry me and my baggage. When it was as good as I could possibly get it I had it pulled very carefully down to the shore by Yahoos under the orders of the sorrel nag and another servant. When everything was ready and the day came for me to leave I said goodbye to my master and his lady and the whole family, my eyes full of tears and my heart weighed down with grief. But his honor, out of curiosity and maybe (if it isn't vain to say so) partly out of affection was determined to see me in my canoe, and he asked several of his neighboring friends to join him. I was forced to wait over an hour for the tide, and then I saw that the wind was luckily blowing towards the island I intended to make for. So I said goodbye to my master again, but as I was going to lie down to kiss his hoof he did me the honor of gently raising it to my mouth. I know how much I have been criticized for mentioning this last detail. My critics think it is most unlikely that such a noble person would give me, such an inferior creature, such a mark of distinction, and I am well aware of how some travellers love to boast about the favors they have been given. But if these critics knew more about the noble and courteous nature of the Houyhnhnms they would soon see they are wrong.

I paid my respects to the rest of the Houyhnhnms who were with his honor, then I got into my canoe and pushed off from the shore.

Chapter XI

[The dangerous voyage undertaken by the author. He arrives at New Holland, hoping to settle there. He is wounded with an arrow by one of the natives. He is captured and forced onto a Portuguese ship. The captain is very polite. The author arrives in England.]

I began this dangerous voyage on February 15, 1714-15, at nine o'clock in the morning. The wind was in my favor; however at first I only used my paddles, but thinking that I would soon be tired, and that the wind might change, I put up my little sail. And so, with the help of the tide, I went on at a speed of, as far as I could guess, five miles an hour. My master and his friends stayed on the shore until I was almost out of sight; and I often heard the sorrel nag (who always loved me) crying out, "Hnuy illa nyha, majah yahoo!" ("Take care of yourself, gentle Yahoo!").

My plan was, if I could, to find some small island, uninhabited, but that could, through my work, give me what I needed to live. This would have made me much happier than to be the first Minister at the greatest court in Europe. That was how horrible I felt it would be to go back to live in society under the government of Yahoos. At least if I was alone as I wished to be I could enjoy my own thoughts, and think with pleasure of the goodness of those inimitable Houyhnhnms, without having the chance to sink back into the vice and corruption of my own species.

The reader may remember what I said, when my crew plotted against me, and imprisoned me in my cabin. I stayed there several weeks without knowing what course we were on, and when I was put ashore in the longboat the sailors told me, with oaths, whether they were true or false, that they did not know what part of the world we were in. However I believe that we were then about 10° southward of the Cape of Good Hope, or about 45° southern latitude; I gathered this from some general conversation I overheard them having, as I suppose they were south-east of their intended course for Madagascar. Although this was only a guess, I decided to steer eastwards, hoping to reach the south-west coast of Australia, and perhaps I would find an island like the one I wished for to the west of it. The wind was coming directly from the west, and by six in the evening I calculated that I'd gone east at least fifty miles. I then saw a very small island about a mile and a half away, which I soon reached. It was nothing more than a rock, with one creek carved out by the force of the storms. I landed my canoe here, and climbing up the rock I could plainly see land to the east, stretching from south to north. I slept all night in my canoe, and continuing my voyage early the next morning I arrived seven hours later on the southeast point of Australia. This confirmed the opinion I have held for a long time, that the maps and charts put this country at least three degrees more to the east than it really is. I told my worthy friend, Mr.Herman Moll the mapmaker, this many years ago and told him my reasons for it, although he has chosen to take the word of other authors.

I saw no natives in the place where I landed, and as I was unarmed I was afraid of going too far inland. I found some shellfish on the shore and ate them raw, not daring to light a fire in case it should seen by the natives. I stayed there three days feeding on oysters and limpets so as not to waste my own stores; fortunately I found a stream of very clean water, which was a great relief. On the fourth day I went a little too far in the morning and saw twenty or thirty natives on a hill not more than five hundred yards away. They were stark naked, men, women, and children, gathered round a fire as I could see from the smoke. One of them spotted me and warned the others; five of them came towards me, leaving the women and children by the fire. I ran as fast as I could for the shore, got into my canoe, and shoved off. The savages, seeing me escape, ran after me and before I could get far enough out to sea they fired an arrow which went deep into the inside of my left knee; I will have a scar until the day I die. I guessed that the arrow might be poisoned, and once I had rowed out of the reach of their darts (it was a calm day) I tried to suck the wound and bandaged it as well as I could.

I didn't know what to do, as I did not dare go back to the same landing place, so I headed north and I was forced to paddle, for although the wind was very gentle it was in my face, coming from the northwest. As I looked out for a safe landing place, I saw a sail to the north-north-east. It got closer by the minute, and I could not decide whether I should wait for them or not. Eventually my hatred of the Yahoo race won out and I turned around and sailed and paddled together to the south and reached the same creek I had set out from in the morning. I would rather have taken my chance with the savages than live with European Yahoos. I pulled my canoe as close in to the shore as I could and hid myself behind a stone by the little stream which, as I have already said, had very fine water.

The ship came within a mile of this creek, and sent her longboat with containers to pick up fresh water (for the place, it seems, was very well-known); I did not see it coming until the boat was almost on shore and it was too late to find another hiding place. When they landed the sailors saw my canoe and, searching through it, it was easy for them to guess that the owner could not be far away. Four of them, well armed, searched every crack and hiding place, until in the end they found me flat on my face behind the stone. They looked on in amazement for a while at my peculiar clothes; my coat made of skins, my wooden soled shoes, and my furry stockings. They concluded from my clothes that I was not a native of place, as they all go naked. One of the sailors, in Portuguese, told me to get up and asked who I was. I understood the language very well and getting to my feet I said that I was a poor Yahoo exiled by the Houhynhnms, and asked them to please let me go. They were surprised to hear me answer them in their own tongue, and they saw from my skin that I must be a European. However they had no idea what I meant by Yahoos or Houyhnhnms, and at the same time they started laughing at my strange accent, which sounded like the neighing of a horse. All the time I was shaking, caught between fear and hatred. I asked them again to let me leave, and started quietly going to my canoe, but they grabbed hold of me, asking what country I was from, where I had come from and many other questions. I told them that I was born in England, from which I had come about five years ago, and at that time their country and mine were at peace. I hoped therefore that they would not treat me as an enemy, since I meant them no harm but was a poor Yahoo looking for some lonely place where he could spend the rest of his unlucky life.

When they began to talk, I thought I'd never heard or seen anything more unnatural; it looked as monstrous as if, in England, a dog or cow was speaking, or a Yahoo in Houyhnhnmland. The good Portuguese were just as amazed by my strange clothes and the odd way I spoke, however they could understand me very well. They spoke to me with great kindness and said that they were sure the captain would carry me back to Lisbon for free, and from there I could go back to my own country. Two of the sailors would go back to the ship, tell the captain what they had seen and receive his orders. In the meantime, unless I would give my solemn oath not to run away, they would tie me up. I thought it was best to go along with their proposals. They were very eager to know my story, but I did not tell them much, and they assumed that my misfortunes had made me stupid. In two hours the boat, which had taken the water back to the ship, returned with the captain's orders that I should be taken on board. I dropped to my knees to try to stop them taking me but it was useless. Having tied me with ropes the men threw me into the boat, from where I was taken onto the ship, and then into the captain's cabin.

His name was Pedro de Mendez; he was a very polite and generous person. He asked me to tell my story, and wanted to know what I would have to eat or drink. He said that I would be treated as well as himself, and said so many nice things that I was amazed to find a Yahoo who could be so polite. However I remained silent and sullen; just the smell of him and his men made me want to faint. Eventually I asked to be given some food from my canoe, but he ordered me a chicken and some excellent wine and then directed that I should be given a bed in a very clean cabin. I would not undress, lying on top of the bedclothes, and in half an hour I sneaked out when I thought the crew was eating and, getting to the side of the ship, I was going to leap into the sea, and swim for my life, rather than stay with Yahoos. But one of the sailors stopped me, and once the captain was informed I was chained in my cabin.

After dinner, Don Pedro came to me and asked what made me try such a desperate thing. He promised me that all he wanted to do was help me in any way he could, and he spoke so movingly that in the end I decided to treat him like an animal which had a little intelligence. I gave him a very short account of my voyage; of the plot against me by my own men; of the country where they had put me ashore and the five years I had lived there. He regarded all this as if it were a dream or hallucination, and I took great offence at this because I had quite forgotten about lying, the unique characteristic of Yahoos in all the countries where they rule, which makes them doubt the truthfulness of others of their own kind. I asked him if it was the custom in his country to say the thing which was not. I promised him that I had almost forgotten what he meant by lying, and if I had lived a thousand years in Houyhnhnmland I would never have heard a lie from the lowest servant. I told him I didn't care whether he believed me or not. However in return for his kindness I would pander to his corrupt nature to the extent of answering any objection he might care to make about my story, and then he would see the truth.

The captain, a wise man, after trying to catch me out in my story in many ways, at last began to believe in my honesty. But he added that since I was so attached to the truth I must give him my word of honor to stay with him on this voyage, without trying to risk my life again, or else he would keep me a prisoner until we arrived at Lisbon. I gave him the promise he asked for, but at the same time insisted that I would sooner go through the greatest hardship than go back to live with Yahoos.

Our voyage passed without any particular mishaps. In gratitude to the captain I sometimes sat with him at his request, and tried hard to hide my hatred of humanity, although it often showed; when it did he let it go without comment. But for most of the day I kept myself in my cabin, to avoid seeing any of the crew. The captain had often begged me to take off my savage clothes, and offered to lend me his own best suit of clothes. I would not accept this offer, disgusted at the idea of covering myself with anything that had been worn by a Yahoo. I only asked him to lend me to clean shirts, which, as they had been washed since he wore them, I believed would not pollute me so much. I changed these every second day, and washed them myself.

We arrived at Lisbon on November 5, 1715. When we landed the captain made me cover myself with his cloak, to prevent the rabble from mobbing me. I was taken to his own house, and at my sincere request he led me up to the highest room backwards. I told him to hide my story of the Houyhnhnms from everybody, because if even a tiny bit of it got out it would not only draw great crowds of people to see me, but would probably put me in danger of being imprisoned or burnt by the Inquisition. The captain persuaded me to accept a new suit of clothes, but I would not allow the tailor to measure me. However, Don Pedro was almost the same size as me, so they fitted me well enough. He kitted me out with other necessary items, all new, which I aired for 24 hours before I would wear them.

The captain was not married, and didn't have more than three servants, none of whom were allowed to wait at table. His whole attitude was so pleasant, added to the very high intelligence for a human which he had, that I really began to tolerate his company. He brought me forward enough that I risked looking out of the back window. By stages I was brought into another room, from which I glanced into the street, but I jumped back in fright. In a week he had persuaded me to come down to the door. I found my fear gradually faded, but my hatred and contempt seemed to increase. Eventually I was brave enough to walk the streets with him, but I kept my nose well blocked with rue or sometimes with tobacco.

In ten days Don Pedro, whom I had told a little about my household, suggested to me as a matter of honor and conscience that I should go back to my homeland and live at home with my wife and children. He told me that there was an English ship in the port about to sail, and he would give me everything I needed. It would be boring to repeat the argument we had. He said it was impossible to find a deserted island like the one I wanted, but I could give orders in my own house and be as isolated as I wished. Eventually I agreed, as it seemed to be the best I could hope for. I left Lisbon on the 24th day of November in an English merchant ship, but I never asked who the captain was. Don Pedro went with me to the ship and lent me twenty pounds. He said a fond goodbye, and hugged me when we parted, which I put up with as best I could. During this last voyage I did not associate with the captain or any of his men; I pretended I was ill and stayed in my cabin. On 5 December 1715 we dropped anchor in the Downs about nine in the morning, and at three in the afternoon I arrived safely at my house in Rotherhithe.

My wife and family welcomed me with great surprise and joy, because they had written me off for dead. However I must admit that the sight of them only provoked hatred, disgust and contempt, which was made worse by knowing how closely related to them I was. Although, since my unhappy exile from the land of the Houyhnhnms, I had forced myself to put up with the sight of Yahoos, and to talk with Don Pedro de Mendez, my memory and imagination was always full of the virtues and ideas of the wonderful Houyhnhnms. When I thought that by having sex with one of the Yahoos I had become a parent of more of them I was filled with shame, confusion and horror.

As soon as I came in the house my wife took me in her arms and kissed me. Having not been used to the touch of that disgusting animal for so many years I fell unconscious for almost an hour. At the time of writing I have been back for five years. During the first year I couldn't stand for my wife or children to be near me; the smell of them was intolerable, and I certainly could not let them eat in the same room as me. To this day they dare not touch my bread, or drink out of the same cup as me, and I will not hold any of their hands. The first money I paid out was to buy two young cart horses, which I keep in a good stable. Apart from them my groom is my favourite person, as I am cheered up by the smell he picks up in the stable. My horses understand me pretty well; I talk with them at least four hours every day. They have never known a bridle or a saddle. They live in great friendship with me and with each other.

Chapter XII

[The author's truthfulness. His intentions in publishing this book. His criticism of those travellers who don't tell the truth. The author denies having any hidden motive in writing. A criticism is answered. How colonies are populated. His native country is praised. The right of the Crown to the countries the author describes is justified. The difficulty of conquering them. The author says goodbye to the reader; explains how he will be living in future; gives the reader good advice, and finishes.]

So, gentle reader, I have given you the true story of my travels for sixteen years and more than seven months. I have taken more care to be truthful than I have to be exotic. I could, perhaps, like others, have amazed you with strange and unlikely stories, but I chose simply to tell you the facts in the simplest manner and style, because my main intention was to inform you, not to entertain. It is easy for those of us who journey to faraway countries, which are seldom visited by Englishmen or other Europeans, to give descriptions of incredible animals on land and sea. But a traveller's mission should be to make men wiser and better, and to improve their minds by showing them bad, as well as good, examples from foreign countries.

I sincerely wish that there was a law that every traveller, before he was allowed to publish an account of his travels, should have to take an oath before the Lord high Chancellor that everything he was going to print was, as far as he knew, completely true. Then the world would not be cheated, as it usually is, by some writers who push terrible lies on the innocent reader in order to make their books sell better. I have read several travel books with great delight in my youth; but having since visited most parts of the earth, and been able to see what lies their accounts were with my own eyes, I have very much taken against these sorts of books, and it angers me to see how mankind's trust is so blatantly abused. So, since my friends were kind enough to think that my poor efforts would be welcomed in my country, I made a rule, which could never be broken, that I would always tell the truth. Indeed I am never attempted to lie while I still have in my mind the lectures and example of my noble master and the other wonderful Houyhnhms whom I was so lucky to hear for so long.

IF FATE HAS MADE SINON MISERABLE, SHE WON'T MAKE HIM A LIAR AS WELL

I am well aware how little respect there is for writings which require neither genius nor education, nor indeed any other talent except a good memory or careful diary keeping. I also know that travel writers, like dictionary makers, are crushed into obscurity by the weight and size of whoever came last and so is on top. And it is very likely that the travellers who visit countries which I have described after me may find my errors (if there are any) and add many new discoveries of their own, and so push me out of fashion, stand in my place, and make the world forget I ever wrote anything. This would of course be more than I could bear, if I was looking for fame: but as all I cared about was the good of the public, I cannot say I'm that disappointed. For who can read of the virtues I have spoken of with reference to the glorious Houyhnhnms without being ashamed of his own vices when he thinks that he is one of the intelligent ruling animals of his country? I shall say nothing about those distant countries where Yahoos rule; the Brobdingnagians are among the best and their wise ideas about morality and government are ones it would do us good to follow. But I shan't speak further about it; I'll leave it to the discerning reader and his own interpretation.

I am very content that this work of mine cannot possibly be criticised; how can anyone object to a writer who only gives the plain facts of things which happened in distant countries where we have no interest, business or diplomatic? I have carefully avoided every fault which ordinary travel writers are often correctly charged. I am not involved with any political party, and write without anger, prejudice, or malice against any man, or group of men, at all. I write for the best reason, to inform and instruct mankind; I may, without vanity, say that I have some superiority over mankind, from the lessons I learned by talking so long with the wonderful Houyhnhnms. I am not writing for money or praise. I never write a word that looks as though it is passing comment on anyone, or can possibly give any offence, even to those who are quickest to take it. So I hope I can justifiably say that I am a perfectly blameless author against whom the tribes of answerers, considerers, observers, reflectors, detectors, and remarkers will never be able to write.

I must admit that it was whispered to me that as a subject of England it was my duty to have given an account to the secretary of state when I first got home, because all lands discovered by a subject belonged to the Crown. But I doubt whether our conquests in the countries I have spoken of would be as easy as those of Ferdinando Cortez over the naked Americans. The Lilliputians I think are not worth the cost of a fleet and an army to invade them and I would question whether it would be wise or safe to attack the Brobdingnagians, or how an English army would cope with the flying island over their heads. The Houyhnhnms do look as though there are not ready for war, a science they know nothing about, and they would be especially vulnerable to missiles. However if I was a minister of state I could never advise invading them. Their common sense, unity, fearlessness and their love of their country would more than compensate for their lack of military skill. Imagine twenty thousand of them charging into the middle of a European army, scattering the ranks, overturning the carriages and grinding the soldiers' faces into mincemeat with terrible kicks from their back legs. They would definitely be like what the poet said about Caesar Augustus: "He is a horse who will kick if you rub him the wrong way." But, instead of thinking how to conquer that great nation I wish they had the ability or inclination to send enough of their people over here to civilise Europe by teaching us the basic principles of HONOR, justice, truth, temperance, public spirit, fortitude, tenacity, friendship, benevolence, and loyalty. We still have the names of these virtues in most of our languages and they can be read in modern, as well as ancient, authors; I know this is true from my own little reading.

But I had another motive, which made me less keen to increase his Majesty's Empire through my discoveries. To tell the truth I had developed a few worries about the way Princes behave in these circumstances. For example, a crew of pirates might be driven astray by a storm; finally a boy in the crow's nest spies land; they go on shore to rob and plunder, they find a harmless people, are given a warm welcome, they give the country a new name, they claim it formally for their King, put up a rotten plank or a stone as a marker, then murder two or three dozen of the natives, and carry off a couple more, by force, as a sample. Then they return home and are pardoned. This is how a new land is acquired and it is claimed to now be the King's by divine right. Ships are sent as soon as possible; the natives are driven out or destroyed; the Princes are tortured to give up their treasure; all acts of inhumanity and lust are permitted until the Earth stinks of the blood of the natives. And this revolting crew of butchers, undertaking such a holy mission, that is a modern colony, sent to convert and civilise a heathen and barbarian people.

But of course this description does not apply to the British nation, who set the example for the whole world in their wisdom, care, and justice in setting up colonies; in their generous funding for the advancement of religion and education; their choice of sincere and able ministers to spread Christianity; their care in filling their provinces with people who are sober in speech and in life from this mother kingdom; their great regard for the machinery of justice, in appointing in all the colonies officers of the highest ability, who could never be corrupted; and above all by sending the hardest working and most virtuous governors, who care about nothing besides the happiness of the people over whom they rule and the HONOR of their master the King.

But as those countries which I have described do not appear to want to be conquered and enslaved, murdered or driven out by colonists, and they don't have great stocks of gold, silver, sugar or tobacco, I humbly decided that they were not proper subjects for our keenness, our bravery, or our attention. However if those more deeply involved with these matters hold a different opinion I am ready to give evidence, when I am called by law, that no European ever visited those countries before me. That is, if the natives are to be believed, unless some argument might arise concerning the two Yahoos who were said to have been seen many years ago on a mountain in Houyhnhnmland.

As for the ceremony of taking possession in the name of my sovereign, it never occurred to me; and if it had, given the position I was in, I would perhaps, for the sake of common sense and self-preservation, have postponed doing so until a more favourable time.

As I have now answered the only objection that anyone can make against me as a traveller, I will here say goodbye to my kind readers and go back to enjoy my own thoughts in my little garden in Rotherhithe; I shall follow those excellent lessons in virtue which I was given by the Houyhnhnms; I shall teach the Yahoos of my own family, as long as I find them to be teachable creatures; I shall look at myself in the mirror often, and so, if possible, I will in time be able to stand the sight of a human being. I shall cry out against the brutality to Houyhnhnms in my own country, and I shall always treat them with respect, for the sake of my noble master, his family, his friends, and the whole Houyhnhnm race, which our ones have the HONOR to be physically identical to, even if their intellects do not match.

Last week I began to permit my wife to have dinner with me, at the far end of a long table; and I let her answer (but as briefly as possible) the few questions I asked her. But as the smell of the Yahoo is still very offensive to me I always keep my nose well blocked with rue, lavender, or tobacco leaves. And although it is hard for an old man to shed his old habits I am somewhat hopeful that in a while I might be able to put up with a neighbour Yahoo in my company, without those fears I have now of his teeth or his claws.

It would be easier to become reconciled with Yahoos in general if they could just be happy with those vices and stupidities which nature has given them. I am not in the least annoyed by the sight of a lawyer, a pickpocket, a colonel, a fool, a lord, a gambler, a politician, a pimp, a doctor, an informer, a blackmailer, an attorney, a traitor and so on; these are all quite natural. But when I see a lump of deformity and disease, both of the body and mind, which also has pride, I find it beyond endurance. I will never be able to understand how such an animal and such a vice could go together. The wise and virtuous Houyhnhnms, who are full of all the virtues a thinking creature can have, have no word for pride in their language, which has no terms to describe anything that is evil, except for those they use to describe the revolting qualities of their Yahoos, and they couldn't see the quality of pride in them because they did not fully understand human nature, as it is seen in other countries where that animal rules. But I, with more experience, could plainly see some basic pride amongst the wild Yahoos.

But the Houyhnhnms, who are ruled by reason, are no more proud of their good qualities than I would be of having a full set of limbs, which no sane man would boast of even though he would be miserable without them. I have spoken at length on this subject because I want to make the company of an English Yahoo tolerable by any means possible; and so I ask that any who are tainted with this absurd vice keep out of my sight.

Made in the USA
Coppell, TX
06 January 2020